Wild Grass

AND

Morning Blossoms
Gathered at Dusk

Wild Grass

AND

Morning Blossoms Gathered at Dusk

LU XUN

Translated by

EILEEN J. CHENG

Edited by

THEODORE HUTERS

The Belknap Press of Harvard University Press

CAMBRIDGE, MASSACHUSETTS

LONDON, ENGLAND

2022

First printing

Library of Congress Cataloging-in-Publication Data
Names: Lu, Xun, 1881–1936, author. | Cheng, Eileen, 1969– editor. |
Huters, Theodore, editor. | Lu, Xun, 1881–1936. Ye cao. English. 2022 |
Lu, Xun, 1881–1936. Zhao hua xi shi. English. 2022
Title: Wild grass ; and, Morning blossoms gathered at dusk / Lu Xun ;
edited by Eileen J. Cheng and Theodore Huters.
Other titles: Morning blossoms gathered at dusk.
Description: Cambridge, Massachusetts : Harvard University Press, 2022. |
Includes bibliographical references.
Identifiers: LCCN 2022001874 | ISBN 9780674261167 (cloth)
Subjects: LCSH: Lu, Xun, 1881–1936—Translations into English. |
LCGFT: Short stories. | Essays.
Classification: LCC PL2754.S5 Y4513 2022 | DDC 895.185109—dc23/eng/20220310
LC record available at https://lccn.loc.gov/2022001874

Contents

Morning Blossoms Gathered at Dusk

Wild Grass

AND

*Morning Blossoms
Gathered at Dusk*

Introduction

Lu Xun (Zhou Shuren, 1881–1936), the "father of modern Chinese literature," is widely considered one of the greatest writers of twentieth-century China.[1] An accomplished scholar, translator, cultural critic, and classical poet, he was also a pioneer of various literary forms. His literary reputation largely hinges on his two short story collections, *Outcry* (1923) and *Hesitation* (1926). Though less known outside of China, the imaginative prose essay collection *Wild Grass* (1927) and the experimental memoir *Morning Blossoms Gathered at Dusk* (1928) showcase Lu Xun's breadth and creativity as a writer and include some of his most brilliant work.

Lu Xun completed *Wild Grass* and *Morning Blossoms* between 1924 and 1926, a particularly fraught period in his personal and public life.[2] China, ruled by competing warlord factions and subjected to imperialist aggression, was wracked by instability and violence. Boycotts and anti-imperialist demonstrations swept through the cities in 1925 after students protesting the killing of a Chinese worker in a Japanese-owned mill in Shanghai were shot and killed by municipal police at the Shanghai International Settlement on May 30. Ten months later, in what Lu Xun referred to as the "darkest day since the founding of the Republic," the Beiyang warlord Duan Qirui (1865–1936) ordered the

1

Figure 1. Sketch of Lu Xun by Tao Yuanqing, 1926. Reproduced from *Lu Xun wenxian tu zhuan* (Illustrated biography and documents of Lu Xun) (Zhengzhou: Daxiang chubanshe, 1998), 93.

killing of anti-imperialist demonstrators at Tiananmen Square on March 18, 1926. Among the forty-seven dead, three were Lu Xun's students from Peking Women's Normal College, whom he memorialized in the essay "In Memory of Liu Hezhen" (1926).[3] For his writings condemning government brutality, Lu Xun was blacklisted. In a nine-month period in 1926, he moved from Beijing to Xiamen to Guangzhou before finally settling in Shanghai in the last decade of his life.

His creative writings, which he referred to as "small, pale white blossoms blooming on the edges of an abandoned hell," flourished in this turbulent period of his life.[4] The political and social issues so clearly represented in his short stories and essays had become, if any-thing, even more pressing. What led him to delve into the worlds of dreams, memory, and the imaginary at this time? What role do these works play in the oeuvre of a "realist" writer?

Some critics have read Lu Xun's memoir as a retreat into a pri-vate garden of memories when political realities became too grim. Indeed, in the preface to *Morning Blossoms,* Lu Xun conveys a sense of helplessness over the political situation and the itinerant life it forced upon him. Engaging in the transcendent world of *Wild Grass* and in-dulging in memories in *Morning Blossoms* might have provided solace, diversion, and an outlet for unleashing creative energies at a chaotic and uncertain time.[5]

The two volumes, however, served as far more than mere dis-tractions. Lu Xun seemed intent on experimenting with new realms of literary expression to articulate different ways of seeing and being in the world. Some critics claim that *Wild Grass* contains its author's philosophy of life—a philosophy as dense, dark, and pessimistic as the pieces themselves. Yet, the collection as a whole is teeming with life. Surreal worlds of dreams and imagination come alive through vivid imagery and hauntingly poetic language—worlds where humans coexist with ghosts, talking animals, and sentient objects, and come face to face with their own corpses. In blurring the distinctions be-tween humans and nonhuman others, in affirming the singularity of each being while acknowledging our interdependence in a vibrant ecological web of existence, *Wild Grass* asks: What does it mean to be human?

As a memoir, *Morning Blossoms* is rooted in the experiences of daily life. Like Lu Xun's stories, the essays depict the cruelty of human society. Yet, philosophically, the memoir echoes the themes of *Wild*

Grass. Readers are ushered into the world of the child—a vulnerable subject not yet fully indoctrinated in societal norms and conventions—whose life is enmeshed with an array of subjects and objects, real and imagined. These vulnerable subjects include the human and nonhuman—family servants, social outcasts, cats, mice, monsters, and spirits—that inhabit the child's world and imagination. By challenging the norms that dictate social life and giving voice and visibility to subjects and objects not often seen or heard in the world of narrative, the memoir echoes the questions posed in *Wild Grass:* What counts as a meaningful existence? Whose lives can be grieved and whose cannot?

Wild Grass and *Morning Blossoms* gesture to a world *beyond*—a polyphonous world where the existence of diverse beings and their struggles to survive are affirmed and shown to be part of our shared predicament of being without a home in the world. Delving into a world *beyond*—exploring dreamscapes and imaginary worlds—is a way of transcending our epistemological limits, allowing for a "pluralistic perspective that recognizes . . . various existential possibilities."[6] Going beyond the focus on the predatory nature of human society in his short stories, Lu Xun explores alternate ways of knowing and imagining the self, others, and the world in literary form. A world of wonder rife with contradictions, in which the mundane appears extraordinary, the bizarre becomes commonplace, and all that was once certain is called into question—such is the world of *Wild Grass* and *Morning Blossoms Gathered at Dusk.*

Eileen J. Cheng

Wild Grass

Bordering on the Divine

Translator's Introduction to
Wild Grass

Lush, lush the grass on the plain	離離原上草
wilting and thriving each year	一歲一枯榮
Not consumed when wildfires burn	野火燒不盡
grow again when spring winds blow	春風吹又生

"Bidding Farewell, Composed to the Grass on an Ancient Plain"
by Bai Juyi (772–846)

賦得古原草送別
白居易

Lake waters run clear in the second month	二月湖水清
Spring birds chirping in every home	家家春鳥鳴
Forest flowers, swept aside, keep falling	林花掃更落
Grass on the path, trampled, still grows	徑草踏還生

"Celebrating a Visit with Wang the Ninth in Springtime"
by Meng Haoran (689–740)

春中喜王九相尋
孟浩然

Wild grass, when it appears in classical Chinese poetry, is portrayed as an essential part of the natural landscape. With a short life cycle of growth, decay, and regeneration, it is often associated with the ephemeral nature of life. Its presence might evoke sadness or regret—over a departure, a short-lived reunion, a passing life. Coming alive every spring, wild grass might symbolize hope, vitality, and new beginnings.

7

Though humble and ordinary, grass thrives in the most inhospitable of terrains. Neglected and abused, it evokes feelings of desolation and isolation. Scorched by fires, trampled by passersby, it regenerates nonetheless. As a metaphor for the human condition, wild grass represents resilience, vitality, and a will to survive against all odds.

⸺

The creative pieces in *Wild Grass* (*Yecao*, 1927) are among the most stylistically brilliant and radically innovative of Lu Xun's writings. A few depict grim social realities similar to those found in his stories, but secular issues, while still present, mostly recede to the background. Readers are invited into the intimate world of nature, dreams, and the imaginary, worlds populated by a gamut of subjects: from the human, fauna, and flora to the inanimate and fantastic. T. A. Hsia calls the work "genuine poetry in embryo: images imbued with strong emotional intensity, flowing and stopping in darkly glowing and oddly shaped lines, like molten metal failing to find a mold."[1] Leo Ou-fan Lee writes that the collection's combination of "formalistic experimentation and psychological probing yields a magnificent harvest of symbolic art."[2]

What role does this eclectic collection play in the oeuvre of a "realist" writer?[3] Some critics claim that *Wild Grass* contains Lu Xun's philosophy of life—a philosophy as dense, dark, and pessimistic as the pieces themselves. In the foreword to the collection, Lu Xun writes:

> Wild grass—its roots are not deep, its flowers and leaves not beautiful. Yet it absorbs dew, water, and flesh and blood of old corpses, robbing each of its existence. Still, while alive, it is trampled on and hacked off until it dies and rots away . . . fires

surge and churn underground. Once the molten lava erupts through the surface, it will burn up all the wild grass and trees, so there will be nothing left to rot.

This raises an existential question: If wild grass is doomed to a life of struggle against an inevitable death, what is the point of its existence? As a philosophical work, *Wild Grass* is a meditation about the meaning of life itself. If we understand life not only as suffering but as a journey unto certain death and decay, then what is the point of living?[4] What does it mean if life itself is conditioned by, and conditional on, death, of the self and others? And what is the point of writing about it at all?

Traces of the classical lyrical and modernist traditions intermingle with Daoist and Buddhist metaphysics in Lu Xun's foray into a shadowy world of darkness, death, and the unknown *beyond*. Exploring the unknown *beyond* is a way of transcending our own epistemological limits, allowing for a "pluralistic perspective that recognizes . . . various existential possibilities" and prepares our minds "intuitively . . . for its inquiry into the unknown."[5] The lines of questioning *Wild Grass* undertakes require what John Keats referred to as "negative capability"—that is, the ability to remain "in uncertainties, mysteries, doubts, without any irritable reaching after fact and reason."[6] Remaining in this state of not-knowing is far from being passive for, as David Jauss puts it, "to resist the mind's tendency to converge on a comfortable certainty requires an arduous active effort."[7] In *Wild Grass,* Lu Xun explores alternate ways of knowing, imagining, and representing the self, the other, and the world in writing—a world of wonder rife with contradictions, in which the mundane becomes extraordinary, the bizarre becomes commonplace, and all that was once certain is called into question.

The Inhuman

Lu Xun wrote the twenty-three pieces in *Wild Grass* between December 1924 and April 1926. Each piece was first serialized in the Beijing literary journal *Threads of Talk* (*Yusi*) and originally titled "Wild Grass," followed by a number indicating its sequence in the series. The preface was completed in 1927, and the complete volume was published that same year.[8]

Wild Grass is often referred to as a collection of "prose poems."[9] The term, however, is somewhat of a misnomer. The collection is an eclectic mix of genres, including prose poems, anecdotes, parables, dream-writing, and short memoirs; it also includes a one-act play and a parody of a classical poem. Going beyond the confines of a uniform genre or style may have given Lu Xun a means to circumvent the limits of form and representation, to better reflect the diversity, complexity, and contradictory nature of the worlds, subjects, emotions, and ideas he wanted to capture in writing.

Like his short stories, the human world in *Wild Grass* is bleak, cruel, and devoid of compassion. Portrayed are the miserable lives of society's abject—the slave, the beggar, the outcast, the prostitute. Even as they suffer, some of the victims are shown supporting their oppressors and / or oppressing their own kind ("Tremors on the Border of Degradation," "The Alms Seeker" "The Clever Man, the Fool, and the Slave"). Bystanders thirst for spectacles of suffering and slaughter, while some victims of abuse relish and flaunt their misery ("Revenge," "Revenge (II)," "The Clever Man, the Fool, and the Slave," "Amid the Pale Bloodstains"). The human world is a veritable living hell.

Wild Grass, however, departs from the almost exclusive focus on the gritty world of humankind in Lu Xun's stories.[10] Diverse subjects

and objects—human and nonhuman, animate and inanimate—
populate *Wild Grass*. Some pieces take the natural world as a point of
departure. "Snow," for instance, asks: What different forms does the
spirit of the rain assume north and south of the Yangtze River? In
"The Preserved Leaf," the narrator's memories of an autumn past are
revived as he comes across a dried leaf, with a hole in its center, pressed
between the pages of a book. The edges of the hole, which had turned
black, looked like "the bright pupil of a staring eye." While its edges
"no longer glistened," the image of this "eye" staring back at the narrator gestures toward the mysterious lives and perspectives of other
beings. While dreaming individuals make frequent appearances in
Wild Grass, the first "dreamer" in the collection is a tiny pink flower
in the opening piece, "Autumn Night." Indeed, the very title of the
volume asks: What might the world look like from the perspective
of wild grass?

While critics have long noted the prominence of darkness and
death in *Wild Grass*, the collection teems with life and pulsates with
sound. In its delineation of a vibrant ecological web of existence and
the suffering shared by all beings in the struggle to survive, and in
its blurring of the distinctions between humans and nonhuman
others, *Wild Grass* invites readers to reflect: What counts as a meaningful life? What does it mean to be human?

The tone is set in the opening lines of the first piece, "Autumn
Night": "Beyond the wall of my backyard, you can see two trees. One
is a jujube tree and the other is also a jujube tree." Each singular being,
like each of these jujube trees, however insignificant in our eyes, has
a unique existence, an existence that is also mutually interdependent
with that of others. Brimming with fruit in the late summer, the trees
attract children, who come to strike off the jujubes. With the arrival
of autumn, the once vibrant trees wither and fall into neglect. Bereft

of fruit and foliage, some branches curve into arcs, nursing scars left from the children's beatings; others stand tall and erect like iron rods that "pierce the odd and high sky, causing the sky to blink his sinister eyes." As each singular life transforms and struggles to survive, each, in its own way, leaves its mark on an often inhospitable world.

Pieces like "Autumn Night" dispel illusions of the superiority of humans in the great chain of being. Amid the misery and suffering of all existence, signs of beauty, courage, and resilience abound in the world of nature, where humans almost always pale in comparison to their nonhuman counterparts. In "Autumn Night," the narrator describing the strength and fortitude of the jujube trees appears as a passive and cowardly observer. Startled by the sound of his own laughter, he retreats to the confines of his room as darkness approaches. He turns up the wick of his lamp, attracting flying insects. As the insects charge fearlessly into the glass chimney to their deaths, the narrator languidly lets out a yawn, lights a cigarette, and "silently pays tribute to these exquisite, emerald heroes."

Humans appear no better in dreams or the supernatural world; they are often animalized as their nonhuman others are humanized. In "The Dog's Retort," the narrator dreams that he is a beggar.[11] Annoyed by a barking dog, the beggar curses it as a "snooty mutt" and tells it to "shut up." To his surprise, the dog politely engages him in civil discourse: it expresses bewilderment over the human propensity to discriminate against their own kind, a skill that dogs have yet to master. Outmatched in rhetoric and forced to confront his own hypocrisy, the beggar flees. In "The Good Hell That Was Lost," humans are shown to be more abominable than the Devil himself. For all its otherworldly concerns, the political subtext of the piece— as a bleak assessment of the secular reforms of Lu Xun's times—is hard to miss. The conditions of this "good" Hell becomes far more oppressive after it is taken over by humankind.

Some of the most creative pieces in *Wild Grass* push the idea of subjectivity beyond the world of the sentient to the world of the imaginary and implausible. "The Good Hell That Was Lost" depicts a hell haunted by humans. "The Shadow's Farewell" depicts a shadow that wants to part from its master. Some subjects defy imagination: a sentient corpse, a talking flame encased in ice ("After Death," "Dead Fire"). These paradoxical subjects inspire readers to think beyond conventional limits and dualities, to see and understand contradiction as a condition of existence itself.

The Limits of Form

Some pieces in *Wild Grass* challenge assumptions of what it means to be human from without by anthropomorphizing nonhuman others; other pieces with first-person narrators question the coherence of a human "self" from within by delineating the existence of multiple "I's." Human subjects are portrayed in various states of existence—as the living, the dead, or the somewhere-in-between or beyond (corpses and ghosts)—and appear in various modes of consciousness—on the verge of sleep, sleeping and dreaming, awake or on the cusp of awakening, and at times flowing through multiple states in the same piece.[12] In essays reminiscing on the past, a writer representing an I-now recalls the experiences of an I-then ("The Kite," "Snow," "The Preserved Leaf"). Most of the seven dream sequences begin with a writer representing the thoughts of an awake-I, recounting the experiences of the I-in-the-dream. At times, the I-in-the-dream is recalling his experiences, only to be interrupted by the I-who-awakens.

What do we mean, then, when we say "I"? And how do we represent this "I" in writing? Through its varied and experimental forms, *Wild Grass* also offers a sustained meditation on writing and representation. Sharing the Daoist, Buddhist, and Western modernist propensity to question representation itself—that is, the delusory nature of form and language and their tendency to reify dualities and absolutes—many pieces in *Wild Grass* deploy form and language in such a manner as to expose their inadequacies, at once affirming, negating, and placing them in a state of suspension. Boundaries of the self and the world appear elastic and permeable, as what lies within and without once perceived borders are blurred and turned inside out.

Dreams are common literary devices used to illustrate the illusory nature of life and the ever-changing nature of forms and beings. Dream sequences are similarly deployed in *Wild Grass*. Multiple I's from the past, present, and future converge in "Tombstone Inscriptions." The I-narrator recounts a dreamscape in which the I-in-the-dream comes across a dilapidated tombstone and a disemboweled corpse. While its face is indistinct, the corpse is, one gathers, yet another iteration of the "I." The barely legible epitaph describes the failure of the once-living corpse's journey in search of himself:

> . . . *gouge out my heart and eat it, wanting to know its true taste.*
> *The pain is so searing, how would I know its true taste?*
> . . . *as the pain subsides, slowly consume it. But the heart now grown old and stale, how could I know its true taste? . . .*
> . . . *answer me, or else leave! . . .*

The human capacity for self-knowledge, the piece suggests, may be inherently limited. Self-introspection, likened to a form of self-cannibalism, might lead not to self-knowledge but to self-dissolution, possibly even to the death of the self.[13] But it might also lead to an epiphany: the self, like the hollow corpse, might just be empty at the core.

"Tombstone Inscriptions" points to a source of human suffering: the futile attachment to form, bodily and textual. Read as a metanarrative on the limits of writing, the cryptic epitaphs—the story itself and the tombstone inscriptions in the dream—fail to live up to their form and function, offering few revelations about the subject they represent. Yet, the fading inscriptions and the decomposing corpse correspond in an uncanny manner: indistinct, not entirely legible, and in the process of continued decay, their remains underscore the ephemeral nature of all forms. In negating the premises of its own form and language and using the very same language to explore different modes of existence, "Tombstone Inscriptions" performatively expresses its own linguistic and ontological reality.

The limits of representation are explored in another dream narrative, "Story of Good Things," this time by questioning the ability of language to capture the "essence" of experiences in and of themselves. The elusive nature of form is metaphorically represented through the moving landscapes that the narrator sees in his dreams and recalls in his memories. The I-in-the-dream describes his boat ride:

> I seem to recall riding a small boat past an ancient road. Things on both sides of the bank—the tallow trees, newly sprouted grain, wildflowers, chickens, dogs, bushes and withered trees, thatched huts, pagodas, monasteries, farmers and peasant women, peasant girls, clothes hung out to dry, monks, straw hats, the sky, clouds, and bamboo—are reflected in the clear turquoise stream; their images sway along with the duckweed and the swimming fish, shimmering as the rays of the sun strike

them with each dip of the oar. All these things and their reflections scatter, sway, expand, and merge into one other. Once merged, they shrink back and then revert to a semblance of their original form. The ragged edges of the reflections merge into one another like summer clouds rimmed by sunlight flashing quicksilver flames.

"Story of Good Things" as a whole illustrates the futility of grasping for permanence in a world that is constantly in flux. Once the I-in-the-dream attempts to "fix" his gaze on the image, it is immediately and violently destroyed, "as if someone had thrown a big rock into the river water. The ripples suddenly rise up, tearing the whole expansive reflection to shreds."[14] The awakened-I attempts to recapture his dream experience through writing, only to find that "not a shard of the shattered reflection remained and all I saw was the dim lamplight."

While the coda of "Story of Good Things" seems to echo the ostensible message of linguistic inadequacy in "Tombstone Inscriptions," the hallucinatory dream within the narrative negates it. In its use of indirect and paradoxical language, "Story of Good Things" recalls the deployment of language in Daoist texts, as it reveals "the paradox of a thinking that is simultaneously suspicious of language while richly employing it in manifold ways."[15] With no subject and no plotline, the dream unfolds through a form, style, and language that differs from the conventional narrative that frames it. Eschewing narrative linearity, the "story" attempts to replicate the experience of pure consciousness through the use of ellipsis, poetic imagery, and stream-of-consciousness narration. The piece's radically modernist style also well captures the Daoist concept of harmony—oneness with the universe—and the Buddhist notion of perfect interfusion—the mutual interdependence and interpenetration of all things.[16] The I-in-the-dream loses himself among the intermingling and ever-changing reflections and experiences the sublime: "Numerous beautiful people and beautiful events weaving into one another like a tapestry of clouds in the sky, fluttering by like a myriad of shooting stars, as the scene unfolds and stretches out into infinity."

The story illustrates the intangible and ephemeral nature of experience made all the more splendid by its fleeting nature, when in a sublime moment, one unexpectedly finds oneself in alignment with the universe—a universe that is otherwise beyond the reach of the conditioned mind. This divine moment, however brief, can nonetheless be revived and recaptured through dreams, memory, and artistic creations that disrupt and transcend conventional understandings of the world. For in spite of lamenting his inability to hold onto the dream images, the narrator writes at the end of the piece: "But I always remember seeing this story of good things on that murky night. . . ."

In "How I Write," Lu Xun describes his state of mind when he wrote the foreword to *Wild Grass*:

> I become calm and silent. The lonely silence concentrates, like wine, lightly intoxicating me. Looking out the back window, I see numerous white spots scattered on the bony mountain peaks—graves—and dark yellow fire—the tile lamp of the *Nanputuo* temple. Before me, the sky and ocean are indistinct. The night, like a black, cottony mass, looks like it is about to assault the depths of my heart. Reclining on the stone barrier and looking afar, I hear the voice of my heart. All around, from the far corners of the earth, it seems that there is infinite sorrow, suffering, decay, and death, randomly mixing into this lonely

silence, adding color, flavor, and fragrance and transforming it into a healing wine.[17]

The writer loses himself in the full intensity of his emotions, manifested and mirrored in the physical landscape. In the moment of communion between man and nature, "I had wanted to write, but was unable to, not knowing where to start. This is what I was referring to in the line 'When I am silent, I feel replenished; as I open my mouth, I sense emptiness.'"[18] It seems that only in silence, and in the act of surrendering oneself fully to experience, can one truly hear one's inner voice and be in communion with the universe. To enunciate the feeling of full presence in that sublime moment—in its randomness, messiness, complexity, and contradictions—it seems, only serves to destroy it, capturing mere fragments of the whole. Yet, as the "Story of Good Things" and *Wild Grass* as a whole show, sparks of that divine moment can be revived and relived through altered states of consciousness or through engagement with works of art, which while conscious of the limits of their own form and language, nonetheless try to transcend them as they gesture to a world *beyond*.

Radical Hope

Despair, like hope, is just a delusion.
Lu Xun, "Hope," in Wild Grass

At the end of the dreamscape in "Tombstone Inscriptions," the corpse sits up and transmits the following message telepathically: "When I've turned to dust, you'll see my smile!" Affirming the inevitable demise and decay of all things, "Tombstone Inscriptions" suggests that the dissolution of corporeal form—and the delusion of the "self" it represents—may not necessarily be a loss, but a form of release.

Echoing the words of the telepathic corpse, Lu Xun in the "Afterword to Graves" refers to himself as an intermediary, or more literally, a "thing-in-between" (zhongjian wu): "In the chain of evolution, everything is an in-between . . . things pass away and pass away, each and everything passes away quickly like time; they are passing away or will pass away—that is all there is to it, and I am perfectly content with it."[19] In the same essay, referring to his writings, he notes:

> I cannot firmly and decisively destroy them, wishing for the nonce to use them to observe the remaining traces from a life that has passed by. I only hope that readers partial to my work merely take this as a souvenir and know that within this small tumulus there is buried a body that was once alive. And after the passage of yet more time it, too, will transform into dust, and the memories will also vanish from the human realm, and I would have accomplished what I set out to do.[20]

The writer plays a constructive role as a bridge from the past to the future. On the "awakened" writers who call out in a new voice, Lu Xun writes that "they should still pass away like time itself, gradually wither away, to be at most a piece of timber or a stone that is part of a bridge, not some goal or model for the future. What is to emerge should be different, even if it is not some divinely gifted sage . . . what emerges should, at the very least, bring with it a new atmosphere."[21] The "new" here is uncertain, but different from the past, a new that is made possible by the in-betweens who live, die, and pave the way for a future they will not be a part of.

A similar affirmation of the capacity of all things—be it a piece of timber or small stone, or an outcast of society—to leave a mark on the world appears in many of the pieces in Wild Grass. The narrator of "Tremors on the Border of Degradation" dreams of himself dreaming. In the first dreamscape, the I-in-the-dream encounters a scene in which a woman sells her body to buy food for her young daughter. Jolted awake, the I-in-the-dream enters a second dreamscape, a continuation of the earlier dream, but after many years have elapsed. The now grown daughter, ashamed of her mother's sordid past, heaps scorn and abuse on the old woman. Amid the jeers of her daughter and her family, the old woman walks out of the shed at night, deep into the boundless wilderness.

The simple story line, ostensibly about an abject woman's oppression, is complicated by the descriptions of the woman's bodily sensations that permeate the multiple layers of the story. In the first dream episode, the woman's body "trembles from hunger, misery, shock, humiliation, and pleasure." The "waves of pleasure, humiliation, misery, shock, and hunger" that "permeate and pulsate through the air" describe not only the woman's emotions and sensations, but also those of her child and "patron" as well. In the second dream episode, after the old woman walks out into the wilderness, her body again convulses as a medley of sensations and emotions overcomes her: "hunger, pain, shock, humiliation, pleasure . . . inflicting suffering, hardship, and dragging in others . . . devotion and estrangement, loving caresses and revenge, nurturance and annihilation, blessings and curses . . ." Removed from civilization, the old woman—naked, alone, and stripped of all identity—enters a realm of consciousness that encompasses all humanity. The boundaries and distinctions between "I" and "others," "oppressor" and "victim," "past" and "present" are blurred and dissolved as she becomes a transparent vessel of pure sensation and experience, her own intertwined with those of all others. The "border" referred to in the title is itself blurred, as the line of degradation borders on the divine. The abject woman's primal wordless scream—"half-human, half-beast, and not of this world"—expresses a full range of emotions that is at once human, bestial, and divine.

Mutually interconnected with all things, the life force of this figure—at once degraded, at once divine—traverses through the past and the present and radiates out into an unfolding future:

> Her entire body—like a once great, noble statue, now wasted and withered—trembles all over. Each tremble resembles a tiny fish scale, each scale undulating like water boiling over a blazing fire. The air grew turbulent in an instant, like roiling waves in a vast sea during a thunderstorm . . . only the trembling disperses outward like the rays of the sun, instantly whirling around the waves in the sky, like a hurricane billowing in the boundless wilderness.

Her trembling body, the tiny "tremors on the border of degradation," emits a life force that pulses out into the universe, crossing and breaking down borders, bearing with it the potential for seismic change.[22]

In another piece, titled "Hope," Lu Xun asserts that "despair, like hope, is just a delusion." "Tremors on the Border of Degradation" and other pieces in *Wild Grass* fluidly cross the borders of hope and despair—neither fully succumbing to nor excluding either—and indulge in uncertainty and the possibilities inherent in that uncertainty. This refusal to succumb to either hope or despair is akin to Jonathan Lear's notion of "radical hope"—a hope that resists any trace of false optimism, yet at the same time recognizes that "given the abyss, one cannot really know what survival means."[23] Like Lu Xun's notion of "resisting despair," radical hope is a "daunting form of commitment" that requires the maintenance of faith "in the world that transcends one's current ability to grasp what it is."[24] As Lu Xun writes, the future might bear "the horror of annihilation," yet might also hold "the hope of regeneration."[25] The kernels of hope in the volume are like the wild grass in Bai Juyi's poem quoted at the outset—not completely extinguished by burning wildfires, coming to life again when the spring wind blows.

In the preface to *Wild Grass*, Lu Xun writes: "My past life has met its demise. From its demise, I derive great joy, because from this I know it once existed." On the collection as a whole, he remarks: "In the interstices of light and darkness, life and death, past and future . . . I offer this clump of wild grass as a testament . . . I hope the demise and rotting of these wild grasses come swiftly. Otherwise, I will not have lived, something even more lamentable than their demise and rotting." In an essay written in later life, Lu Xun likens his role as a writer to a street vendor: "I am just hawking my wares at the roadside deep into the night; all that I have are but some small nails and a few tiles and dishes. But I hope, and even believe, that some people will find something useful in their midst."[26]

So too the case of the in-betweens in *Wild Grass*, all of which bear testimony to a past that has gone and a present in the process of disappearing. This present, destined to decay, nonetheless leaves marks on a world fraught with uncertain possibilities. Representations that aspire toward truth are by nature partial and mark the absence of what was once present. At the same time, they may reflect in the present specters of that which has ceased to exist. While the significance of Lu Xun's writings might fade in time, they might, like the rusty nail or broken tile hawked by a street vendor, serve a purpose far larger than their humble appearance suggests. Tombstone inscriptions, however faded and incomplete, might allow glimmers of the past to flicker alive. A writer's words, like the shadow that refuses to follow its "master," might linger on after the master has departed; or, like the arhat made of snow, might grace their divine presence on the world before disappearing. Or, like the dead flame encased in ice, Lu Xun's writings might one day yet smolder alive, reignited in the hands of a discerning reader, to illuminate the past and the present, to serve as a guide for a future in the making.

Through its diverse subjects in between multiple borders, at times in suspension, at times in dissolution, at times residing in the interstices, *Wild Grass* provides a multiperspectival lens through which Lu Xun's vision unfolds. His status as an in-between—neither "this" nor "that" and without a home in the world—at times made him feel ill at ease. But refusing to capitulate to a world defined by dualities and embracing his state of in-between-ness as a writer allowed him to transcend "this" or "that" and observe the complexities and contradictions of his life and times with a critical eye and to chronicle them with brilliant insight. As a creative writer, residing in the interstices enabled him to see beyond a world defined by conventional limits, to create the bizarre, surrealistic, and splendid world of *Wild Grass*.

Echoing his celebration of the child and childlike heart-mind (*tongxin*) in some of his essays and in his memoir *Morning Blossoms Gathered at Dusk,* several pieces recount children's creative spirit and propensity to delight in the world of the everyday, nature, and the divine: flying kites outdoors in the spring, building arhats out of snow in the winter ("The Kite," "Snow"). Children's connection to nature and absorption in their own world of make-believe and play provide a contrast to the tainted minds of adults, who seem to find perennial entertainment through inflicting or witnessing the pain and suffering of others ("Revenge," "Revenge (II)"). *Wild Grass* itself can be seen as Lu Xun's tapping into the childlike heart, indulging in imaginative and creative expression to explore a world of the surreal and fantastic.

In form and style, the collection reflects and represents the complexity of the world composed of myriad forms. Diverse ideas, styles, and generic, literary, and linguistic conventions—indigenous and foreign, old and new—intermingle freely and often messily. The individual pieces in *Wild Grass* can, like single blades of grass, function on their own and are often read as stand-alone pieces, generating a wide variety of readings.[27] Yet, the pieces also read meaningfully as part of a whole, as a web of intertexts. Some pieces engage one another sympathetically through shared or overlapping narrative structures, images, and themes, or reappearing phrases, subjects, and objects. The figure of the beggar is alluded to in three essays ("The Alms Seeker," "The Dog's Retort," "The Passerby"). The four seasons, symbolizing the cycle of birth and death, and of a life in constant flux, is a thread linking many of the pieces ("Autumn Night," "Snow," "The Kite," "The Preserved Leaf"). "Lip rouge" used to describe flowing reflections in the water ("Story of Good Things"), the disappearing lip rouge on the melting arhat ("Snow"), and the flushed cheeks of the prostitute ("Tremors on the Border of Degradation") reinforce the theme of impermanence. With its wide array of intertextual engagements—among the individual pieces in the volume as well as with texts outside of it—it is not surprising that the individual pieces in *Wild Grass* and the collection as a whole can be abstruse and esoteric, yet also insightful and profound.[28]

In Lu Xun's first short story collection, *Outcry,* he adopts the metaphor of an indestructible iron house—with no windows and doors, its sleeping inhabitant slowly suffocating to death—to describe the social and political conditions of his time.[29] Is there a way of escaping the iron house? *Wild Grass* offers no definitive answers, yet its depiction of a world with permeable walls and borders, a world of infinite possibility conjured through imagination, dreaming, and artistic engagements, suggests one way of coping with this feeling of entrapment. While these metaphysical meditations on a world of enchantment and the tapping into the childlike mind through creative writing offer no concrete solutions to secular problems, they may have provided Lu Xun momentary inspiration, solace, and reprieve when the walls of his own world became too constricted. Perhaps in this case, imagining a dimension "beyond" the iron house is preferable to being awakened to face a suffocating death within it.

Were it located in the world of *Wild Grass,* perhaps the walls of the iron house would be permeable, or perhaps, as in "Dead Fire," it would all be just a nightmare from which the narrator would awaken from, gasping. Or perhaps, like the burning iron house parable in the *Lotus Sutra,* the Buddha would, through skillful means, usher the inhabitants out of the house and into a great chariot. That great chariot might deliver them to salvation—or perhaps, as in "Dead Fire," roll off into a valley after crushing the people in its way.

But in the tangible human world, subjects and objects in suspension inevitably descend and dreamers awaken. In part due to the political exigencies of the time, Lu Xun's radical aesthetic experiments ground to a virtual halt after the completion of *Wild Grass,* as he turned his pen almost exclusively to the writing of polemical essays— his "daggers and spears" that addressed the pressing social issues of the day head on.[30]

That is not to suggest that *Wild Grass* does not echo some of Lu Xun's earlier "outcries" nor foreshadow his later "descent" back to the world of the iron house;[31] nor is it to say that *Wild Grass* does not entertain the remote possibility of an awakened few destroying the iron house. This very possibility is interspersed in a few pieces where the world of dreams and the imagination collide with the human realm. In "Such a Fighter," an ever-vigilant warrior clings to his spear in the face of the empty battle formation before him, ready to fight invisible enemies. The eponymous "passerby" turns his back against the past and forges a new path with his bloody feet, in spite of being told that all that lies ahead is a field of graves. Allusions to bloodshed linked to political events of the time creep with increasing urgency into the last two pieces, both written after the March 18 incident, which deeply affected Lu Xun. It is also accompanied by a faint hope in the possibility of a few to inspire change. In the penultimate piece, "Amid the Pale Bloodstains," a rebellious fighter—who "sees clearly through all the ruins and desolate graves" and "remembers all the intense and endless agony, and looks squarely at all the accumulated layers of congealed blood"—rises "to either revitalize or destroy humankind."

The collection begins with "Autumn Night" and ends with "Awakening." This last piece may signal Lu Xun's own self-conscious "awakening" from the dreamy world of *Wild Grass,* as he assumes the role of a transitional writer paving the way for the next generation. The essay opens with the sounds of hovering airplanes on bombing missions, alluding to the warlord infighting in Beijing where Lu Xun resided at the time. He writes: "I often feel a slight anxiety, as if I were witnessing the onslaught of 'death,' yet, at the same time, I also feel intensely the very presence of 'life' itself." As he edits the manuscripts submitted by young writers, "the souls of these unpretentious youths rose up . . . one after another," invigorating him. "Troubled, moaning, and outraged" by the social inequities before them, "their souls have been beaten coarse by the assault of sandstorms . . . I am more than willing to kiss this invisible, colorless coarseness that is dripping with blood."

Out of the blue, a splendid garden scene appears before him: "Exotic flowers are in full-bloom, serene, rosy-cheeked girls frolic about at leisure without care. A crane cries out, lush white clouds float up en masse. . . . All this, naturally, is mesmerizing." The suffering, outrage, and courage of the youths, however, pulls him back to reality, and Lu Xun writes: "But I never forget for a moment that I am living in the human realm."

Eileen J. Cheng

Preface to the
English Translation of
Wild Grass (1932)

《野草》英文譯本序

Through a friend, Mr. Y. S. Feng sent his English translation of *Wild Grass* for me to look at and asked me to say a few words about it.[32] A pity that I don't know English, so all I can do is just say a few words. I hope, however, that the translator will not fault me for complying with only half of what he had hoped for.

These twenty or so short prose pieces, as noted at the end of each one, were written in Beijing between 1924 and 1926 and published

---

First published in Lu Xun's essay collection in *Two Hearts* (*Er xin ji,* 1932). Lu Xun, *Lu Xun quanji* (Complete works of Lu Xun), 18 vols. (Beijing: Renmin wenxue, 2005), 4:365–366.

The English translation of *Wild Grass* for which this preface was written was never published. The manuscript had been submitted to the Commercial Press but was destroyed when the press was bombed by the Japanese in the Battle of Shanghai on January 28, 1932 (see *LXQJ* 4:366n1). The pieces Lu Xun cites in this preface are mostly written in the "realist" vein, which may have reflected more his literary sensibilities at the time he wrote it—as a leading voice of the League of Left-Wing Writers and a promoter of proletarian literature.

successively in the journal *Threads of Talk*. They are, for the most part, little more than impromptu reflections. Since it was difficult to say things directly at the time, the wording is sometimes rather ambiguous.

Now to point out a few examples: I wrote "My Lost Love" to satirize the poems on failed love affairs in fashion at the time; I wrote part one of "Revenge" because I detested the large numbers of by-standers in our society; astonished by the passivity of our youths, I wrote "Hope." "Such a Fighter" reflected my attitude toward those writers and scholars who supported the warlords; "The Preserved Leaf" was written for those who loved me and wanted to protect me. After the Duan Qirui government gunned down an unarmed crowd, I wrote "Amid the Pale Bloodstains"; at the time, I had already gone into hiding at another location. When the Fengtian and Zhili warlord factions were at war, I wrote "An Awakening," and from then on, I could no longer reside in Beijing.

So, one can say that these are mostly small, pale white blossoms blooming on the edges of an abandoned hell, so of course one can't expect them to be beautiful.

But this hell must also be eradicated—this was conveyed to me by the demeanor and voices of a few ruthless and eloquent heroes whose ambitions have yet to be realized. And so I wrote "The Good Hell That Was Lost."

Later on, I no longer wrote such things. In times when things are changing daily, such writings, and even such thoughts, are no longer allowed to exist. I think this may perhaps be for the better. This preface to the English translation should conclude here as well.

November 5, 1931

Figure 2. Cover illustration of *Yecao* (Wild grass), designed by Sun Fuxi. Reproduced from *Lu Xun sanwen ji: Yecao* (Lu Xun's collected essays: *Wild Grass*) (Shanghai: Shanghai wenyi chubanshe, Shanghai Lu Xun jinianguan, 1990).

Inscriptions

題辭

When I am silent, I feel replenished; as I open my mouth, I sense emptiness.

My past life has met its demise. From its demise, I derive great joy,[33] because from this I know it once existed. The life that has passed has rotted away. From its rotting, I derive great joy, because from this I know that this life was not empty.

The mud of life dumped on the ground. Trees do not grow from it, only wild grass. For this, I am to blame.

Wild grass—its roots are not deep, its flowers and leaves not beautiful. Yet it absorbs dew, water, and flesh and blood of old corpses, robbing each of its existence. Still, while alive, it is trampled on and hacked off until it dies and rots away.

But I'm at ease, joyful. I will laugh, I will sing.

I take pride in my wild grass, but I detest the ground they adorn.

First published in issue 138 of *Threads of Talk* (*Yusi*) on July 2, 1927. Lu Xun, *Lu Xun quanji* (Complete works of Lu Xun), 18 vols. (Beijing: Renmin wenxue, 2005), 2:163–165. The preface was removed on the seventh printing of the volume in 1931 due to censorship but included in subsequent editions of *Wild Grass* published after 1941.

Fires surge and churn underground. Once the molten lava erupts through the surface, it will burn up all the wild grass and trees, so there will be nothing left to rot.

But I'm at ease, joyful. I will laugh, I will sing.

How quiet and solemn heaven and earth are, I'm unable to laugh and sing. Even if heaven and earth weren't so quiet and solemn, perhaps I still wouldn't be able to laugh and sing. In the interstices of light and darkness, life and death, past and future, I offer this clump of wild grass as a testament—to my friends and foes, humans and beasts, those whom I love and those whom I do not.

For my own sake and for the sake of my friends and foes, humans and beasts, those whom I love and those whom I do not, I hope the demise and rotting away of these wild grasses come swiftly. Otherwise, I will not have lived, something even more unfortunate than their demise and rotting away.

Away with you, wild grass, along with my inscriptions!

April 26, 1927, written at the White Cloud Pavilion in Guangzhou

Autumn Night

秋夜

Beyond the wall of my backyard, you can see two trees. One is a jujube tree, and the other is also a jujube tree.

The night sky above them is odd and high. I have never seen a sky this odd and high in my life. It is as if he wanted to part from the human world so that people would no longer see him when they lift up their faces. But for now, he is exceedingly blue, blinking his dozens of sparkling star-eyes, looking on coldly. The edges of his mouth reveal traces of a knowing smile as he scatters a thick layer of frost on the grasses and wildflowers in my yard.

I don't know the actual names of those grasses and wildflowers or what people call them. I recall a certain kind that had tiny pink flowers, one still blooming now, but even tinier than before. In the cold night air, she shivers as she dreams—dreaming of the arrival of spring, dreaming of the arrival of autumn, dreaming of a skinny poet wiping his tears off her last petals and telling her that though autumn will come and though winter will come, afterward, spring will still follow,

First published in issue 3 of *Threads of Talk* (*Yusi*) on December 1, 1924. Lu Xun, *Lu Xun quanji* (Complete works of Lu Xun), 18 vols. (Beijing: Renmin wenxue, 2005), 2:166–168.

as butterflies flit about and honey bees hum songs of spring once again. And so she smiles, though crimson from the cold and still shivering.

The jujube trees—they have just about lost all their leaves. Previously, one or two children would still come to strike them, but now not a single jujube remains, and even the leaves have all fallen off. The tree knows of the dreams of the tiny pink flower—that after the autumn will come spring. He also knows the dreams of the fallen leaves—that after spring will still be autumn. His leaves have just about all fallen off and though only branches remain, they are comfortably stretched out, no longer arched as they had been when the tree was full with fruit and foliage. But a few remaining branches are drooping, protecting the wounds on the trunk sustained from the sticks used to strike off the jujubes. A few of the longest and straightest branches quietly, like iron rods, pierce the odd and high sky, making the sky blink his sinister eyes. They pierce the full round moon in the sky, making the moon blanch in embarrassment.

The sky, blinking his sinister eyes, turns an even more intense blue and feels more ill at ease. It is as if he wanted to part from the human world, to avoid the jujube trees, leaving only the moon behind. But the moon, too, has stealthily hidden itself in the east. With nothing left to them, the branches still quietly, like iron rods, pierce the odd and high sky, intent on dealing him a fatal blow, no matter how the sky flashes his many seductive eyes.

"*Wa!*" a cry—an inauspicious bird on its night roam flies by.

I suddenly hear laughter in the middle of the night, muffled, as if afraid of rousing those asleep—yet the air from all around echoes in laughter. It is the middle of the night and no one else is around. I immediately make out this sound is inside my mouth, and chased by the sound of this laughter, I immediately retreat to my room. I quickly turn up the wick of the lamp.

The glass pane of the back window *dings* as numerous flying insects recklessly crash into it. Not long after, a few make their way in, probably through the holes in the paper screen. Once they are in, the glass lamp chimney, too, starts to *ding* as they crash into it. One charges in from above and encounters the flame, and I believed at the time that the flame was real. Two or three rest on the paper lampshade, taking a breather. The shade had been newly changed the night before. The snow-white paper had been pleated into a wavelike pattern, and painted on one of its corners is a sprig of scarlet gardenias.

When the scarlet gardenias bloom, the jujube trees, their green stalks curving into arcs, will again dream their tiny pink flower dreams. . . . Again I hear the midnight laughter. I hastily set my own mood aside to look at the little green bugs, dead on the white paper lampshade. Big heads with little tails like sunflower seeds, their bodies—only half the size of a wheat kernel—an adorable, pitiful green.

I let out a yawn, light a cigarette, and blow out a puff of smoke. Facing the lamp, I silently pay tribute to these exquisite emerald heroes.

September 15, 1924

The Shadow's Farewell

影的告別

When you sleep until you have lost all sense of time, then your shadow will come to bid farewell, saying those words—

Things that displease me are in Heaven—I don't want to go there. Things that displease me are in Hell—I don't want to go there. Things that displease me are in that future golden world of yours—I don't want to go there.

It is you, though, that displease me.

Friend, I don't want to follow you anymore, I don't want to stay. I don't want to!

Alas, alas, I don't want to, I would rather wander in the void.

I am a mere shadow, I want to leave you and sink into darkness. Yet the darkness will swallow me, and the light will make me vanish.

But I don't want to wander between darkness and light, I would rather sink into darkness.

Yet I end up wandering between darkness and light, I don't know if it's dusk or dawn. For now, I will raise my ashen hand, pretending

First published in issue 4 of *Threads of Talk* (*Yusi*) on December 8, 1924. Lu Xun, *Lu Xun quanji* (Complete works of Lu Xun), 18 vols. (Beijing: Renmin wenxue, 2005), 2:169–170.

to drink a cup of wine. When I have lost all sense of time, I will go far away on a solitary journey.

Alas, alas, if it were dusk, the darkness of the evening would naturally come to submerge me—or else I would vanish in the daylight, if it were now dawn.

Friend, the time is near.

I will wander in darkness in the void.

You are still expecting a gift from me. What can I give you? Nothing, just more of the same darkness and emptiness. But I wish it were mere darkness, which might vanish in your daylight; I wish it were mere emptiness, which would not occupy space in your heart.

I want it to be like this, friend—

I go far away on a solitary journey, to the darkness where neither you nor any other shadows exist. Only when I am submerged in darkness will that world be entirely mine.

September 24, 1924

The Alms Seeker

求乞者

I walk alongside the tall, dilapidated wall, treading on loose dust. A few other people are walking on their own. A light breeze stirs. The unwithered leaves on the branches of the tall trees hanging over the wall sway above my head.

A light breeze stirs, dust all around.

A child seeks alms from me. He, too, is wearing a lined jacket and doesn't look to be in a particularly sorry state. He kowtows as he blocks my way and wails pitifully as he chases me.

I despise his tone of voice and attitude. I loathe the fact that he isn't miserable—it's almost as if he was playing a game. I am annoyed by his pitiful wails as he chases me.

I walk on. A few other people are walking on their own. A light breeze stirs, dust all around.

A child seeks alms from me. He, too, is wearing a lined jacket and doesn't look to be in a particularly sorry state. But he is dumb and gesturing with palms outstretched.

First published in issue 4 of *Threads of Talk* (*Yusi*) on December 8, 1924. Lu Xun, *Lu Xun quanji* (Complete works of Lu Xun), 18 vols. (Beijing: Renmin wenxue, 2005), 2:171–172.

I particularly loathe this gesturing of his. And maybe he isn't dumb at all, and it's all a mere ploy for seeking alms.

I don't give him alms. I don't have a charitable heart. But I am superior to the almsgivers—I give the alms seeker annoyance, suspicion, and hatred.

I walk alongside the collapsed mud wall, broken bricks piled in the gaps, nothing in the walls. A light breeze stirs, the autumn chill penetrates my lined jacket, dust all around.

I consider how I will seek alms: If I utter cries, what tone of voice should I use? If feigning dumb, what gestures should I use? . . .

A few other people are walking on their own.

I will receive no alms and encounter no charitable hearts. I will receive in return annoyance, suspicion, and hatred from those who deem themselves superior to the almsgivers.

I will seek alms by doing nothing and through silence! . . .

I will at least receive emptiness.

A light breeze stirs, dust all around. A few other people are walking on their own.

Dust, dust . . .

. . .

Dust . . .

September 24, 1924

My Lost Love

我的失戀

—A new doggerel in the ancient style[34]　　— 擬古的新打油詩

The one I love lives on a hillside;　　我的所愛在山腰；
long to seek her, but it's far too high,　　想去尋她山太高，
lower my head, at a loss, tears dampen
　　my robe.　　低頭無法淚沾袍。

My love bestows me a butterfly scarf;　　愛人贈我百蝶巾；
what shall I give in return: an owl.　　回她什麼：貓頭鷹。
She thence turns on me and pays me
　　no heed.　　從此翻臉不理我，
Wherefore? It alarms me so.　　不知何故兮使我心驚。

The one I love lives in a bustling street;　　我的所愛在鬧市；
long to seek her, but it's packed
　　with crowds,　　想去尋她人擁擠，
raise my head, at a loss, tears dampen
　　my ears.　　仰頭無法淚沾耳。

First published in issue 4 of *Threads of Talk* (*Yusi*) on December 8, 1924. Lu Xun, *Lu Xun quanji* (Complete works of Lu Xun), 18 vols. (Beijing: Renmin wenxue, 2005), 2:171–172.

My love bestows me a double
    swallow portrait;
what shall I give in return: candied haws.
She thence turns on me and pays me
    no heed.
Wherefore? It confuses me so.

The one I love lives by a riverside;
long to seek her, but the waters are deep,
cock my head, at a loss, tears dampen
    my lapels.

My love bestows me a gold watch chain;
what shall I give in return: cold medicine.
She thence turns on me and pays me
    no heed.
Wherefore? It unnerves me so.

The one I love lives in a mansion;
long to seek her, but I have no car,
shake my head, at a loss, tears pour forth.

My love bestows me a bouquet of roses:
what shall I give in return: a red-banded
    snake.
She thence turns on me and pays me no
    heed.
Wherefore?—Oh, just let her go.

愛人贈我雙燕圖；
回她什麼：冰糖壺盧。

從此翻臉不理我，
不知何故兮使我糊塗。

我的所愛在河濱；
想去尋她河水深，

歪頭無法淚沾襟。

愛人贈我金表索；
回她什麼：發汗藥。

從此翻臉不理我，
不知何故兮使我神經衰弱

我的所愛在豪家；
想去尋她兮沒有汽車，
搖頭無法淚如麻。

愛人贈我玫瑰花；

回她什麼：赤練蛇[3]。

從此翻臉不理我。
不知何故兮——由她去罷。

October 3, 1924

Revenge

復仇

Human skin is probably not even half a millimeter thick. Hot crimson blood, pulsing underneath, courses through blood vessels even more tightly packed than the dense swarms of inchworms crawling up the garden wall, radiating warmth. People then seduce, excite, and attract one another with this warmth, giving their all in hopes of acquiring intimacy, kisses, and embraces, so they can experience the intoxicating joy of life.

But with a mere thrust of a sharp blade, one can cut through this thin, peach-colored layer of skin and see the hot crimson blood spurt out swift as an arrow, immediately bathing the murderer in all its warmth. Then, the expiring of icy-cold breath and the sight of pale white lips would induce the murderer into a trancelike state as he experiences the transcendent, ultimate joy of life. The victim, himself, is immersed in this transcendent, ultimate joy of life for eternity.

Thus, the two of them with their bare-naked bodies, each gripping sharp blades, face off against each other in the vast wasteland.

First published in issue 7 of *Threads of Talk* (*Yusi*) on December 29, 1924. Lu Xun, *Lu Xun quanji* (Complete works of Lu Xun), 18 vols. (Beijing: Renmin wenxue, 2005), 2:176–177.

The two of them on the verge of embracing, on the verge of slaughtering one another . . .

Passersby rush over from all around, in dense swarms, like inchworms crawling up the wall, like ants carrying a piece of salted fish head. They are decked out in smart clothes but empty-handed. Yet they rush over from all around, craning their necks to relish the spectacle of this embrace or slaughter. They are already anticipating the fresh taste of sweat or blood on their tongues to follow.

But the two of them remain facing each other, in the vast wasteland, their bare-naked bodies, each gripping sharp blades. They neither embrace nor slaughter one another and show no signs of embracing or slaughtering one another either.

The two of them remain this way until eternity, their supple bodies already on the verge of withering, yet showing no signs of embracing or slaughtering one another whatsoever. So the passersby get bored. They feel boredom seep into every pore of their bodies, feel the boredom seep from their hearts and out through every pore, creeping over the vast wasteland and seeping into the pores of others. Then their throats and tongues feel parched, their necks tired. Finally, they look at one another and slowly wander off, feeling withered to the point of losing all interest in life.

So then only the vast wasteland is left. And the two of them with their bare-naked bodies, each gripping sharp blades, remain standing, their bodies withered. Their corpselike gazes relish looking at the withered bodies of the passersby, relish this bloodless slaughter, both immersed in the transcendent, ultimate joy of life for eternity.

December 20, 1924

Revenge (II)

復仇（其二）

He believed himself to be the son of God, the king of the Israelites, so he went to be crucified.

Soldiers dressed him in a purple robe, set a crown of thorns on his head, and saluted him. And they lashed his head with a stick of reed, spat on him, and then knelt and worshipped him. The mocking over, they stripped off the purple robe and left him wearing his own clothes as before.

See how they lashed his head, spat on him, worshipped him . . .

He was unwilling to drink the wine mixed with myrrh. He wanted to savor, with a clear head, how the Israelites treated the son of their God, to prolong the time he could pity their future and hate their present.

All around was hostility—to be pitied, to be damned.

Ding, ding, the sharp tip of each nail pierced into his palms. Ah, that these pitiful, accursed people were going to crucify the son of their God—this eased his pain. *Ding, ding,* the sharp tip of each nail

First published in issue 3 of *Threads of Talk (Yusi)* on December 1, 1924. Lu Xun, *Lu Xun quanji* (Complete works of Lu Xun), 18 vols. (Beijing: Renmin wenxue, 2005), 2:178–180.

pierced into the soles of his feet, crushing one of the bones, the pain penetrating to the marrow. Yet, that these accursed people are killing the son of their very own of God—this soothed his pain.

The cross was erected—there he hung in the void.

He didn't drink the wine mixed with myrrh. He wanted to savor, with a clear head, how the Israelites treated the son of their God, to prolong the time he could pity their future and hate their present.

The passersby insulted and cursed him; the head priests and the scribes, too, tormented him. Even the two thieves crucified along with him sneered at him.

See, even those crucified along with him . . .

All around was hostility—to be pitied, to be damned.

As he felt the pain in his hands and feet, he savored the tragedy of these pitiful people crucifying the son of God as well as the joy of the son of God about to be crucified by these accursed people.

Suddenly, the intense pain of his broken bones shot through him to the marrow, and he was intoxicated with great joy and great compassion.

His abdomen quivered with waves of pain from the pity and the curses.

All around was darkness.

"Eloi, Eloi, lama sabachthani?" (which translates as: My God, my God, why hast thou forsaken me?)

God had forsaken him so, in the end, he was still a "son of man" after all—but the Israelites crucified even this "son of man."

The blood-soaked stains and bloody stench on the bodies of those crucifying the "son of man" reeked far more than those crucifying the "son of God."

December 20, 1924

Hope

希望

My heart feels exceptionally lonely.

Yet my heart is at peace: no love nor hate, no joy nor sorrow. No color nor sound either.

I have probably grown old. My hair is already white—isn't this a plain fact? My hands shake—isn't this a plain fact? Then my soul's hands must also be shaking; its hair must also be white.

Yet this was many years ago.

Before this, my heart was once filled with voices singing gory songs—blood and iron, flames and poison, regeneration and revenge. Then suddenly, all of these things emptied out. But at times, I would deliberately fill the void with a futile, self-deceptive hope. Hope, hope, I used this shield of hope to resist the onslaught of the dark night of emptiness, even though behind this shield was still the dark night of emptiness. And even so, my youth gradually wasted away.

Did I not, long ago, know that my youth had already slipped away? But I believed that the youthful vitality outside my body still

First published in issue 10 of *Threads of Talk* (*Yusi*) on January 19, 1925. Lu Xun, *Lu Xun quanji* (Complete works of Lu Xun), 18 vols. (Beijing: Renmin wenxue, 2005), 2:181–184.

existed: the stars, the moonlight, the fallen butterfly corpses, flowers in the dark, the owls' inauspicious calling, the cuckoo bird's spitting of blood, indistinct laughter, the dance of love in the air . . . even though these signs of youth are forlorn and nebulous, they still represent youth nonetheless.

But why am I so lonely now? Is it the case that even this youthful vitality outside my body has slipped away, and that most of the world's young people have grown old and feeble?

Then it is up to me to wrestle with this dark night of emptiness. I lay down the shield of hope and hear Petőfi Sándor's (1823–49) song of "Hope":

> What is hope? A whore:
> she seduces everyone and gives all away,
> When you have squandered many treasures—
> your youth—she then abandons you.

Seventy-five years have passed since this great lyric poet and Hungarian patriot died on a Cossack soldier's sharp spear for his ancestral homeland. Tragic indeed was his death, but even more tragic is that his poetry still hasn't died to this day.

But, wretched life! One as rebellious and brave as Petőfi had to, in the end, halt his tracks before the dark night and turn around to gaze back at the distant Orient. He said:

Despair, like hope, is a delusion.

If I still have to drag out an ignoble existence by means of this "delusion" that is neither light nor dark, then I would still want to go in search of that forlorn and nebulous youth that has slipped away, outside my body though it may be. Because once this youth outside me is extinguished, then the twilight years within me will also wither away.

Yet, at present, there are no stars and no moon, no fallen butterfly corpses, no indistinct laughter or dance of love in the air. And yet the young people are all at peace.

Then it is up to me to wrestle with this dark night of emptiness. Even if I'm unable to locate the youthful vitality outside my body, at least I will strike out at the twilight years within me. Yet where is the dark night now? At present, there are no stars and no moon, not even indistinct laughter nor the dance of love in the air. Yet the young people are all at peace, and before me there is not, it would seem, even an actual dark night.

Despair, like hope, is a delusion.

January 1925

Snow

雪

Rain in the temperate south never turns into hard, icy, glistening snowflakes. Well-informed people find it monotonous; perhaps the rain, too, finds it unfortunate? Snow in the Jiangnan region is exquisitely moist and beautiful—it is the vague hint of spring; it is the skin of a healthy young maiden. In this snowy wilderness, there are blood-red camellias, white plum blossoms with single-layered petals tinged with green, and dark yellow, bowl-shaped wintersweet blossoms. Beneath the snow are clumps of cold, green weeds. There are certainly no butterflies; whether honeybees come to suck nectar from the camellias or plum blossoms, I can't quite recall. But before my eyes now, amid the winter flowers blooming in the snowy wilderness, I can seemingly make out many honeybees flying about to and fro and hear them buzzing noisily.

The children are breathing on their little fingers, red from the cold, like purplish baby ginger. Seven or eight of them have gathered

First published in issue 11 of *Threads of Talk* (*Yusi*) on January 26, 1925. Lu Xun, *Lu Xun quanji* (Complete works of Lu Xun), 18 vols. (Beijing: Renmin wenxue, 2005), 2:185–186. Lu Xun here is reminiscing about the snowy days of his childhood as he writes about winter in "the north"—referring to Beijing, where he was residing at the time.

to make a snow arhat.[35] They are unsuccessful, so one of the fathers has come to help. The arhat they build is much taller than the children, though nothing more than a small mound piled on top of a larger mound and hard to make out whether it's a gourd or an arhat in the end. But it is spotlessly white and gorgeous. The moist snow holds its shape and the entire figure glistens luminously. The children use longan seeds to make eyeballs and someone had stolen lip rouge from one of their mother's cosmetics boxes to paint on the lips. So *this* time, it's a big arhat for real. And there it sits, with sparkling eyes and scarlet lips, on the snow-covered ground.

The following day, a few children still come to visit him, clapping their hands, bowing to him, and laughing with glee. But eventually, he is left sitting all alone. The sunny days come and melt his skin, and the cold nights coat him in a layer of ice, transforming him into an opaque crystal. A succession of sunny days turns him into something unrecognizable and the lip rouge on his mouth also fades completely.

In the north, however, the snowflakes, after swirling about, never stick together. Like powder or sand, they scatter on the rooftops, the ground, and the withered grass—just as it is now. Some of the snow on the rooftops has long vanished from the warmth of the fires lit by the homes' inhabitants. Under the clear sky, a whirlwind suddenly descends and the rest of the flakes flutter about vigorously. They sparkle and glisten in the sunlight, like a thick mist enshrouding a flame, swirling, rising, and filling up the whole sky—making the sky glisten as it swirls and rises.

In the boundless wilderness, in the bitter cold universe, glistening as it swirls and rises, is the spirit of the rain . . .

Indeed, it is the lonely snow, the dead rain, the spirit of the rain.

January 18, 1925

The Kite

風箏

The winter season in Beijing—the ground still covered in snow, bare, ashen tree branches forming Y-shaped forks in the clear sunny sky, a few kites fluttering in the distance—leaves me in awe and dejected.

Kite season in my hometown is in the early spring, in February. Raise your head when you hear the *sha sha* sound of the kite reels turning and you might see a greyish crab kite or a powder-blue centipede kite. Or a lonely tile-shaped kite without a reel, flying low, all by itself, looking frail and pitiful. Yet by this time, the willows on the ground will have already sprouted, and the wild peach trees will have already emitted early buds—and all this, harmonizing with the childrens' decorations in the sky, create a portrait of the warmth of spring. But where am I at present? I am surrounded by the harshness of bitter winter, yet the hometown I had bid farewell to and the spring that had slipped away so long ago have begun rippling in this sky.

First published in issue 12 of *Threads of Talk* (*Yusi*) on February 2, 1925. Lu Xun, *Lu Xun quanji* (Complete works of Lu Xun), 18 vols. (Beijing: Renmin wenxue, 2005), 2:187–189.

But I was never fond of flying kites. Not only was I not fond of it, in fact, I detested kites, considering them playthings for good-for-nothing kids. My younger brother was just the opposite. He was probably around ten years old at the time, sickly and skinny beyond measure, and most fond of kites. Since he couldn't afford to buy one and I had forbidden him from flying one, all he could do was stare blankly at the sky in wonder, sometimes for hours on end, his little mouth agape. If a crab kite in the distance suddenly descended, he would cry out in alarm. If two entangled tile kites broke free, he would jump up and down with glee. This behavior of his was, in my eyes, foolish and despicable.

One day, it suddenly struck me that I hadn't seen much of him for several days. Then I recalled spotting him in the backyard gathering dried bamboo stalks. A thought dawned on me, and I ran to the rarely visited storage shed and pushed the door open. As expected, I discovered him among the dusty objects there. He was sitting on a small stool, facing a big square bench. He then stood up in a panic, turned pale, and cowered in fear. Propped against the big square bench was the bamboo frame of a butterfly kite, the paper yet to be pasted on. On the bench was pair of kite reels for the butterfly eyes, decorated with red paper strips, the job just about completed. Pleased with uncovering his secret, I was also furious that he had deceived me, surreptitiously and painstakingly devoting himself to making playthings for good-for-nothing kids. I immediately reached out and broke off one of the butterfly's wings, then threw the kite reels on the floor and trampled them flat. When it came to age and physical strength, he was no match for me. So of course I achieved total victory, then strutted out proudly, leaving him standing despondently in the shed. How he was afterward, I neither knew nor cared.

But my comeuppance finally came, long after we had parted ways—when I was already middle-aged. I had the misfortune of coming across a foreign book on the subject of children quite by chance—only then did I learn that playing games is the most appropriate activity for children and that toys are like angels to them. And so this scene of childhood psychological abuse that I had never given a thought to for the last twenty years suddenly unfolded before my eyes. It was as if my heart had transformed into a piece of lead, which sank of its own great weight.

Though my heart sank, it didn't break—it merely sank and sank of its own great weight.

I knew how to make it up to him though: give him a kite, approve of him flying it, encourage him to fly it, fly it together with him. We would shout, run, and laugh—yet by this time he, like me, had long since grown a beard.

I knew of another way to make it up to him: seek his forgiveness, then wait for him to say: "I don't hold it against you in the least." Then my heart would surely feel lighter—this was indeed a workable plan. On one occasion when we met—our faces then already carved with numerous wrinkles betokening the hardships of life—my heart was heavy. We gradually began broaching the subject of old childhood memories, and I recounted this episode, attributing it to my youthful muddle-headedness. "I don't hold it against you in the least," I thought he would say, and so I would be forgiven immediately, and my heart would feel lighter from then on.

"This actually happened?" he said with a surprised laugh, as if hearing a story about someone else. He didn't remember a thing about it.

Forgotten completely, no resentment whatsoever—what, then, was there to forgive? Forgiveness in the absence of resentment is nothing but a lie.

What was there left to hope for? My heart would have to go on sinking under its own great weight.

Now, the spring in my hometown has resurfaced in the air of this alien locale—presenting me memories of a childhood long gone yet also bringing along a sorrow I can't quite get a grip on. Better just hide myself in the harshness of the bitter winter—but now here I am, clearly besieged by the bitter winter, imparting its utterly formidable coldness.

January 24, 1925

Story of Good Things

好的故事

The lamp flame gradually dwindled, indicating that not much kerosene remained. The kerosene wasn't the old trusted brand, and its smoke had long left dark stains on the glass chimney. The sound of exploding firecrackers reverberated all around, and tobacco smoke surrounded me. It was a murky night.

I closed my eyes and leaned against the back of the chair. My hands, gripping a copy of *A Primer for the Beginning Learner,* rested on my knees.

In the haze, I saw a story of good things.

This story is at once beautiful, refined, and captivating. Numerous beautiful people and beautiful events are weaving into one another like a tapestry of clouds in the sky, flying by like a myriad of shooting stars, as the scene unfolds and stretches out into infinity.

I seem to recall riding a small boat past an ancient road. Things on both sides of the bank—the tallow trees, newly sprouted grain, wildflowers, chickens, dogs, bushes and withered trees, thatched huts,

First published in issue 13 of *Threads of Talk* (*Yusi*) on February 9, 1925. Lu Xun, *Lu Xun quanji* (Complete works of Lu Xun), 18 vols. (Beijing: Renmin wenxue, 2005), 2:190–192.

pagodas, monasteries, farmers and peasant women, peasant girls, clothes hung out to dry, monks, straw hats, the sky, clouds, and bamboo—are reflected in the clear turquoise stream; their images sway along with the duckweed and the swimming fish, shimmering as the rays of the sun strike them with each dip of the oar. All these things and their reflections scatter, sway, expand, and merge into one other. Once merged, they shrink back and then revert to a semblance of their original form. The ragged edges of the reflections merge into one another like summer clouds rimmed by sunlight flashing quicksilver flames. All the rivers I cross are like this.

The story I see now is like this as well. With the blue sky reflected in the water as a backdrop, all the things are intermingling and weaving into one another and into one expanse, forever vibrant, forever expanding, no end in sight.

The few thin stalks of hollyhock underneath the wilting willow tree by the stream must have been planted by the village girls. Bright red and red-speckled flowers floating about in the water suddenly scatter and lengthen out like long strands of lip rouge, but without any smudging. The thatched huts, the dogs, the pagodas, the peasant girls, the clouds . . . all are floating about. The bright red flowers, once lengthened, turn into vigorously flowing red silk sashes. The sashes weave into the dogs, the dogs into the white clouds, the white clouds weave into the peasant girls . . . in a split second, they shrink back again. But the reflection of the red-speckled flowers has already scattered and lengthened and is about to weave into the pagodas, the peasant girls, the dogs, the thatched huts, and the clouds.

The story I see now comes into focus: beautiful, refined, captivating, and now, distinct. In the clear blue sky are countless beautiful people and beautiful events, I see each and every one of them, I know each and every one of them.

I am about to fix my gaze on them all . . .

Just as I am about to fix my gaze on them all, I am suddenly jolted awake and as I open my eyes, the cloud tapestry becomes wrinkled and disarrayed, as if someone had thrown a big rock into the river water. The ripples suddenly rise up, tearing the whole expansive reflection to shreds. Reflexively, I hastily grab on to the copy of *A Primer for the Beginning Learner* that almost drops to the floor, some shattered shards of rainbow-colored reflections still remaining before my eyes.

I'm really fond of this story of good things, and I want to chase after the shards of shattered reflections while they remain, to make the image whole and preserve it. I toss the book aside, lean forward, and reach my hand out to grab a pen. But not a shard of the shattered reflection remains, and all I see is the dim lamplight. I am no longer in the small boat.

But I always remember seeing this story of good things on that murky night . . .

February 24, 1925[36]

The Passerby

過客

Time: Dusk on a certain day

Setting: A certain place

Characters:

OLD MAN—about seventy years old, white hair and beard, in a long black robe.

GIRL—about ten years old, jet-black hair, black eyes, in a long, black-and-white checkered gown.

PASSERBY—between thirty and forty years old with a troubled and uncompromising appearance, a somber gaze, black mustache, disheveled hair; his short black jacket and pants are in tatters, bare feet in worn out shoes. A sack hangs from his arm, and he is supported by a bamboo cane as tall as he is.

To the east are a few trees and broken tiles; to the west is a desolate, downtrodden mass graveyard. In between are tracks of what appears

First published in issue 17 of *Threads of Talk* (*Yusi*) on March 9, 1925. Lu Xun, *Lu Xun quanji* (Complete works of Lu Xun), 18 vols. (Beijing: Renmin wenxue, 2005), 2:193–199.

to be, but may not actually be, a path. The door of a small mud hut
opens out to these tracks. Beside the door is a dead tree stump.

(*The GIRL is about to help the OLD MAN sitting on the*
tree stump get up.)

OLD MAN: Child. Hey, child! How come you stopped?

GIRL: (*looking to the east*) There's someone walking toward
us—have a look.

OLD MAN: No need to look at him. Help me inside. The
sun is about to set.

GIRL: I . . . want to have a look.

OLD MAN: Ay, child! Every day you see the sky, the earth, the
wind. Aren't these things beautiful enough? Nothing is as
beautiful as these things, yet you insist on seeing whoever
it is that's coming. Things that appear after sunset won't do
you any good . . . why don't we just go inside?

GIRL: But he's already come so close to us. Ah, it's a beggar.

OLD MAN: A beggar? Unlikely.

(*From the east, a PASSERBY hobbles out from among the trees. After*
hesitating for a moment, he slowly walks toward the OLD MAN.)

PASSERBY: Sir, how are you this evening?

OLD MAN: Ah, fine! Luck is with us. How are you?

PASSERBY: Sir, I'm sorry to impose, may I ask you for a cup
of water? I'm so thirsty from walking, and there is neither
pond nor puddle around here.

OLD MAN: Oh, yes, yes. Please have a seat. (*To the GIRL*)
Child, fetch some water and make sure the cup is clean
(*the GIRL silently walks into the mud hut*).

OLD MAN: Sir, please have a seat. How may I address you?

PASSERBY: Address me? I don't know. For as long as I can
     remember, I have been all on my own, so I don't know
     what my name is. Along my journey, people address me
     as they please, by all sorts of names I can no longer recall
     clearly. Not to mention that I've never heard myself called
     by the same name twice.

OLD MAN: Ah, ah. Then where are you from?

PASSERBY: *(hesitates slightly)* I don't know. For as long as I
     can remember, I have been walking like this.

OLD MAN: Right. Then, may I ask you where you are going?

PASSERBY: Of course. But I don't know. For as long as I can
     remember, I have been walking like this, walking to a cer-
     tain place, a place that lies just ahead. The only thing I
     remember is that I have been walking a long way and now
     I have arrived at this spot. I will keep going that way
     (pointing west), up ahead!

*(The GIRL comes out, carefully carrying a wooden cup in both hands
and hands it to him)*

PASSERBY: *(takes the cup)* Many thanks, young lady *(drinks the
     water in two gulps and returns the cup)*. Many thanks, young
     lady. This is truly a kindness rarely seen. I really can't
     thank you enough!

OLD MAN: You shouldn't feel such gratitude. It won't do
     you any good.

PASSERBY: Indeed, it won't do me any good. But I have re-
     covered some strength now, and I will be on my way. Sir,
     you probably have been living here for quite some time,
     do you know what lies ahead?

OLD MAN: Ahead? Graves are ahead.

PASSERBY: (*surprised*) Graves?

GIRL: No, no, no. There are all sorts of wild lilies and wild roses there—I often go there to play and have a look at them.

PASSERBY: (*looks to the west, appears to be smiling*) That's right. Those places have all sorts of wild white lilies and wild roses—I have often gone there to play and have a look at them as well. But they're graves (*faces the OLD MAN*). Sir, what lies ahead after you walk to the end of the graveyard?

OLD MAN: After you walk to the end of the graveyard? That I don't know. I've never gone there.

PASSERBY: You don't know?

GIRL: I don't know either.

OLD MAN: I only know what's to the south and to the north, and to the east, which was the way you came. That's the place I'm most familiar with and perhaps the best place for those like you. Please don't mind my saying so, but in my opinion you are already exhausted, so why don't you just turn around, since even if you proceed, there's no guarantee that you'll be able to walk to the end.

PASSERBY: No guarantee that I can walk to the end? . . . (*in deep thought, suddenly startled*). That's not possible! I just have to keep on going. If I go back, there is no place where things don't have names, no place without landlords, no place without eviction and entrapment, no place without superficial smiles and crocodile tears. I detest them all, I won't turn back.

OLD MAN: That isn't necessarily so. You may still encounter genuine tears from the depths of people's hearts and from those who feel compassion for you.

PASSERBY: No, I don't want to see tears from the depths of their hearts. I don't want them to feel compassion for me.

OLD MAN: In that case, then, you (*shaking his head*) have no choice but to go on.

PASSERBY: Yes, I have no choice but to go on. Not to mention that there is also a voice ahead of me that urges me on, beckons me, so I'm unable to rest. A pity that my feet have long been worn out from walking—they are covered with blisters and have been bleeding profusely (*raises his foot to show the OLD MAN*). So I no longer have enough blood; I need to drink some blood. But where is blood to be found? I don't want to drink just anybody's blood, either. So all I can do is drink some water to supplement my blood. There has always been water to be found along the way, so I haven't really felt a lack. It's just that I'm physically too weak right now, possibly because there's too much water in my blood. Today I didn't encounter so much as a small puddle, which is probably why I have walked less than usual.

OLD MAN: That's not necessarily so. The sun is setting—why don't you have yourself a little rest, like me?

PASSERBY: But the voice up ahead is telling me to go on.

OLD MAN: I know.

PASSERBY: You know? You know that voice?

OLD MAN: Yes, it seems to have called out to me in the past as well.

PASSERBY: Is it the same voice that's calling me now?

OLD MAN: That I don't know. It called out to me only a few times, and I ignored it, so it stopped calling, and so now I don't recall it very clearly anymore.

PASSERBY: Oh, you ignored it . . . (*in deep thought, suddenly startled, listens attentively*). No! It's better that I go on. I can't rest. How abominable that my feet have long been worn out from walking (*preparing to walk*).

GIRL: For you! (*passes over a piece of cloth*) To wrap your blisters.

PASSERBY: Thank you (*takes the cloth*), young lady. This truly is . . . this truly is a kindness rarely seen. This will allow me to walk a longer distance (*sits down on the broken bricks, about to bind the cloth on his ankle*). But, no! (*struggling to get up*). Young lady, I'm returning it to you, it's too small for binding. Not to mention that I have no way of repaying such excessive kindness.

OLD MAN: You shouldn't feel such gratitude. It will do you no good.

PASSERBY: Indeed, this will do me no good. But to me, there's nothing more precious than this act of charity. Look, is there anything on me that can compare to this?

OLD MAN: You shouldn't take it so seriously.

PASSERBY: Indeed, but I can't help myself. I'm afraid this is what will happen to me: if I receive someone's charity, I might become like a vulture who upon seeing a corpse, hovers over it, wishing to see its destruction with my very own eyes; or perhaps I might curse everything, wishing everything other than the corpse to be destroyed, myself included, because I deserve to be cursed. But I don't possess that much strength, and even if I did, I wouldn't wish for the corpse to have such a fate, because it probably wouldn't wish for such a fate. This is as it should be. (*To the GIRL*) Young lady, this piece of cloth of yours is really fine, but it's a little small. I'm returning it to you.

GIRL: (*startled, retreats*) I don't want it anymore! You take it with you!

PASSERBY: (*appearing to laugh*) Oh, oh . . . is it because I've held it?

GIRL: (*nods, points to his pocket*) You can put it in there and take it with you when you go play.

PASSERBY: (*retreats dejectedly*) But carrying this burden on me, how can I walk?

OLD MAN: You haven't been able to rest, so you aren't able to carry it. Rest a while and it'll be fine.

PASSERBY: Right, rest . . . (*reflecting, suddenly startled, listens carefully*) No, I can't! It's best that I keep going.

OLD MAN: You still don't want to rest?

PASSERBY: I'd like to rest.

OLD MAN: Then you should rest a little while.

PASSERBY: But I can't . . .

OLD MAN: You still feel it's better to keep going after all?

PASSERBY: That's right. It's better to keep going.

OLD MAN: Well then you'd best go on.

PASSERBY (*stretching from his waist*): All right, then I will take my leave. I'm very grateful to you both. (*To the GIRL*) Young lady, I'm returning this to you—please take it back.

(*The GIRL, frightened, draws back her hands and is about to duck into the mud hut.*)

OLD MAN: Take it with you. If it gets too heavy, you can just throw it away in the graveyard.

GIRL (*steps forward*): Oh, no, that won't do!

PASSERBY: Oh, no, that won't do!

OLD MAN: Well, then just hang it on a wild lily or wild rose.

GIRL (*claps hands*): Ha ha! Good idea!

OLD MAN: Oh, oh . . .

(*silence for a moment*)

OLD MAN: Well, farewell then. I wish you peace. (*stands up, turns toward the GIRL*) Child, help me inside. Look, the sun has long set (*turns around toward the door*).

PASSERBY: Thanks to you both. Peace to you both (*pacing back and forth in deep thought, suddenly taken by surprise*). But I can't! I must go on. I best be on my way . . . (*raises his head, walks resolutely toward the west*).

The GIRL helps the OLD MAN into the mud hut and immediately shuts the door. The PASSERBY hobbles into the wilderness, the dark night trailing behind him.

March 2, 1925

Dead Fire

死火

I dreamed of myself sprinting on an ice-mountain.

It is a tall, imposing ice-mountain, reaching up to the icy sky. The sky is filled with frozen clouds, each shimmering like a fish scale. At the foot of the mountain is an ice-forest, branches and leaves of its trees resembling pine and cypress. All is icy cold, all is ash white.

But all of a sudden, I fall into a valley of ice.

Above, below, all around is icy cold and ash white. But on the ash white ice are countless red shadows, tangled together like a web of corals. I look down under my feet—a flame is there.

It is a dead fire. Fiery in form but immobile, it is completely frozen, like a coral branch. On the tip of the flame is a puff of congealed black smoke, its charred and withered appearance leading me to suspect that it had just been released from the inferno of existence. And so, the flame's reflections on the surrounding walls of ice reflect back on one another, transforming into innumerable shadows, turning the valley of ice into a coral red.

Ha ha!

First published in issue 25 of *Threads of Talk* (*Yusi*) on May 4, 1925. Lu Xun, *Lu Xun quanji* (Complete works of Lu Xun), 18 vols. (Beijing: Renmin wenxue, 2005), 2:200–202.

When I was a child, I was fond of gazing at the foamy waves stirred up by motorboats and the fiery flames shooting up from blazing furnaces. Not only was I fond of gazing at them, I also wanted to see them clearly. Alas, they were ever-changing, never keeping a fixed form. No matter how intently I stared, I could never retain a fixed image.

Dead flame, I finally have you now!

I pick up the dead fire. As I am about to examine it closely, its icy cold burns my fingers. But I simply endure the pain and stuff it into my pocket. In an instant, the entire valley of ice turns ash white. At the same time, I think about how to get out of the valley of ice.

A stream of black smoke shoots out from my body, coiling up like a collared reed snake. In an instant, the entire valley of ice is engulfed in surging red flames, like a great conflagration hemming me in. I look down—the dead fire, now ignited, burns a hole through my robe and flows out onto the icy ground.

"Hey, friend! You awakened me with your warmth," he says.

I greet him immediately and ask his name.

"I was first abandoned in the valley of ice," he replies off-topic. "Those who abandoned me have long perished and gone. I was nearly frozen to death by the ice. If you hadn't reignited me with your warmth, I would have perished before too long."

"Your awakening pleases me. I was just thinking about how to get out of the valley of ice. I'd like to bring you along so that you never have to freeze again and so you can burn on for eternity."

"Oh, no! Then I'll burn out!"

"Your burning out would make me sad, so I'll just leave you here then."

"Oh, no! Then I'll freeze to death!"

"Then, what's to be done?"

"But what about you, what will you do then?" he asks back.

"As I've said: I want to get out of this valley of ice . . ."

"Then I might as well burn out!"

All of a sudden, he shoots up like a red comet and we both leave the valley of ice. A large stone cart speeds over unexpectedly and I am, in the end, crushed to death under its wheels—but not before seeing the cart tumble into the valley of ice.

"*Ha ha!* None of you will come across the dead fire ever again!" I said with a smug laugh, as if this were just what I wanted.

April 23, 1925

The Dog's Retort

狗的駁詰

I dreamed of myself walking along a narrow alley, clothes tattered, like a beggar.

A dog starts barking from behind.

I look back with contempt and curse:

"*Hey!* Shut up! You snooty mutt!"

"*Hee hee!*" he laughs, then says: "Not at all—I'm ashamed that I'm no match for humans in that regard."

"What!?" I'm outraged, feeling this the greatest of insults.

"I'm ashamed that I still can't tell copper from silver, still can't tell officials from ordinary citizens, still can't tell masters from slaves, still can't tell . . ."

I flee.

"Wait! Let's talk some more . . ." From behind, he loudly urges me to stay.

I keep on running, fleeing as fast as I can until I have fled the dreamscape and am lying in my own bed.

April 23, 1925

First published in issue 25 of *Threads of Talk* (*Yusi*) on May 4, 1925. Lu Xun, *Lu Xun quanji* (Complete works of Lu Xun), 18 vols. (Beijing: Renmin wenxue, 2005), 2:203.

The Good Hell That Was Lost

失掉的好地獄

I dreamed of myself lying in a bed out in the frigid wilderness, right next to Hell. The uniformly low yet orderly moans of all the ghosts harmonize with the angry roars of the flames, the bubbling of the boiling oil, and the clanging of the iron pitchforks, creating an intoxicating symphony, as if proclaiming to all three realms: All is at peace down in Hell.

Before me stands a great man, handsome and compassionate, his whole body radiating light—but I know he is the Devil.

"Everything has come to an end, come to an end! The pathetic ghosts have lost their good Hell!" He cries indignantly, then sits down and recounts to me a story he knew of—

"When Heaven and Earth were the color of honey—that is, the time when the Devil had emerged victorious over God and wielded absolute power over all things—he had Heaven, the human world, and Hell under his domain. So he personally descended to Hell and sat in Hell's very center, his whole body radiating bright light, illuminating all the gathered ghosts.

First published in issue 32 of *Threads of Talk* (*Yusi*) on June 22, 1925. Lu Xun, *Lu Xun quanji* (Complete works of Lu Xun), 18 vols. (Beijing: Renmin wenxue, 2005), 2:204–206.

"Hell had fallen into neglect for a long time: the sword trees had lost their luster, the boiling oil had ceased to bubble at the edges, the great flames merely gave off a few puffs of pale smoke now and then. At a distance, the mandrake flowers were still blooming, though the blossoms were tiny and pathetically pale—and no wonder, since the ground had been thoroughly scorched by wildfires and was thus no longer fertile.

"The ghosts awakened in the midst of the cold oil and lukewarm fire, much seduced by the pathetic pale blossoms of Hell illuminated by the bright light radiating from the Devil. They suddenly recalled the human world, and after remaining in silent contemplation for who knows how many years, emitted a stentorian cry denouncing Hell to the human realm.

"Humankind then rose up in response, righteously speaking out and battling the Devil. Sounds of war far louder than thunder permeated the three realms. After deploying grand schemes and setting massive traps, the Devil was at last forced out of Hell. The final victory came when the flag of humankind was also erected over the gates of Hell!

"While the ghosts were still cheering, the emissary from the human realm who had come to set Hell in order had arrived and sat in the center of Hell and, assuming the dignified air of humankind, berated all the ghosts.

"By the time the ghosts emitted another stentorian cry denouncing Hell, they had come to be regarded as turncoats of humankind. Condemned to a life of eternal damnation, they were led to the center of the Sword Tree Forest.

"Humankind thus wielded absolute authority over Hell, their power even greater than that of the Devil. They put in order that which had fallen into neglect, first giving Ox-head Ah Pang the highest emolument of Grand Pasture. Moreover, they added fuel to the fire, sharpening Blade Mountain, completely changing Hell's appearance by washing it clean of its former decadent aura.

"The mandrake flowers withered at once. The oil bubbled as before, the blades were as sharp as before, and the fire as hot as before. All the ghosts groaned and thrashed about as before, so much so that they had no time to recall the good Hell that was lost.

"This is the success of humankind, the misfortune of the ghosts . . .

"You are suspicious of me, my friend. Indeed, you are human! I'm going to go seek out wild beasts and demons . . ."

June 16, 1925

Tombstone Inscriptions

墓碣文

I dreamed of myself facing a tombstone, reading the inscriptions carved on it.

The tombstone appears to be made of sandstone, crumbling at numerous spots and overgrown with moss. Only a few phrases remain:

> . . . *in a frenzy of boisterous singing catch a chill, in the skies see an abyss. In all eyes see a void, in no hope find redemption* . . .
> . . . *a wandering spirit transforms into a serpent, mouth with venomous fangs. Bites not others, but bites itself, dies in the end* . . .
> . . . *leave!*

I go around behind the tombstone—only then do I see a lone grave, bereft of vegetation and fallen into disrepair. Through a big crack, I glimpse a corpse, chest and abdomen completely caved in, no heart nor liver within. Yet the face shows no trace of joy or sorrow but is hazy, as if shrouded in smoke. In my apprehension, I turn

First published in issue 11 of *Threads of Talk* (*Yusi*) on June 22, 1925. Lu Xun, *Lu Xun quanji* (Complete works of Lu Xun), 18 vols. (Beijing: Renmin wenxue, 2005), 2:207–208.

around, but not before seeing the remaining phrases on the backside of the tombstone—

> . . . *gouge out my heart and eat it, wanting to know its true taste.*
> *The pain is so searing, how could I know its true taste?*
> . . . *as the pain subsides, slowly consume it. But the heart now*
> *old and stale, how could I know its true taste?* . . .
> . . . *answer me, or else leave!* . . .

I'm about to leave. But the corpse sits up in the grave. Its lips don't move, but says—

"When I turn to dust, you'll see my smile!"

I flee, dare not look back, terrified to see him in pursuit.

June 17, 1925

Tremors on the Border of Degradation

頹敗線的顫動

I dreamed of myself dreaming.

I don't know where I am, but before me is a night scene inside a small, tightly sealed cottage. Yet I can also see the forest of dense greenery on the rooftop.

The lamp chimney on the wooden table, freshly wiped, lights up the room, making it exceptionally bright. In the bright light, on the dilapidated bed, beneath the unfamiliar, hairy, burly lump of flesh is a thin, frail body, trembling from hunger, pain, shock, humiliation, and pleasure. The full figure's flaccid yet supple skin is smooth, both pale cheeks flushing lightly, like lip rouge coated on lead.

The lamp flame also shrinks back in fear as the east turns light.

Yet waves of pleasure, humiliation, pain, shock, and hunger still permeate and pulsate through the air.

First published in issue 35 of *Threads of Talk* (*Yusi*) on July 13, 1925. Lu Xun, *Lu Xun quanji* (Complete works of Lu Xun), 18 vols. (Beijing: Renmin wenxue, 2005), 2:178–180.

"Ma!" A girl about two years old—startled awake by the opening and shutting of the door—cries out from a corner of the room partitioned off by a straw mat.

"It's still early—sleep a little longer!" her mother says anxiously.

"Ma! I'm hungry and my stomach hurts. Is there anything we can eat today?"

"Yes, we have food today. When the griddle-cake seller comes around in a little while, Mama will buy you some." Gratified, she clutches the silver piece in her palm even more tightly, her soft, low voice trembling with dejection as she walks toward the corner of the room to look at her daughter. She moves the straw mat aside, picks up her daughter, and lays her on the dilapidated bed.

"It's still early—sleep a little longer." With no one to share her troubles, she raises her eyes to gaze at the sky above the dilapidated roof as she speaks.

Suddenly another huge wave billows up in the sky, colliding with the first, swirling and forming a vortex, engulfing everything in its path, including me. I can't breathe.

I wake up moaning. Outside the window, the whole sky is the silvery color of moonlight—dawn, it seems, is a long way away.

———

I don't know where I am, but before me is a night scene inside a small, tightly sealed cottage. I know it is a continuation of my earlier unfinished dream, except many years have elapsed. Both the interior and exterior of the cottage are now very tidy. Inside, a young couple and their flock of children, filled with hate and contempt, are confronting an old woman.

"We can't face the world, all because of you!" the man snarls. "You might feel like you brought her up, but in fact, you ruined her. She would have been better off had she starved to death as a child!"

"Made me suffer this whole lifetime—you!" the woman cries.

"And you had to drag me into this too!" the man cries.

"Oh, and you had to drag all of them into this too!" the woman cries, pointing to the children.

The youngest one, playing with a reed, brandishes it in the air like a sword right then and shouts:

"Kill!"

The corners of the old woman's mouth are twitching. In an instant, she goes into a daze then becomes tranquil; not long after, she calmly stands up, like an emaciated stone statue. She opens the door and walks out, striding out into the deep night, leaving the cold jeers and vicious laughter behind her.

She walks on far into the deep night, walks on until she reaches a vast, boundless wilderness. All around is wilderness, above her nothing but the high sky, where neither a single insect nor bird flies past. She is stark naked, standing in the middle of the wilderness like a stone statue. In a split second, her past flashes before her eyes—hunger, pain, shock, humiliation, pleasure, and then she trembles; inflicting suffering, misery, dragging in others, then she convulses; kill, then she becomes calm . . . then again, in an instant, everything blends together—devotion and estrangement, loving caresses and revenge, nurturance and annihilation, blessings and curses . . . she stretches out both hands toward to the sky, as a language half-human, half-beast, and not of this world, and thus without words, flows from her lips.

As she utters the wordless language, her entire body—like a once great and noble statue, now wasted and withered—trembles all over. Each tremble resembles a tiny fish scale, each scale undulating like water boiling over a blazing fire. The air grows turbulent in an instant, like roiling waves in a vast sea during a thunderstorm.

She then raises her eyes to the sky, and her wordless language breaks off into complete silence. Only the trembling radiates outward like the rays of the sun, instantly whirling around the waves in the sky, like a hurricane billowing in the boundless wilderness.

It was a nightmare, and I had felt something pressing me down—but even then, I knew it was my hands, which I had placed on my chest. In my dreams, I had used every ounce of my strength to move aside the weight of those heavy hands.

June 29, 1925

An Argument

立論

I dreamed of myself in an elementary school lecture hall—I was preparing a composition and consulting the teacher on how to make an argument.

"It's difficult!" The teacher looks at me, squinting through the rims of his glasses, and says: "Let me tell you a story.

"A certain family gave birth to a boy—the entire household was thrilled beyond measure. They brought him out to show guests when he was one month old—probably, as one would expect, in hopes of garnering some auspicious wishes.

"One said: 'This child will be rich in the future.' He then received thanks.

"One said: 'This child will be an official in the future.' He then received some compliments in return.

"One guest said: 'This child will die in the future.' He was then severely beaten by the entire family.

First published in issue 35 of *Threads of Talk* (*Yusi*) on July 13, 1925. Lu Xun, *Lu Xun quanji* (Complete works of Lu Xun), 18 vols. (Beijing: Renmin wenxue, 2005), 2:204–206, 212–213.

"That he will die is a certainty. That he will be rich and noble might be a lie. Yet, the liar is rewarded, and the one who states the truth suffers a beating. You . . ."

"I'd like to neither lie nor suffer a beating. What, then, should I say, teacher?"

"Well, then, you'd better say, '*Aiya!* Oh, this child! Just look at him! How . . . Oh my! *Ha ha! Hehe!*

"*He, hehehehe!*"[37]

July 8, 1925

After Death

死后

I dreamed of myself dead on a road.

Where this is, how I got here, how I died, I have no idea. At any rate, by the time I realize I am dead, I am already lying there dead.

I hear cries of magpies, followed by crows. The air is cool and refreshing—though there is a slight whiff of soil—it's probably dawn now. I try to open my eyes, but they won't budge, as if they didn't belong to me. Then, I try to raise my hand and the same thing happens.

A sharp jab of terror suddenly pierces my heart. While alive, I had speculated for the fun of it: if death were a matter of the motor nerves ceasing to function while one's consciousness remained intact, how much more horrifying that would be than being completely dead! Who would have known that my premonition would be spot-on and that I myself would now be living proof of it?

I hear footsteps, probably people walking on the street. A wheelbarrow pushes past my head. It's probably carrying a heavy load—the

First published in issue 36 of *Threads of Talk* (*Yusi*) on July 20, 1925. Lu Xun, *Lu Xun quanji* (Complete works of Lu Xun), 18 vols. (Beijing: Renmin wenxue, 2005), 2: 214–218.

clickety-clack sound it emits annoys me so, even making my teeth grate. I feel my eyes fill with crimson—the sun must have risen. My face, then, is facing east. But it doesn't really matter. I hear the sound of people's *chitter-chatter*—they have come to observe the spectacle. They kick up some dirt, which flies into my nostrils, making me want to sneeze—in the end, though, I don't. I merely feel the urge.

Once again the sound of footsteps, one after the other, all stopping nearby, then more murmuring. More spectators have gathered. I suddenly really want to hear their comments, but at the same time, I think about how all my talk when I was alive—about how criticism isn't worth a cent and the like—probably contradicted what I truly believed. Newly dead and exposed already. I listen anyway, but I didn't get the point in the end, as the gist is no more than this:

"Dead? . . ."

"Oh—uh . . ."

"*Hmmph!* . . ."

"*Tsk . . . Ay!* . . ."

I'm absolutely delighted because I haven't heard a single familiar voice this whole time. Otherwise, it would make them sad or glad or give them some gossip to add to their after-meal chats, wasting a lot of precious time—all of which would have made me feel very sorry indeed. Now, no one has seen me, so no one is affected. Good! It seems that I haven't let anyone down in the end.

But something, probably an ant, is climbing up my spine, making me itch. I can't move at all, so I can't get rid of it. Under normal circumstances, I could get it off by just twisting my body. And now, *another* one is climbing up my thigh! *What do you bugs think you're doing? Vermin!*

Things get even worse. With a buzz, a fly lands on my cheek, and after taking a few steps, it flies off again, opens its mouth, and licks the tip of my nose. Annoyed, I think: *My good fellow, I'm no great personage, no need for you to forage my corpse to find fodder for your commentaries*—but then I can't speak. It then runs down the bridge of my nose and licks my lips with the cold tip of its tongue. I don't know if this is an expression of affection or not. Then a few others congregate on my eyebrows, shaking the root of each hair with every step they take. So unbearably annoying to me—so utterly unbearable.

Suddenly, a gust of wind blows and something from above covers me. They all fly off together and before departing, even say—

"What a shame! . . ."

I almost pass out from rage.

A heavy *thud* and vibrations from the ground as wood is thrown onto the earth suddenly awakens me. I feel the patterned weave of the reed mat pressing against my forehead. But when the reed mat is lifted off, I immediately feel the heat of the sun's rays again. And I hear someone saying—

"Why did he have to die here? . . ."

The voice sounds close to me—he must be bending over me. But then, just where *should* one die? I used to think that though people may not have the right to live as they please on this earth, at least they have the right to die as they please. Now I know this isn't the case and how hard it is to satisfy the will of the public. A shame that it has been some time since I have had paper or pen, but even if I did, I still wouldn't be able to write, and even if I could, there would be nowhere to publish. Better to just cast aside such thoughts.

Someone comes to lift me up. I don't know who it is. I hear the sound of a knife being removed from its sheath, so probably the police are here as well, this *here* that I wasn't supposed to have died at. My body is turned over several times, then I feel myself lifted up and set down again. I hear the sound of something being covered and nails being hammered. But, strangely, only two nails. Is it the case that only two nails are used to seal a coffin here?

I think: *Hemmed in by six walls and nailed down from the outside. What utter defeat—alas, how pathetic!*

It's stuffy in here! . . . I think.

Yet I am actually much calmer than before, though I don't know whether I have been buried or not. Against the back of my hand I feel the patterned weave of the straw mat and think that this corpse-mat isn't so bad after all. A pity that I don't know who spent the money on me! But how despicable, the punks who put my body in the coffin! A corner of the back of my shirt is wrinkled, and they didn't smooth it out. Now pressing down against it is making me most uncomfortable. Things handled so carelessly, just because you think the dead are completely unaware? *Ha ha!*

My body seems much heavier than when I was alive, so it's extremely uncomfortable when it presses down against the crease of my shirt. But I think: *I'll get used to it before long; or, as my corpse is about to rot, it won't be such a bother anymore. So it's just best to calmly contemplate things for the moment . . .*

"Hello, sir? Are you dead?"

It is quite a familiar voice. When I open my eyes to look, it is the young clerk from the *Boguzhai* rare bookshop. It has probably been more than twenty years since I last saw him, but he still looks the same. I also look at the six-sided walls around me—much too crude and shabby, no finish work done to them at all, the sawn edges still rough.

"No worries, no problem at all," he says, unwrapping the dark-blue cloth bundle. "Here is a Ming edition of the *Gongyang* commentary. It's the Jiajing imprint and I've come to deliver it to you. Please keep it. This is . . ."

You! I fix on his eyes with astonishment and say. *Are you really such an idiot? Look at my present state, would I still be reading a Ming edition or any other for that matter?*

"Have a look, no worries."

I immediately shut my eyes because I'm more than a little annoyed at him. There's a pause and no sound, so he's probably left. But then an ant climbs up my neck and finally up my face, circling my eyes.

I never imagined that a person's thinking can still change after death. But just then, some force shatters my inner calm; at the same time, a profusion of dreams appears before my eyes. A few friends wish me peace, while a few enemies wish me ruin. Yet, I just keep on muddling on, neither at peace nor ruined, failing to live up to the expectations of either side. Now I have died off like a shadow, unbeknownst even to my enemies—I'm unwilling to give them an ounce of pleasure, even if doing so wouldn't cost me a thing . . .

I feel like I am about to cry out with joy. This is probably my first cry after death. But in the end, no tears come. All I see is a momentary flash before my eyes and then I sit up.

July 12, 1925

Such a Fighter

這樣的戰士

We need such a fighter—

Not a fighter as benighted as an African aborigine carrying a snow-bright Mauser rifle. Not one as weary as a soldier of the Chinese Green Banners bearing a pistol.[38] He doesn't rely on any armor—whether made of leather or scrap iron—for protection. He has only himself and a spear, like those wielded and thrown by barbarians.

He walks into an empty battle formation. Everyone he meets nods at him in the same manner. He knows that this nod is the enemy's weapon—a weapon that kills without bloodshed.

Many fighters have perished under it—like an artillery shell, it renders the brave warriors powerless.

Above those heads hang all sorts of banners, embroidered with all sorts of fine-sounding titles: philanthropist, scholar, litterateur, elder, youth, dandy, gentleman . . . Beneath are all sorts of outerwear, embroidered with all sorts of fancy decorations: scholarship, morality, national essence, will of the people, logic, justice, Oriental civilization . . .

First published in issue 58 of *Threads of Talk* (*Yusi*) on December 21, 1925. Lu Xun, *Lu Xun quanji* (Complete works of Lu Xun), 18 vols. (Beijing: Renmin wenxue, 2005), 2:219–220.

Yet he raises his spear.

They raise their voices in unison, swearing that their hearts are located in the center of their chests, unlike those whose hearts are off to one side. Breastplates are placed in front of their chests to protect their hearts, serving as proof of their conviction that their hearts are located in the center of their chests.

Yet he raises his spear.

He smiles, and aiming to one side, hurls his spear and pierces directly into their hearts.

Everything collapses and falls to the ground, leaving only outerwear that has nothing inside of it. Emptiness has fled victoriously because it has now become the offender, guilty of killing off the philanthropists and their ilk.

Yet he raises his spear.

He takes big strides into the empty battle formation and again encounters the same nods, all sorts of banners, all sorts of outerwear . . .

Yet he raises his spear.

In the end, he finally grows old and feeble, and dies in the empty battle formation. In the end, he is not a fighter, but emptiness is the victor.

In such a realm, nobody hears the battle cry: Peace.

Peace . . .

Yet he raises his spear!

December 14, 1925

The Clever Man, the Fool, and the Slave

聰明人和傻子和奴才

The Slave wants nothing more than to find someone to vent his sorrows to. This is all he wants, and this is all he can do. One day he meets a Clever Man.

"Sir!" he says sadly, his tears forming a single line as they stream from the corners of his eyes. "As you know, the life I lead is not fit for a human. I can't count on a single meal a day. Even if I have one, it may be nothing more than sorghum husks that even dogs and pigs won't eat—and just a small bowl of it at that . . ."

"This really is pathetic," the Clever Man says, also in a dejected manner.

"Isn't it so!" He brightens up. "And the work—there's no rest night or day. At dawn I fetch water and at night I cook. Mornings I run errands and evenings grind the grain. When it's sunny I wash the clothes, and when it's rainy I raise an umbrella. In the winter I keep the furnace burning and in the summer wave a fan. In the middle of

First published in issue 60 of *Threads of Talk* (*Yusi*) on January 4, 1926. Lu Xun, *Lu Xun quanji* (Complete works of Lu Xun), 18 vols. (Beijing: Renmin wenxue, 2005), 2:221–223.

the night I stew snow fungus and serve the master when he's gambling—I never get a share of the winnings, and sometimes I even get whipped.

"*Ay, ay* . . ." the Clever Man sighs, the rims of his eyes reddening slightly, as if about to shed tears.

"Sir! I can't put up with this any longer. I have to find some way out, but what way is there? . . ."

"I think things will get better for you . . ."

"Is that so? If only it were so. But having vented my sorrows to you, sir, and gained your sympathy and solace, I'm now feeling much better. So there is justice in the world after all . . ."

But after a few days, he feels aggrieved again and, as before, goes in search of someone to vent his sorrows to.

"Sir!" he says, tears streaming from his eyes. "As you know, the place I live in is worse than a pigsty. My master doesn't treat me like a human being. He treats his lapdog thousands of times better."

"The bastard!" the person cries out, surprising the Slave. This person is a Fool.

"Sir, I live in a small dilapidated shack, damp and dark, swarming with bedbugs. When I sleep, I'm bitten all over. The foul stench assails my nose, and there's not a window in any of the walls . . ."

"Why don't you have your master put a window in?"

"How is that possible? . . ."

"Then take me there to see it!"

The Fool follows the Slave to his shack and starts smashing the mud wall with his hands.

"Sir! What are you doing?" the Slave exclaims in shock.

"I'm smashing a hole to make a window for you."

"You can't do that! The Master will berate me!"

"Forget him!" The Fool continues smashing.

"Somebody come help! A robber is destroying our shack! Come quickly! If you don't come right away, he will smash a hole right through it! . . ." He cries and screams as he rolls around on the ground.

A group of slaves come out and drive the Fool away.

Hearing the shouting, the last one to slowly make his way out is the Master.

"There was a robber who came to destroy our shed. I was the first one to raise a cry, then all of us drove him away together," he said respectfully and with a note of triumph.

"You did well," the Master praised him.

That day, many people came to express their sympathy, the Clever Man among them.

"Sir, this time, because I performed a great service, the Master praised me. Earlier, you said that things would get better for me—you really showed foresight . . ." he says happily, looking as if he were full of hope.

"Isn't it so . . ." the Clever Man replies, seeming pleased for him.

December 26, 1925

The Preserved Leaf

蠟葉

Reading *Collected Poems from Goose Gate* under lamplight, I suddenly come across a dried maple leaf pressed between the pages.

This makes me recall a particular day in late autumn last year. A heavy frost had descended the night before, most of the tree leaves had fallen and scattered about, and the small maple tree in the courtyard had also turned red. I paced around and about the tree, carefully examining the leaves' colors, having never paid them such attention when they were still a lush green. Not all the leaves had turned red—most were simply a pale crimson, while a few still showed dark green patches against a scarlet background. A lone leaf had a small hole bored through by a bug, and the rim of the hole had turned black. Surrounded by the motley of red, green, and yellow, it looked like the bright pupil of a staring eye. I thought to myself: This is a blighted leaf! So I picked it off and wedged it between the pages of my newly purchased *Collected Poems*. I probably wanted to preserve this mottled, decayed leaf that was on the verge of falling for a little longer, so that it wouldn't be scattered with all the rest.

First published in issue 60 of *Threads of Talk* (*Yusi*) on January 4, 1926. Lu Xun, *Lu Xun quanji* (Complete works of Lu Xun), 18 vols. (Beijing: Renmin wenxue, 2005), 2:224–225.

Yet on this particular night, it lies before my eyes, yellowed and waxen, that pupil no longer glistening as it had the year before. I'm afraid that in a few more years, when the original color vanishes from memory, I will also have forgotten the reason why it was wedged in the book in the first place. It seems that the riot of colors on that blighted leaf, right on the verge of falling—and still a verdant green at that—could only have been encountered in that brief moment. When I look out the window, even the trees most tolerant of the bitter cold have long been stripped of their leaves, let alone the maple tree. In late autumn, I imagine there must have been blighted leaves like this one that I picked last year, but a pity that I didn't have the leisure to admire the autumn colors this year.

December 26, 1925

Amid the Pale Bloodstains

淡淡的血痕中

—Commemorating a few of the dead, the living, and the yet
to be born

The present Creator is still a coward.

He stealthily transforms Heaven and Earth, yet dares not destroy
this world. He stealthily makes all living things wither and die, yet
dares not preserve their corpses for long. He stealthily makes people
shed blood, yet dares not let the bloodstains retain their fresh color.
He stealthily makes humankind suffer, yet dares not let people remember their suffering forever.

He considers only the needs of those like him—the cowards and
weaklings among humankind—in his designs. He uses ruins and desolate graves to accentuate the grand mansions; he uses time to dilute
the pain and bloodstains. Each day he pours out a cup of slightly
sweetened bitter wine and gives it to humankind—not too much, not

First published in issue 75 of *Threads of Talk* (*Yusi*) on April 19, 1926. Lu Xun, *Lu Xun
quanji* (Complete works of Lu Xun), 18 vols. (Beijing: Renmin wenxue, 2005), 2:226–227.

too little, just the right amount to slightly intoxicate, so that the imbibers can still cry and sing, so that they seem at once sober and drunk, knowledgeable yet ignorant, wanting to die, yet also wanting to live. He has to make sure that all beings want to keep on living—he still lacks the courage to completely destroy humankind.

A few ruins and desolate graves scattered over the earth are reflected in the pale bloodstains. In the midst of it, the people are savoring a faint sense of sorrow, their own and that of others. But they are unwilling to cast it aside, believing it is, after all, better than emptiness. Each one refers to himself as "a person punished by heaven" to justify their ruminating over that faint sense of sorrow—their own and that of others. They are suffocating, quietly fearing the arrival of new sorrows. The newness terrifies them, yet also makes them thirst for an encounter.

These are the good citizens of the Creator. This is how he needs them to be.

A rebellious warrior has arisen among humankind. He stands erect, sees clearly through all the ruins and desolate graves—those already transformed and those existing in their original state. He remembers all the intense and endless agony and looks squarely at all the accumulated layers of congealed blood. He has a deep understanding of all that is dead, living, and yet to be born. He sees through the Creator's tricks. He will rise up, either to revive or destroy humankind—these good citizens of the Creator.

The Creator, the weak coward, ashamed, hides himself. And so, the countenance of Heaven and Earth, in the eyes of the warrior, transforms.

April 8, 1926

Awakening

一覺

Planes on bombing missions, as if following a school day routine, fly overhead every morning in Beijing. Each time I hear their engines cleaving the air, I sense a kind of slight anxiety, as if I were witnessing the onslaught of "death." Yet at the same time, I also feel intensely the very presence of "life" itself.

After the faint sounds of an explosion here and there, the planes emit a *whirring* drone and eventually fly off. There may well have been casualties, yet all under heaven seems more peaceful than before. Outside the window, the new leaves of the white poplar trees shimmer a deep gold in the sunlight, and the flowering plum blooms even more radiantly than the day before. After I tidy up the newspapers strewn all over the bed and wipe off the pale dust that had gathered on the desk since the previous night, my small, square study is now spick and span as before.

For some reason, I start editing the manuscripts of young writers that have been accumulating in my possession for some time now.

First published in issue 11 of *Threads of Talk* (*Yusi*) on April 10, 1926. Lu Xun, *Lu Xun quanji* (Complete works of Lu Xun), 18 vols. (Beijing: Renmin wenxue, 2005), 2:228–231.

I would like to put them all in order once and for all. As I read them in order of submission, the souls of these unpretentious youths rise up before me, one after another. They are remarkable and pure—*ah,* yet they are troubled, moaning, and outraged, and have, in the end, become coarsened, these lovable youths of mine.

Their souls have been beaten coarse by the assault of sandstorms, but I love them because they are human souls. I am more than willing to kiss this invisible, colorless coarseness that is dripping with blood. In a dimly perceptible scene in a splendid garden, exotic flowers are in full bloom, serene, rosy-cheeked girls frolic about at leisure without care. A crane cries out, lush white clouds float up en masse . . . All this, naturally, is mesmerizing, but I never forget for a moment that I am living in the human realm.

All of a sudden, I recall a certain incident: two or three years ago at Peking University, I saw a young man whom I didn't know enter the instructors' common room. He handed a package of books to me and then left without a word; when I opened it, I saw it was a copy of the journal *Shallow Grass.* Amid the silence, I was able to gather much meaning. And *ah,* how rich this gift! A pity that *Shallow Grass* is no longer published, it seems that it had merely served as a precursor to the journal *Sunken Bell.* And in the endless expanse of blowing sand, the *Sunken Bell* tolls on all by itself, resonating within the depths of this sea of humanity.

I recall that Tolstoy wrote a short story after being profoundly moved by the sight of a thistle, which bore a single flower even after having been all but plucked to death. But when plants desperately extend their roots down into the arid desert, to absorb water from springs deep in the recesses of the earth to form an emerald forest, they do so instinctively as a means of survival. Yet the sight makes the parched and weary traveler rejoice at having found a place to rest for a short time, something that at once inspires such gratitude and sorrow!?

"Without a Title" in the *Sunken Bell*—which serves in lieu of an introduction—reads: "Some say that our society is like a swath of desert. Were it really a desert, though desolate, it is tranquil nonetheless; though a little lonely it may feel, it can nonetheless impart upon you a sense of the boundless. Oh, why must it seem so chaotic, so gloomy, so fantastically mutable!"

Indeed, the souls of these youths tower before my very eyes— they have already been coarsened up, or are about to be coarsened up. Yet I love these bleeding and silently suffering souls, because they make me feel that this is a human world, and that we are living in this human world.

As I am editing the manuscripts, the sun sets in the west, but the light from the lamp allows me to continue. All kinds of signs of youth and vitality flash before my eyes, one after another, though everything around me is shrouded in dusk. Exhausted, I hold a cigarette between my fingers. Amid unnameable thoughts, my eyes close quietly, and I see a long dream. I wake with a start, everything still shrouded in dusk. The hazy smoke rises up into the stagnant air like small summer clouds, slowly transforming into indescribable shapes.

April 10, 1926

Figure 3. Lu Xun in Shanghai, March 6, 1928. Reproduced from *Lu Xun wenxian tu zhuan* (Illustrated biography and documents of Lu Xun) (Zhengzhou: Daxiang chubanshe, 1998), 144.

Morning Blossoms Gathered at Dusk

Figure 4. Cover illustration of *Zhao hua xi shi* (Morning blossoms gathered at dusk), designed by Tao Yuanqing. Reproduced from *Lu Xun sanwen ji: Zhao hua xi shi* (Lu Xun's collected essays: *Morning Blossoms Gathered at Dusk*) (Shanghai: Shanghai wenyi chubanshe, Shanghai Lu Xun jinianguan, 1990).

Vulnerable Subjects

Translator's Introduction to
Morning Blossoms Gathered at Dusk

Longing for my love in the morning	朝亦有所思
Longing for my love at dusk	暮亦有所思
Ascending the tower, gazing toward you	登樓望君處
Lush, lush, floating clouds fly by	藹藹浮雲飛.
Floating clouds cover Yang Pass	浮雲遮卻陽關道
At nightfall, who knows what I hold in my bosom	向晚誰知妾懷抱
Jade well, green moss, in the spring courtyard corner	玉井蒼苔春院深
Fallen Paulownia blossoms on the ground, unswept	桐花落地無人掃
"Longing for My Love"	有所思
by Liu Yun	劉雲

In contrast to the strength and resilience of wild grass, flowers are often associated with beauty, fragility, and vulnerability in classical Chinese poetry. Radiant blossoms might symbolize feminine beauty. A fallen flower might represent an abandoned woman—alone, pining for her youth or a departed lover—or serve as a reminder of the ephemerality of life. In the tradition of literary transvestism, male poets would adopt a feminine voice and persona to represent their own vulnerability or politically marginalized status.[1]

The title and cover image of Lu Xun's (1881–1936) memoir, *Morning Blossoms Gathered at Dusk* (*Zhao hua xi shi*, 1928) (Figure 4), ostensibly draws on these classical allusions. The cover features a woman dressed in flowing robes wandering in a private garden. Both cover and title evoke a state of quietude and a feeling of nostalgia, conjuring up an image of a lone poet reflecting on the passage of youth and / or reminiscing on more idyllic times. Yet, if the home is imagined to be a place of warm affective ties and a repository of fond childhood memories, *Morning Blossoms* does not quite live up to expectations. While warm recollections surface here and there, the memoir depicts a childhood and adolescence marked by disappointment. "Morning blossoms gathered at dusk"—whether a literal reference to fallen flowers, an allusion to the marginalized status of the narrator or other characters in the memoir, or a comment on the anachronistic paradox of recalling memories from the past in the present—confronts an uncomfortable truth of existence: of living itself as an experience of disillusion, displacement, and being without a home in the world.

Nostalgia without a Home

The ten pieces in *Morning Blossoms Gathered at Dusk,* written within a nine-month period in 1926, were first serialized in the journal *Wilderness Monthly* (*Mangyuan yuekan*). Each piece was originally titled "Recollecting Old Matters" (Jiu shi chong ti), followed by a number indicating their sequence in the series. The preface was completed in 1927, and the volume published under the new title *Morning Blossoms Gathered at Dusk* the following year.[2]

Lu Xun wrote *Morning Blossoms* in his mid-forties. Some critics have read his memoir as a writer's retreat into a private garden of memories when political realities became too grim. Indeed, in the preface to the volume, Lu Xun conveys a sense of helplessness over the political circumstances and the itinerant life it forced upon him. Trivial pursuits such as admiring the miniature gardenia on his desk and editing manuscripts, he writes, "while akin to a living death," were nonetheless effective distractions. By extension, indulging in fond memories may provide comfort and solace during chaotic times. As Lu Xun writes: "For a period of time, I would frequently recall the fruits and vegetables that I ate as a child in my hometown: water chestnuts, broad beans, water bamboo shoots, musk melons—all so delectable and mouth-watering, they seduced me into a nostalgic yearning for home."

Yet, appearances are rarely so simple in Lu Xun's writings. Further reflection undermines his sense of nostalgia, as he writes later in the preface: "It was only afterward, on tasting them again long after my departure, that I found nothing remarkable; only in the realm of memory did the old flavors still linger. Perhaps they will keep on deluding me for a lifetime, constantly inducing me to look back to the past."

Lu Xun recognizes the seductive allure of "home," of remembrances that may reflect a yearning for a different time and place from the present rather than an accurate recollection of the past.[3] While not bereft of fond memories, *Morning Blossoms* actively resists the lure of nostalgia. In contrast to the poetic title and the idyllic image on the book cover, the memoir recounts a childhood and adolescence marked by suffering, loss, and death.

Why return to traumatic memories at a time when one desperately longs for "a bit of serenity amidst the chaos"? Clues might be found in the autobiographical preface to *Outcry* (1923), in which Lu Xun explains the reasons for the bleak tone of his first short story collection:

> When I was young, I, too, had many dreams, most of which I later forgot, but I see nothing in this to regret. While the thing called memory can fill one with delight, there are also, ineluctably, times when it makes one feel lonely. What is the point of tethering the loose threads of one's thoughts to those lonely bygone days? My agony, however, stems from being unable to forget completely; some of the things I am unable to forget completely have now become the source for *Outcry*.[4]

Writing short stories, Lu Xun suggests, serves as a creative outlet for working through painful memories neither fully processed nor forgotten.[5] A few of the life-defining events alluded to in the preface to *Outcry*—notably his father's illness and death and his decision to abandon his medical studies—are fleshed out in more detail in *Morning Blossoms*. Writing directly about traumatic memories may have been an attempt to escape their haunting presence and in turn, to break free of the patterns of thought and behavior conditioned by them.[6]

As Lu Xun writes in the foreword to *Morning Blossoms*, he needed time and distance to reflect more objectively on the episodes of his life and to engage in "merciless" dissection—of himself, his hometown, and society at large.[7] These self-reflections, like those of the protagonist of his first short story, "Diary of a Madman" (*Kuangren riji*, 1918), are also attempts to understand the world, to arrive at some deeper truths about self and society. Far more than a personal memoir, *Morning Blossoms* challenges traditional images of home and family and examines the effects of loss and trauma on both a personal and societal level. Anti-nostalgic in sentiment, among the questions it poses: What if "home" is not just a place of comfort, belonging, and warm affective ties, but also a site of abuse and dysfunction from which one wants to flee? What about those without a home? Can the "homeless" ever find a place where they belong in the world? As the lure of the home is dispelled, the narrator and we, as readers, confront an uncomfortable truth of existence: that living itself is an experience of disillusion, displacement, and being without a home in the world.

Memoir without a Subject

Morning Blossoms, which Lu Xun classifies as a creative work, is a series of experiments with form. A radically self-conscious and imaginative stylist, Lu Xun did not confine himself to the limits of genres. Well aware of the vagaries of memory and how the present mediates our remembrance of things past, he is not particularly concerned with factual accuracy. As he writes in the preface to his memoir, episodes "are transcribed from my memory and may deviate slightly from actual fact, but this is how I remember things now."

Rather, Lu Xun seems intent on experimenting with a new realm of literary expression as he explores the inner world of memories. The preface notes that "the forms of the essays probably appear as a mishmash," written as they were at different times and locales. Yet the assortment of forms and styles, which defy simple continuity and cohesion, well captures the messy, random, and subjective qualities of memories. A work about displacement, the memoir itself exploits the gaps in time and space as it reconstructs the narrator's sense of the past.[8] What are memories, after all, if not reminders of our own belatedness and perpetual dislocation—physically and temporally—from the episodes of our lives that we hope to recollect?

Like *Wild Grass, Morning Blossoms* questions a stable notion of the "I." Writing the memoir necessitates a kind of disembodiment and self-suspension, as the I-now stands outside of itself to narrate the experiences of an I-then. The narrative intrusions by the I-now vary in degrees (sometimes minimal, sometimes substantial), and may appear in the beginning, middle, or end of a piece or interspersed throughout. Similar to traditional biographies, the memoir frequently blurs the lines between fact and fiction. Experiences of the child or young adult recollected by the I-now are often accompanied by dramatized scenes and dialogue that unfold in real time. Threads of the past are interwoven with those of the present, with varying degrees of relevance, and at times in seemingly random ways. Some memories are hazy and fragmented, while others appear more distinct and complete. Trivial and mundane experiences—reading books, playing in the garden, boyhood pranks and antics—are interspersed with recollections of major life events—the father's illness and death, departure from one's hometown, study abroad in Japan, the death of a friend.

Each essay, which revolves around a certain episode in the narrator's life, functions as a stand-alone piece. The collection as a whole, sequenced more or less chronologically, has an internal order that loosely coheres. It traces the child's experiences growing up in an elite family and his young adult years, albeit with large gaps in between. The subject is not a moral exemplar, and the memoir is not a triumphant coming-of-age story. Rather, *Morning Blossoms* ends abruptly with the young adult subject struggling to navigate his way in a cruel and unjust world. The preface provides little closure or structure to frame the volume. The middle-aged writer of the preface presents himself as an aimless and itinerant writer in a state of arrested development, haunted by memories of his past as he faces an uncertain future.

Few autobiographical specifics about the subject are revealed—there are no descriptions of an illustrious clan, and the subject, parents, or other family members are seldom identified by given name. The locale of the hometown is not mentioned, no dates of events are given. No particularly distinctive features, personality traits, or talents of the subject stand out. The vignettes on childhood—reading and hearing folk tales and myths, exploring in the garden, playing at the neighbors, and navigating the complicated world of adult rules—revolve around interests and experiences that would have been familiar to children from elite families and do not appear particularly remarkable.

The plethora of seemingly trivial childhood experiences may seem lackluster to readers expecting to find clues or a riveting account that explains Lu Xun's path to literary greatness. As with his stories that have autobiographical overtones, the subject and the experiences depicted in the memoir, while bearing resemblances to the author's own, should not, as has often been the case, simply be equated to the life of Zhou Shuren per se. That the memoir is deliberately lacking in specificity and is marked by its ordinariness makes it all the more a universal story: it is a lament for the every-child—in particular, children whose inner curiosity, imagination, and affinity with the natural world are suffocated by their environment and upbringing. In its focus on the child's inner mind and life, *Morning Blossoms* stands in stark contrast to the Confucian depictions of children in elite biographies: the child, typically silent or spoken for, is given voice.

A World without Children

Early pieces in the memoir celebrate the figure of the child and offer readers a child's view of the world—albeit one filtered through the memory of the adult narrator.[9] Innocent and without guile, connected to nature and open to the divine, the child possesses an innate curiosity and expansive imagination.[10] The world in the child's eyes is one in which all beings, real and imagined, are interconnected, where human, fauna, and flora coexist and intermingle freely with a world of monsters, ghosts, and spirits. Left to his own devices, the child's impulse is to fully immerse himself in and engage this world of infinite possibilities, one of wonder, danger, and delight through sensorial, imaginative, and aesthetic experiences. His mind nourished by nature and a wide variety of oral folktales and storybooks, the boy is in turn inspired to create worlds of his own through imagination, play, and artistic pursuits.

Why this celebration of the child and the child's inner world?[11] *Morning Blossoms* harkens back to a discourse on the "childlike heart-mind" (*tongxin*, translated as "childlike heart" from here on), where the figure of the child is viewed as inherently good and in tune with nature. According to the Ming philosopher and iconoclast Li Zhi (1527–1602), whose works gained renewed interest in the 1920s, we should all strive to retain this pure childlike state. In his well-known treatise "On the Childlike Heart," he writes: "If the childlike heart is lost, then one loses sincerity; if sincerity is lost, then one loses the genuine person (*zhenren*)."[12] In other words, the childlike heart is what makes us human.

A central thread that runs through all of Lu Xun's works is the notion of "cultivating the human" (*liren*).[13] Sharing Li Zhi's celebration of the childlike heart and appealing for the cultivation of "genuine persons," Lu Xun's memoir offers a scathing attack on Confucian child-rearing and pedagogical practices as forms of dehumanization.[14] In Confucian thought, the family is the primary model of order. Filial piety is thus regarded as the key to maintaining harmonious relationships and order in the family, society, and the cosmos at large. *Morning Blossoms,* however, shows how the child's indoctrination in this "virtue" alienates him from his childlike mind as he is forced to submit unconditionally to familial rules and hierarchy at a tremendous psychic cost.

In *"The Illustrated Twenty-Four Filial Exemplars,"* the classic primer referred to in the title forms a stark contrast to the beloved monster tales that ignite the child's curiosity and imagination. Considered de rigueur in a child's moral education, the tales of filial sacrifice fill the young bibliophile with distaste and dread.[15] The boy finds stories such as "Old Lai Amusing His Parents," in which an old man acts like an infant to entertain his elderly parents, dull and contrived. The story's premise—that children should please their elders unconditionally, however fake and degradingly they have to behave—offends his sensibilities.

In other exemplar tales, the home and the family, far from safe havens, appear rife with danger and abuse. In "Guo Ju Buries His Son," a filial son buries his infant to ensure that his elderly mother has enough food to eat. After reading the story, the child is seized with fear as his parents argue over their limited resources. Anticipating his own possible burial, he begins to view his grandmother as a threat to his existence. What might be interpreted as systemic violence against children depicted in the tales—abuse, infanticide, cannibalism—are condoned and lauded as virtuous acts of filial piety. That such barbaric and predatory behaviors are cloaked under the pretense of civility echo the message found in the first piece of the memoir, "Dogs • Cats • Mice": that humans—the educated, in particular, so fond of preaching false morality—are really no better, and perhaps much worse, than beasts.

In tune with the message conveyed by "Diary of a Madman," *"The Illustrated Twenty-Four Filial Exemplars"* shows how cannibalism, literally and figuratively speaking, starts in the home.[16] The child's upbringing and education nurture in him a "slave mentality" that Lu Xun had long derided, as the child is forced, through psychological indoctrination and a system of discipline and punishment, to conform to arbitrary rules and authority without question. The father-son relationship—viewed as sacrosanct in the realm of Confucian ethics—is distant, as the child is shown to be intimidated and fearful of his father. In "Fair of the Five Fierce Gods," the boy's gleeful anticipation of attending one of the grandest temple fairs in his county is replaced with trepidation as soon as the cold and laconic patriarch appears on the scene. A strict disciplinarian, the father forbids his son from joining the outing unless he memorizes the lines from his primer, *A Brief Mirror of History*. While the terrified child is able, in the end, to recite the incomprehensible lines, gone is his initial sense of wonder and enchantment. As the I-now writes, he remembers little about the fair or the lines he was forced to memorize, as only the fear and dread instilled by his father's threat of punishment still remain. The I-now writes: "Even now when I recall this episode, I still wonder why my father had to make me memorize those lines at that particular moment."[17]

The cruelty of this system is further borne out in "Father's Illness," as the tables are turned on the dying patriarch in an incident that inflicts psychological scars far more devastating than the memory of the sabotaged outing. The narrator recounts a scene where he, as the eldest son and in a forced show of filial piety, is urged by an intermediary on etiquette to shout out at his father's deathbed.

> "Father! Father!" I started calling out.
>
> "Louder! He can't hear you. Quickly, why aren't you calling out?!"
>
> "Father!!! Father!!!"

His face, which had calmed down, suddenly tensed up. He opened his eyes ever so slightly, as if experiencing some pain.

"Call out! Call out!" she urged me.

"Father!!!"

"What? . . . don't shout . . . don't . . ." he said softly and then started drawing rapid breaths. After some time, things returned to normal, and his breathing calmed down.

"Father!!!" I kept calling out until he drew his last breath.

The boy's internalization of the norms of filial piety places him in a predicament. While moral exemplars went to great lengths to extend their parents' lives, he secretly wishes his father a quick death to ease his suffering. Unable to defy etiquette, the child robs his father of a peaceful passing. The narrator feels an intense sense of guilt, which remains unresolved three decades later. He writes: "Now I can still hear my own voice from that time. Every time I hear it, I felt that this was the greatest wrong I ever did my father."

The child's emotions and concern for his father are smothered by prescribed etiquette. Unspoken words, unspoken wishes, and unspoken apologies—these losses are beyond redemption. Yet, by giving voice to these thoughts, however belated, the adult narrator is able to reconnect with that inner child. The revelation of such long-repressed feelings and their lingering effects on the adult psyche also impresses upon readers the long-term damage that these purported norms of "civilized" behavior wreak. In portraying the misery, suffering, and violence that the father and child inflict on each other, wittingly or unwittingly, *Morning Blossoms* exposes the sinister nature of a dysfunctional familial system. Even the patriarch, the perceived authority figure and beneficiary of this system, is victimized in the end, in a seemingly endless cycle of tyranny and oppression.

"From the Garden of Myriad Grasses to the Three Flavors Studio" shows how this process of indoctrination continues through formal education. The child's "paradise"—the garden of his home, filled with beloved plants and creatures, real and imagined, which nurtures his soul and imagination—provides a contrast to the sterile atmosphere of the Confucian academy he is forced to attend. Memorizing incomprehensible classics by rote, day in and day out, and forced to submit to authority without question, the child still maintains his irrepressibly curious mind, indulging in playful antics and finding creative ways to tap into the inner-spirit and delight in the world. As the pressures of academic life and adulthood mount, however, the narrator's curiosity and spontaneity are increasingly stifled. "Trivial Recollections" depicts how stultifying instruction methods persist as well in the "modern-style" schools the young adult later attends.

If "Diary of a Madman" metaphorically exposes Chinese society as cannibalistic, *Morning Blossoms* shows how this pernicious system comes about and continues to reproduce itself. The child's family, his upbringing, education, and social norms all condition him to accept and exist on the terms of an inhuman world. The adult he becomes is increasingly alienated from his childlike heart and the "genuine person" within as he, in effect, becomes an unwitting cannibal, submitting to and perpetuating the norms of a tyrannical system. Caught in this vicious cycle and in this inhospitable and inhuman world, all are victims, and all of us are vulnerable.

Vulnerable Subjects

Morning Blossoms is ultimately an existential meditation on the human condition. The world of the elite child, nameless and faceless, is intricately interwoven with a wide array of subjects and objects, real and imagined, that shape his existence. The motley crew of vulnerable beings includes animals, children, servants, and social outcasts. By giving voice and visibility to subjects and objects not often heard or visible in narrative, the memoir poses the following questions: What does it mean to be human? Whose lives are visible and whose are not? And, as Judith Butler asks—whose lives are grievable and whose are not?[18]

The memoir's unconventional nature is apparent from the first, and ostensibly out of place, essay, "Dogs • Cats • Mice." In arguably the least interesting piece in the collection, Lu Xun takes pains to denounce the "estimable gentlemen" he was feuding with at the time of writing.[19] For their pretentious claims of upholding "truth" and "righteousness" while turning a blind eye and even tacitly supporting the oppression of their own people, the educated elite are, in Lu Xun's eyes, worse than beasts. The essay begins by mocking his literary adversaries' facile attempt at slandering him by calling him a "cat-hater," then takes unexpected detours, first tapping into the subject's fascination with cat-related animal lore before travelling back in time to recount the child's delight in the world of fantastic animal tales and affection for his pet mouse. It turns out that a tragic childhood episode, among the subject's first taste of loss, may have contributed to Lu Xun's cat-hating: the young boy's nanny, Ah Chang, leads him to believe that their house cat had killed his beloved pet; only later does he find out that his mouse had, in fact, been stomped to death by Ah Chang herself. This revelation sets the stage for the rest of the memoir and drives one of its main points home: that one can truly begin to understand one's present only by delving into the past.

Similar themes of loss, death, and betrayal appear with seemingly increasing intensity in the essays that follow. As mentioned earlier, in "Father's Illness," the son shouts out until the patriarch draws his

last breath, in violation of the dying man's last wishes. In the eponymous essay "Fan Ainong," the narrator reconstructs the life and death
of his friend, whom he believes was driven to suicide by societal forces.
In the world of the memoir, each of these lives—the pet mouse, the
patriarch, the social outcast—is at once singular and interconnected
with the narrator's life and that of others. Each life is meaningful and
worthy of commemoration. Each and every one of these lives, big
and small, is grievable.

Morning Blossoms, as with many of Lu Xun's other works, turns
elite literary conventions on their head, bringing to light the plight
of society's abject. By making the child the focus of the memoir, Lu
Xun brings readers into the world of other vulnerable beings who
make up the fabric of the boy's life. In ironic contrast to biographies
of elite men and the memoir's cover—featuring an elite woman in
flowing robes wandering in a garden—the two most memorable
characters in the child's life are women from the lower classes. While
they seldom make a presence in elite biographies, *Morning Blossoms*
shows the dominant roles these women play in the child's life.
Mrs. Yan, whose home is the neighborhood gathering place, appears
in two of the eight essays, including as the enforcer of etiquette in
"Father's Illness." Relishing children's company, she is permissive with
their antics and often joins in their fun. She also introduces them to
some more unseemly sides of life—giving the uncomprehending boy
his first glimpse of pornography and encouraging him to steal jewelry to buy coveted toys. The illiterate nursemaid, Ah Chang, appears
in four of the eight essays and not as a mere extra. At least within the
world of the memoir, her impact on the life of her young charge seems
to far outweigh those of other family members, who are either distant or make few appearances.[20]

Unlike Lu Xun's short stories, the memoir's focus is not exclusively on the cruel society that victimizes the weak and the poor.

Through the eyes of the young child, a vulnerable subject not yet fully indoctrinated in class-consciousness, readers see beyond the stereotypical images of the lower classes. Ah Chang is not a one-dimensional suffering peasant, but a colorful, larger-than-life personality. Indeed, in many episodes where the dominant and sometimes domineering Ah Chang appears, the child often plays a subordinate role. Big in build, she appears superstitious, fond of gossip, and controlling in some vignettes. A pet-killer and tiresome rule-enforcer, she is at times regarded with fear, hatred, and contempt by the child. In other vignettes, she is strong, resourceful, straightforward, and caring. A purveyor of tall tales and enchanting folklore that captivates her young charge, she also acquires a deeply coveted book of monsters—*The Classic of Mountains and Seas*—for the boy, inspiring respect, awe, and fondness, along with his lifelong hobby of collecting illustrated books.

The composite portrait of the very memorable Ah Chang—comical, full of flaws, yet strong and endearing nonetheless—is drawn with compassion, care, and fondness by the I-now. Reminiscent of Lu Xun's depiction of unreliable narrators in his short stories, the end of the essay, however, turns the spotlight on the narrator's limitations. The child in the memoir is completely oblivious to rigid class distinctions and his own elite biases, which the I-now makes painfully clear. The irony, the I-now writes, is that in spite of the dominant role that Ah Chang played in his childhood, he knew neither her real name nor her life story, offering only the following speculation: "All I know is that she had an adopted son and was probably widowed from a young age."

In commemorating the lives of figures such as Ah Chang even as he highlights the partiality of his accounts, Lu Xun attests that there has been a life—"a life worth noting, a life worth valuing and preserving, a life that qualifies for recognition."[21] While the "real" life story of Ah Chang beyond what the child sees, and the adult remembers, remains a mystery to the end, the essay points to the countless, nameless others whose lives have been at once objectified, simplified, and rendered socially invisible in the world of the real and the world of narrative. This portrait of Ah Chang seen through the eyes of the child and filtered through the adult narrator's reflection is a singularly colorful and flawed character, living a life filled with contradiction—sorrow and joy intertwined with unspoken misery and tragedy—a life that we can recognize and sympathize with, a life that is all too human.

Cultivating the Human

Morning Blossoms shows how one's identity is not bounded but inextricably intertwined with the lives of others. We are, in Judith Butler's words, "from the start and by virtue of being a bodily being, already given over, beyond ourselves, implicated in lives that are not our own."[22] The following existential question is also posed in Lu Xun's memoir: How are we to coexist with, relate to, and represent others whose lives are enmeshed with our own?

Indeed, many pieces in the memoir, like "Ah Chang and *The Classic of Mountains and Seas*," "Professor Fujino," and "Fan Ainong," read more like biographical sketches. Going beyond the human world, "Wu Chang [Life Is Unpredictable]" is an account of the "life" of the human-like spirit of Wu Chang as he appears in books and village plays, a welcome and comforting presence in the imagination and lives of the child and the villagers. Depicted are the singular lives of individuals (and spirits)—those who might otherwise be overlooked—courageously toiling on in the face of an inhospitable world.

The last two essays, "Professor Fujino" and "Fan Ainong," pick up on a theme introduced in the first essay and a subtext of the memoir as a whole: the roles and responsibilities of intellectuals and writers as agents of social change. Unlike the previous essays, which focus mostly on his childhood, the last two essays trace the narrator's young adult life as he studies abroad in Japan and then returns to his hometown. The child in the memoir, though not particularly remarkable, is an endearing and sympathetic figure for the most part; the young man he becomes is much less so. Exposed to the harsh realities of adult life and having more fully assimilated into the ways of the world, his mind exhibits few traces of the curiosity and imagination it did in childhood. Indeed, the often self-mocking middle-aged narrator is at times ashamed as he depicts himself, in hindsight and through the eyes of others, as an immature, opinionated, and arrogant young man.

In "Professor Fujino" and "Fan Ainong," the young narrator at first, like those around him, views these unconventional men with disdain. While these last two essays appear as "merciless dissections"—of the subject's own shortcomings, magnified by the strengths of his teacher and friend—their focus is not on the narrator per se; rather, he appears as an ancillary character, a foil to the admirable intellectuals memorialized. "Fan Ainong" shines a light on the eponymous character's remarkable qualities. The seemingly misanthropic Fan— honest to a fault, uncompromising in his principles, with an utter disregard for convention and superficial displays—appears, by the end of the essay, as a far more worthy character than the image-conscious and at times hypocritical narrator. A loyal friend, Fan readily encourages the narrator to escape, even as Fan himself has no options but to remain in their hometown with dwindling prospects. The depiction of Fan's fondness for drink, childlike spirit, and spurned talents harkens back to a lineage of eccentrics whose ambitions were thwarted.[23] The narrator's speculation that his friend's death was a possible suicide adds an aura of mystique to Fan's life and shifts the blame for his tragic fate on a society that preys on the weak and ostracizes nonconformists. In so doing, Lu Xun recasts the mold of Fan Ainong from a forgettable misfit to a misunderstood rebel, a true patriot, and a "genuine person" who lived a tragic but remarkable life—a life worth remembering and recording.

Likewise, the beginning of the penultimate essay paints a less than flattering image of Professor Fujino as seen through the eyes of his students and the impressionable young adult narrator. Unremarkable in stature, disheveled in appearance, with a strange accent and little regard for common social graces, the Japanese anatomy professor is often the butt of students' jokes. Yet, the essay reveals what lies beneath the unglamorous surface: the dignity and fortitude of a selfless individual toiling on with little regard for his own self-image or fame, singularly devoted to his studies and forwarding the cause of humanity.

In a man-eat-man world where the subject often feels bereft of a home, the narrator finds a measure of comfort, affection, and belonging in the company of a kindred spirit—a bond that goes beyond time and space, as the memory of his teacher continues to inspire him. At the end of "Professor Fujino," with a note of sentimentality uncharacteristic of Lu Xun's writings, the narrator concludes:

> For some unknown reason, I would often think of him. Among those whom I consider my teachers, he is the one who gave me the most encouragement and the one I feel most grateful to. I often think of how his passionate hopes for me, his tireless teaching, on a smaller scale was for China, in hopes that China would develop modern medical studies; on a larger scale, it was for scientific research, that is, his hope that modern medical studies would be transmitted to China. In my eyes and in my

mind, his character is a great one, even though his name isn't known by many people.[24]

The adult narrator's bonds with Fan Ainong and Professor Fujino display a form of sociality not driven by domination and submission, but by benevolence and care for the other. Critical as he was of the Confucian virtue of filial piety, Lu Xun's mission of "cultivating the human" evokes Confucian notions of reciprocity and benevolence. In the Confucian *Analects,* one who practices benevolence exhibits the following quality: one, who "wanting to establish himself (*liji*), establishes others (*liren,* earlier translated as "cultivating the human"); wanting himself to achieve, enables others to achieve."[25]

In contrast to the unnamed literary adversaries cursorily mentioned in "Dogs • Cats • Mice," Professor Fujino embodies the image of an intellectual exemplar and a "genuine person."[26] Unlike the "estimable gentlemen," hypocritical and more concerned with maintaining their own elite status than with fighting for a more egalitarian society, Fujino's actions are driven by personal integrity and an inner moral compass.[27] He is an embodiment of a universal human spirit that opposes all forms of oppression. Unimpeded by racial barriers and social hierarchies, the Japanese teacher encourages and inspires his Chinese student to succeed and carry on in his pursuit of realizing a more human and just society for all.[28] In the unlikely figure of a Japanese professor, the narrator finds an intellectual exemplar, a humanitarian, a nurturing paternal figure, and a genuine friend.

While the essay's narrator laments not repaying his friend and teacher in kind, Lu Xun the writer does, in fact, reciprocate, albeit in delayed fashion, with gifts of his own. His commemorative pieces might be thought of as "nobody memoirs," which Thomas Couser notes "may confer unexpected immortality on a hitherto anonymous, but noteworthy, person. If it focuses on someone other than the author, the conveying of immortality can be an important and generous gift."[29] By the time he wrote these biographical sketches, Lu Xun had become a well-established name in the literary field. He underscores his autobiographical subject's ordinariness as he allows the characters of the two unlikely heroes to shine. In its deconstruction of the self and its recognition and reconstruction of the lives of others who have been critical to the development of the yet-evolving self, Lu Xun's memoir bestows just such generous gifts. Like fallen blossoms gathered at dusk, these vulnerable subjects, whose names might have otherwise languished in obscurity, are not forgotten. The memory and significance of their ephemeral existence lives on in those whose lives they have touched and in those inspired by Lu Xun's moving tributes to them.

✹

謝朝華於已披，　啟夕秀於未振
陸機 文賦

Cast aside the morning blossoms already withered,
to make way for dusk buds yet to bloom
Lu Ji, "Rhapsody on Literature"

In "Rhapsody on Literature," Lu Ji (261–303) celebrates the mysterious nature and power of creativity. While a writer must be able to engage past literary conventions, he argues that the good writer must also go beyond them. In the verse quoted above, Lu Ji appeals to readers to cast aside the old conventions (morning blossoms) to make way for new forms of literary expression (dusk buds). In spite of the ironic twist on Lu Ji's literary masterpiece in the title of his memoir, Lu Xun's composition is true to the spirit of "Rhapsody"—

informed by past conventions, yet not encumbered by them. In *Morning Blossoms,* Lu Xun deliberately experiments with new realms of literary expression, breaking through old forms, styles, and conventions to articulate a way of relating to the self, the other, the world, and the act of representation itself.[30]

In the world of the memoir, not only do we see the presence of a diverse array of subjects usually invisible in the writings of the elite; these subjects, while at times shown to be reticent and conforming to unspoken rules of decorum, also assert their own voice and speak on their own terms. The frequent inclusion of direct dialogue and depictions of recitations lends a particularly aural quality to the memoir. A cacophony of voices blends together, sometimes in unison and sometimes in contrast, as students and teachers in the private academies and the "modern" classrooms recite classical Chinese verses and English and German phrases, much of it senseless mumbo-jumbo to the uncomprehending narrator and his classmates ("From the Garden of Myriad Grasses to the Three Flavors Studio," "Trivial Recollections"). In the absence of patriarchs and superiors, readers hear the laughter and chatter of children and the voice of Mrs. Yan and Ah Chang speaking and telling tall tales in colorful vernacular. The direct speech of Professor Fujino—in his quaint and halting drawl—and the unadorned and at times salty language of Fan Ainong are refreshing contrasts to the high-sounding rhetoric of the estimable gentlemen in "Dogs • Cats • Mice." The inclusion of different voices, speech, accents, languages, and linguistic registers adds color, tone, and variety to what otherwise might appear a monotonic world, lending the memoir a polyphonous quality.

Through his scrupulous resistance to totalizing narratives, his refusal to portray a stable, all-knowing subject, his merciless self-dissection, and the inclusion of the lives and voices of a variety of "forgettable" others, Lu Xun was writing a memoir of a different sort—a memoir about an evolving self whose life is inextricably intertwined with the lives of others. The subject's identity is at once singular and relational, his fate at once individual and communal, in a narrative in which each being struggles to survive in an inhospitable world.

Lu Xun's mission as an intellectual and writer chronicling the life of his times was to shine a new light on the past and the present that may illuminate an alternative path to the future, a path that is still unfolding. As much as he claimed to abhor the idea of being seen as a "guide" or "mentor" for youth, he was well aware of his growing influence and stature. He was all too aware that the present is hopelessly enmeshed in the past and that the life of the self is inextricably intertwined with that of others—others whose lives are vulnerable, just like our own. In reconstructing a past self through the eyes of a merciless I-now and the eyes of others, the memoir creates a self that is continuously unfolding to himself, as the different perspectives and parts of the subject coalesce in the mind of the self-reflective narrator. The memoir, in Lu Xun's hands, then, also becomes what Janet Varner Gunn refers to as "an instrument of discovery and not merely a record of what 'really' happened,"[31] a process of revelation that readers, too, bear witness to. In writing his memoir, Lu Xun may have hoped that readers, too, would engage in similar acts of introspection and retrospection. While confronting the memories of loss, one's own complicity in perpetuating an oppressive system, and our status as vulnerable subjects living in an uncertain and inhospitable world may be painful, it may also serve as a catalyst for self-knowledge and in turn, personal and social transformation.

Confronting one's homelessness and grieving loss—of childhood innocence, youthful dreams, and an idealistic vision of home—allows for the possibility that one's thoughts no longer be possessed and limited by them. Lu Xun's memoir then, in coming to terms with his past and with his sense of dislocation, enables new ways of conceptualizing the self, the home, and one's place in the world. What does it mean, then, to live in a human world? In spite of the seemingly pessimistic tone of *Morning Blossoms,* it nonetheless sounds some notes of hope and gives us glimpses of a world of the possible. That is, the human world is one where the childlike-heart can be nourished and allowed to thrive; where relationships are not defined by roles or rigid hierarchies; where adults can learn from children; where paternal figures, abject subjects, and perceived enemies can also be allies and friends; and where sociality is not based on hierarchies and systems of domination and submission, but on benevolence and reciprocity, and in turn, the fostering of "genuine persons." In cultivating one's innate connection with the self, the other, and the world, and striving to enable the same for others, lies the possibility of a more humane world. A place where, as in the world of *Wild Grass,* all lives are intertwined and interdependent, yet each life is also singular, meaningful, and therefore grievable.

Lu Xun saw himself as an intermediary, helping to expose the inner workings of an oppressive society in hopes of paving the way for a more human world for all. In a rare, hopeful declaration of his mission as a writer, he said he wanted to "shoulder the gate of darkness, to free them ["the children"] to a bright, open space, where they can thenceforth pass their days happily and live respectably as human beings."[32] A realm, presumably, where all beings can find some sense of belonging in the world.

Eileen J. Cheng

Introductory Note

小引

I often long for a bit of serenity amid the chaos, but it is by no means easy to find. At present, things are so bizarre and my mind so disordered. When one reaches a point in life where nothing but memories remain, life itself has probably become rather pointless. But there may even be times when no memories are left at all. There are norms for writing in China, yet world affairs still spiral on their own circuitous course. A few days ago, when I left Sun Yat-sen University, I thought of how I had departed Xiamen University four months earlier. Hearing the droning of planes overhead, I unexpectedly recalled the planes circling daily over Beijing just a year ago.[33] At the time, I even composed a short piece called "Awakening." Now, not even a trace of such an "awakening" remains.

The weather in Guangzhou gets hot real early. The rays of the setting sun shine through the west-facing window, making me reluctant to don even a thin layer of clothing. I have never seen a plant

First published in volume 2, issue 10, of the journal *Wilderness* (*Mangyuan*) on May 25, 1927. Lu Xun, *Lu Xun quanji* (Complete works of Lu Xun), 18 vols. (Beijing: Renmin wenxue, 2005), 2:235–237.

like the miniature gardenia that sits on my desk now—immerse a section cutting in water and out sprout lovely green leaves. Admiring the green leaves and editing old manuscripts can be considered small accomplishments after all. Doing such trivial things, while akin to a living death, is quite effective at dispelling the scorching heat.

I finished editing *Wild Grass* the day before yesterday. Now it's on to *Recalling Old Matters,* serialized in the journal *The Wilderness,* the title of which I've changed to *Morning Blossoms Gathered at Dusk.* Flowers picked while still fresh with dew are naturally more colorful and fragrant, but I'm unable to pick them in the morning. Just as I'm unable to immediately and magically transform the bizarre and disordered feelings I have at this moment into bizarre and disordered essays. But perhaps one of these days when I look up at the passing clouds, they will flash before my eyes.

For a period of time, I frequently recalled the fruits and vegetables that I ate as a child in my hometown: water chestnuts, broad beans, water bamboo shoots, musk melons. All of them so delectable and mouthwatering, they seduced me into thinking of home. Afterward, on tasting them again long after my departure, I found nothing remarkable about them; only in the realm of memory did the old flavors still linger. They may, perhaps, keep on deluding me for a lifetime, constantly inducing me to look back to the past.

These ten pieces are transcribed from my memory and may deviate slightly from actual fact, but this is how I remember things now. The forms of the essays are probably a mishmash, as the writing process was intermittent and dragged out over a period of nine months or so. The surroundings varied as well: the first two essays were written under the eastern wall of my residence in Beijing; the middle three were composed when I was taking refuge in a hospital and in a carpenter's workshop;[34] the last five on the top floor of the Xiamen University Library after the scholars there had expelled me from their clique.[35]

May 1, 1927, recorded by Lu Xun at the
White Cloud Tower in Guangzhou

Dogs • Cats • Mice

狗 • 猫 • 鼠

Starting last year, I seem to have heard certain people say that I am a cat-hater. The evidence, naturally, was in that piece of mine, "Rabbits and Cats." Since this was a case of self-incrimination, of course there was nothing more I could say, but it didn't bother me in the least. Once this year came around, however, I started getting more than a little worried. I often can't help dabbing my brush in ink, but

First published in volume 1, issue 5, of the journal *Wilderness* (*Mangyuan*) on March 10, 1926. Lu Xun, *Lu Xun quanji* (Complete works of Lu Xun), 18 vols. (Beijing: Renmin wenxue, 2005), 2:238–249. The first part of this essay is peppered with quotes from Lu Xun's adversaries, which he uses to mock them in return. Among Lu Xun's most vicious "pen battles" at the time of writing was with the "estimable gentlemen"—a term used here and other pieces to refer to members of the Contemporary Review Group (*xiandai pinglun pai*) and Crescent Moon Society (*xinyue she*), most of whom had been educated in England and America. Here, his primary targets include the academic and critic Chen Xiying (also known as Chen Yuan, 1896–1970), the writer Lin Yutang (1895–1976), and the poet Xu Zhimo (1897–1931), who were involved in a dispute at the Peking Women's Normal College, where Lu Xun had once taught. In 1924–1925, the students and the principal of the college, Yang Yinyu (1884–1938), were embroiled in a struggle over students' rights to participate in political protests. In the fall of 1925, the principal expelled a number of activist students, including Xu Guangping (1898–1968), Lu Xun's student and later his common-law wife. Lu Xun, who had by then resigned from the college, supported the students, while Chen Xiying and Xu Zhimo sided with Yang.

for certain individuals, though, it seems that what I write and publish hits a sore spot more often than it scratches an itch. If I'm not careful, I might even end up offending some famous personage or eminent professor, or worse yet, the likes of those "elders who bear the responsibility for guiding youth"[36]—which would be extremely dangerous indeed.

Why so? Because these big shots are "not to be trifled with."[37] In what sense are they "not to be trifled with?" When overcome with rage, they might publish a letter in the papers declaring: "See! Don't dogs hate cats? Mr. Lu Xun admits that he hates cats, yet he still says that 'dogs that have fallen into the water' should be beaten!"[38] The ingenuity of this "logic" lies in the use of words from my own mouth to prove that I am a dog, so anything I say—even indisputable facts such as two times two equals four or three times three yields nine—will be refuted. Since everything I say is wrong, naturally nothing incorrect comes out of those gentlemen's mouths—whether it be two times two equals seven or three times three yields a thousand.

So now and then I pay close attention to the "motives" driving their animosity. It isn't a case of me daring to vainly imitate the fashion nowadays of scholars appraising works based on authorial motive, but merely a way for me to exonerate myself. The way I see it, these matters would probably have come rather effortlessly to an animal psychologist, but the pity of it is that I don't have any expertise in this field. Eventually, however, I discovered an answer from Dr. O. Dähnhardt's *Folktales from Natural History*. This is supposedly what happened: the animals called a meeting to discuss important matters. Birds, fish, and beasts all gathered together, with the sole exception of the elephant. The animals decided to choose an escort to bring over the elephant, and the dog drew the lot for the mission. "How do I find the elephant? I've neither known nor seen one before," the dog asked. "That's easy," the animals said, "the elephant has a hunched back." The dog went on his way and came across a cat, which immediately arched its spine. The dog treated it as an honored guest, and they journeyed back together. The dog introduced the arched-spined cat, saying: "Here's the elephant!" All jeered at the dog, and from then on, dogs and cats became enemies.

Although it hasn't been very long since the Germans left the forest, their scholarship and arts are already very impressive; even the binding of their books and craftsmanship of their toys are much beloved. But this particular fairytale is really unremarkable, and the explanation for the feud between the cat and the dog is also rather pointless. In arching its back, the cat was neither trying to disguise itself nor deliberately putting on airs; the fault lies with the dog for being undiscerning. Nevertheless, it can still count as a reason for the enmity between dogs and cats. But my hatred of cats is altogether different.

In truth, such rigid distinctions between humans and beasts need not be made. Though the animal world is not as pleasant and free as the ancients imagined, there is much less fussy posturing than in the human realm. Animals behave according to their natures and instincts. To them, right is right and wrong is wrong, and there's nothing to dispute. Maggots may be unclean, but they don't profess to be morally superior to others; predatory birds and beasts prey upon weaker animals and one might very well call them merciless, but they never wave a banner of "truth" and "righteousness" and expect their victims to express admiration or praise for them up to the very moment they are devoured. Once humans could stand erect, it was of course a great step forward; once they could talk, this was another great stride. Once they could write and create compositions, this was, of course, yet another great stride. But this was also the undoing of humankind, for this was the start of empty talk. Nothing against empty talk, but there are times when people are oblivious to the fact that their words contradict their thoughts. In such cases, compared to animals that can only growl, people should feel ashamed indeed. If there truly is a Creator on high who looks upon all creatures equally, he might perhaps find these clever human antics gratuitous. It would be like our going to the zoo and seeing monkeys somersaulting and female elephants curtseying—though the sight of them might elicit laughter, we might feel uncomfortable, even sad, all the same, because it seems that they'd be better off without such superfluous cleverness. But since we are now human, we have no choice but to "ally with our cliques to attack the Other,"[39] and so we imitate each other's speech and converse and argue as custom dictates.

Now speaking of the reasons for my hatred for cats, I feel that I have ample reason to do so, and I hate them openly and righteously. Firstly, a cat's temperament differs from other beasts. When a cat captures a sparrow or mouse, it is unwilling to kill it with one bite; it has to toy with the prey to its heart's content—releasing it, catching it again, then releasing it once more—finally devouring it only when it has tired of the game. This is quite similar to the ill-disposition of humans—to delight in the misfortune of others and to prolong the torture of the weak. Secondly, isn't the cat in the same family as the lion and the tiger? Yet why does it have such a fawning disposition? Perhaps it is limited by what nature has granted it. If its body were ten times bigger, one can hardly imagine what kind of attitude it would exhibit. Yet, while these explanations seem as though they are being made up as I take up my pen, they also do seem to me to be the actual reasons that came to mind at the time. But a more reasonable explanation may be the cries cats emit when mating—the whole process is so elaborate and the racket they make so annoying, especially when I'm reading or sleeping at night. On these occasions, I use a long pole to attack them. When dogs mate in the street, idlers often use a wooden stick to thrash them. I once saw a copper plate etching called the "Allegorie der Wollust" [Allegory of Lust]" by Pieter Bruegel the Elder depicting just such a scene, so it seems that such actions are common the world over, from ancient times to now.

Ever since that pig-headed Austrian scholar Freud advocated psychoanalysis—I've heard it translated as "heart examination" by Mr. Zhang Shizhao, which, though simple and archaic sounding, is truly hard to understand—some of our famous personages and eminent professors who are vaguely familiar with the term have appropriated it, inevitably associating it with sexual desire. I'm not going to deal with the matter of beating dogs, but as for my beating cats, it is purely on account of their howling, I have no malicious intent otherwise. I have faith that my capacity for jealousy has limits, after all, which I have to make clear at the outset in this era of ours where people are taken to task at the drop of a hat. For example, before humans mate, there is also an elaborate process; new fashions include writing love letters—if few, called "a bunch," if many, a big "bundle."[40] In the olden days, there were things like "requesting the name," "sending betrothal gifts," and kowtowing and bowing. When the Jiangs of Haichang held a wedding ceremony in Beijing last year, they kept on bowing this way and that for a full three days. They even printed a red-covered book titled *On Wedding Rituals,* and in the preface held forth at great length: "In all fairness, anything called ritual should be elaborate. If the goal was simplicity, what need for ritual? . . . So those devoted to ritual can make it thrive! They should not sink to the level of commoners who do not perform rituals!"

This, however, didn't anger me in the least because it didn't require my presence. So you can see that the reason for my hating cats is really very simple—because they keep making a racket within ear-shot. As for the various rituals people observe, those not involved can simply ignore them and I, for one, couldn't care less; but if someone were to command me to listen to the recitation of love letters or to engage in ritual bowing right when I am about to read or sleep, then in the name of self-defense I will use a long bamboo pole to resist. And then there are the acquaintances I don't normally see who send me red invitations out of the blue with phrases such as "The daughter of our house is departing," "Our young son is getting married," "Respectfully requesting you witness the ritual," or "The presence of your honored family is welcome" printed on them. These phrases contain "insidious insinuations" that make me feel guilty were I not to spend money on their account—I'm rather displeased with this as well.

However, these are all things that have happened recently. As I recollect, my hatred for cats came long before I could enunciate all these reasons for it, when I was perhaps around ten years old. I still remember it clearly now, and the reason was extremely simple: for the mere fact that it ate mice—that is, it ate the adorable little shadow mouse I was raising.

I've heard that in the West, people don't like black cats, but I don't know if this is actually the case or not. The black cat in Edgar Allan Poe's short story, however, really is a bit scary. The cats in Japan have a predilection for turning into spirits, and the cruelty with which the legendary "cat witch" devours people is even more terrifying. Though China had "cat-spirits" in ancient times, I seldom hear of cats engaging in demonic behavior and wreaking havoc. It's as if they have lost their ancient powers and started behaving. It's just that in my childhood I always felt that cats had a demonic air and I didn't have any fond feelings for them. One summer evening when I was young, I was lying on a small table under a big osmanthus tree, cooling myself in the breeze while my grandmother was sitting by the table waving her plantain fan, telling me stories and having me guess riddles. Suddenly I heard the scratchy sounds of claws on the tree, and with the sound came a pair of eyes flashing in the darkness, taking me by surprise and cutting off my grandmother's story. She began telling another story about cats.

"Did you know that the cat was the tiger's teacher?" she asked. "How would children know that the cat is the tiger's master? In the beginning, the tiger didn't know how to do a thing, so it decided to be the cat's apprentice. The cat then taught it how to pounce, catch, and eat prey—just the way cats catch mice. After the lessons were over, the tiger thought it had mastered all the skills and that no animals could rival it. Only its teacher, the cat, was mightier; if it killed off the cat, then it would be the mightiest. The tiger made up its mind and prepared to pounce on the cat. The cat had long known of its intentions and leaped up into a tree. The tiger could do nothing but squat under the tree and gaze up at the cat. The cat hadn't passed down all its skills to the tiger—it had yet to teach the tiger how to climb trees."

How fortunate, I thought, and luckily, the tiger was impatient by nature, otherwise, it might have come climbing down that osmanthus. Still, it was all very scary, so I wanted to go indoors and sleep. The night grew even darker, the osmanthus leaves rustled audibly, and a light breeze stirred. The straw mat must be cooler by now, I thought, so I would be able to fall asleep without tossing and turning.

Under the faint glow of the bean-oil lamp, in a room a few centuries old, lies a world where mice run amok on the beams, scampering about and squealing, putting on airs even more arrogant than those of "famous personages and eminent professors." We kept a cat but were not responsible for feeding it. Though my grandmother and the others often hated the mice for gnawing through the cabinets and stealing our food—these were hardly great crimes in my book and had nothing to do with me. Plus, it's likely that these misdemeanors were the work of large rats; no one could blame it on the little mice I adored. These little mice crawl about on the ground, are about as big as a person's thumb, and aren't all that scary. We called them "shadow mice," an altogether different species from the great rats that live exclusively on rooftops. Two paper cutouts were pasted in front of my bed. One was "Pigsy Becomes a Son-in-law"—the cutout was all long snout and big ears, which I felt was not much to look at. The other, "The Mouse Wedding," however, was adorable. The mice— from the groom to the bride, to the bridegrooms and bridesmaids, to the guests and the officiant—all had sharp cheeks and slender legs, each resembling stern scholars, except that they wore red shirts and green pants. I felt that only the mice I so adored could put on such a grand ceremony.

Nowadays things are much cruder. The human bridal processions one encounters on the streets are little more than advertisements for sexual intercourse, so I don't pay them much attention. But at the time, I was so overcome by the desire to see the ceremony of "The Mouse Wedding" that even if it were like that of the Jiang family from Haichang, going on for three consecutive days, I probably wouldn't have found it tiresome.[41] I was always reluctant to go to sleep on the eve of the fourteenth of the first month of the lunar calendar, as it was the night I would wait for the mouse procession to emerge from under my bed. But all I would see were a few naked mice parading about as usual, and they didn't appear to be putting on a wedding ceremony. This lasted until I could no longer stay awake and would fall asleep, quite let down. By the time I peeled my eyes open, dawn would have already broken and the Lantern Festival would be upon us. Perhaps the mice clan wedding rituals involve neither sending out invitations to solicit gifts nor welcoming onlookers, no matter how much they truly want to witness the procession. As I thought this to be their long-established custom, there was nothing to protest.

The greatest enemy of mice is not, in fact, cats. After spring, when you hear the mice squealing *"za! za za za za!"*—referred to as "mice counting coppers"—you can tell that the terrifying mouse butcher has arrived. These sounds reflect the mice's despair and horror—even encountering a cat would not elicit such a cry. A cat, no doubt, is scary, but there are many ways of escaping a cat, and there's not much it can do once the mouse darts into a small hole. Only that terrifying butcher—the snake—the circumference of its long slender body almost the same as that of a mouse, can follow it wherever it goes. The snake can pursue it for quite a long time, and it's almost impossible for the mouse to escape. By the time one hears the "counting coppers" sound, the mouse has probably already run out of options.

On one occasion, I heard just this kind of "copper-counting" sound coming from an empty room. When I pushed the door and entered, I saw a snake on a beam and on the floor, a mouse, blood dripping from the corner of its mouth, the rib cage on both sides still heaving up and down. I picked it up and laid it in a cardboard box. Only after a long while did it come to and was gradually able to eat, drink, and crawl around. The next day, it seemed as if it had recovered, but it didn't run away. Placed on the floor, it would scamper towards people and crawl up their legs, all the way up to their knees. Placed on the dining table, it would eat food scraps and lick the bowls' edges. Placed on my desk, it would frolic about freely. On seeing the inkstone, it would lick the ground ink. This both surprised and delighted me. I had heard my father speak of a kind of "ink monkey" found in China, no bigger than a person's thumb, its whole body covered with glossy, jet-black fur. It sleeps in brush containers and jumps out at the sound of ink being ground. It waits for the person to finish writing and put the brush away, then licks off all the remaining ink on the inkstone before leaping back into the brush container. How I longed to have such an ink monkey, but all in vain. When I asked where one could be found or purchased, no one knew. "Consolation is better than nothing," so this little mouse became my ink monkey—though it wasn't always willing to wait for me to finish writing before licking the ink.

I don't remember clearly anymore, but this went on for a month or two. One day, I suddenly felt lonely, as if I had lost something. My little mouse often frolicked about in front of me on the table or on the floor. Yet for a good portion of this particular day, it was not to be seen. Everyone had finished lunch and it still hadn't come out—normally, it would have appeared by this time. I waited and waited and still, it didn't appear.

Mama Chang, the female servant who had always looked after me, probably feeling I had waited miserably for far too long, whispered something softly to me. Immediately outraged and saddened, I resolved to become the cats' enemy. She said that the shadow mouse had been eaten by the cat the night before!

When I lose what I love and my heart feels empty, I want to fill it with malicious thoughts of revenge!

My revenge began with the striped cat we raised and gradually grew in scope to include all the cats I encountered. At first, I merely chased them or attacked them. Later on, my methods became more ingenious, hurling rocks at their heads or luring them into an empty room and beating them into submission. This war I waged against them persisted for quite some time, and then it seemed that cats no longer came near me. But however impressive my triumphs over

them were, I could hardly be considered a hero. Not to mention that
there just aren't all that many people in China who have spent their
entire lives waging war against cats, so I might as well just completely
omit the parts about my military strategies and feats.

But many days later, or maybe even well after the better part of
a year, I received unexpected news out of the blue: the shadow mouse
had not been killed by the cat after all—Mama Chang had killed it
with a stomp of her foot as it tried to climb up her leg.

This certainly never occurred to me before. I don't remember
what my thoughts were at the time, but my feelings toward cats did
not, in the end, become more congenial. When I arrived in Beijing,
a cat injured my baby rabbits so my enmity toward them was renewed,
and I used even more cruel tactics against them. The topic of my "cat
hatred" circulated from that time on. Yet, all these things have long
passed and my attitude has changed such that I am now quite polite
to cats. I only shoo them away when circumstances call for it, but I
never beat or harm, let alone kill them. This is the progress I have
made in recent years. As I gained more experience, I suddenly became aware that nine out of ten people naturally despise cats for
stealing fish, carrying off birds, and making a racket at night. However, if I were to get rid of these despicable things on the behalf of
other people, and beat, harm, or kill them, this would immediately
arouse people's pity, and their hatred would be transferred unto me.
And so my current method is that if I encounter a cat wreaking havoc
and annoying others, I go out and stand by the door and loudly curse:
"*Shush!* Scram!" When things quiet down, I return to my study. This
way, I'm able to retain my right to protect the home from foreign
aggression. In fact, Chinese generals and soldiers often employ this
tactic, never getting rid of all the bandits or eradicating the enemy
completely, lest they no longer be valued or even be stripped of their

posts once they are no longer needed. I think that if I can promote this tactic widely, there might be hope for me yet to become an "elder" who "guides youth." But at present, I still haven't made up my mind whether to go through with it or not as I'm still studying and deliberating the matter.

February 21, 1926

Ah Chang and *The Classic of Mountains and Seas*

阿長與山海經

Mama Chang, as I've mentioned already, was the maidservant who raised me or, to put it more grandly, my nanny. My mother and many others addressed her this way since it seemed a little more courteous. Only grandmother called her Ah Chang.[42] Normally I called her *"amah"* without even adding "Chang." But when I detested her—like the time I found out that she had killed my shadow mouse—I would call her "Ah Chang."

Where we lived, there was no one with the surname Chang. She was dark-skinned, plump, and short so the character "長 *chang*" (long) wasn't a descriptive term either. Nor was it her given name, as I recall that she herself had once said that her name was young lady *so-and-so*. Just exactly what *so-and-so* it was, I have now forgotten, but at any rate, it wasn't "young lady Chang." And I never knew her real surname. I recall that she once told me how this term

First published in volume 1, issue 6, of the journal *Wilderness (Mangyuan)* on March 25, 1926. Lu Xun, *Lu Xun quanji* (Complete works of Lu Xun), 18 vols. (Beijing: Renmin wenxue, 2005), 2:250–257.

of address came about: a long, long time ago, our family had a maidservant with a tall build—a real "Ah Chang." Later on, she went back home so this "young lady *so-and-so*" of mine came to take her place. Yet, because everyone had gotten used to that term of address, no one bothered to change it, so from then on *she* became "Mama Chang."

It's not a good thing to talk behind people's backs, but if I were to speak candidly, I can only say that I really didn't admire her much at all. What I hated most was that she often liked to *chitter-chatter* and whisper things in hushed tones to others. She would raise her forefinger, wag it about in the air or point it to the tip of her own—or the other person's—nose. Whenever there was some minor trouble brewing in our home, I couldn't help suspecting that it had something to do with this *chitter-chatter*. She also prevented me from moving about: if I were to so much as pluck a blade of grass or turn over a rock, she would say I was being naughty and threaten to report it to my mother. When summer arrived, she would stretch out both arms and both legs as she slept, forming the character "大" (big) smack in the center of the bed, squeezing me to the edge with no room to turn over. Sleeping in the corner of the mat for so long, I would get broiling hot. When I shoved her, she didn't move; when I shouted at her, she didn't hear me.

"Mama Chang, you're so plump, the heat must bother you so. Your sleeping posture at night probably isn't very good, is it? . . ."

Mother once asked her after hearing me complain many times. I knew her intent was for Ah Chang to give me a little more space. Ah Chang didn't say a word. Yet that night when I woke up from the heat, the character "大" was still splayed across the whole bed, and one of her arms was draped over my neck. I felt that there was really nothing that could be done about it.

But she knew a lot about the rules of etiquette—rules I found exasperating for the most part. One of the most joyous times of the year, is, of course, New Year's Eve. After bidding farewell to the old year, I would receive New Year's money from the elders. Wrapped in red paper and placed beside my pillow, I had only to wait until the next day before spending it as I pleased. Head on my pillow, I would gaze at the red envelopes, imagining the little drum, knife, gun, clay figures, and candied Buddhas I would buy the next day. But then she would come in and place a lucky tangerine at the head of my bed.

"Lad, remember this well!" she said very solemnly. "Tomorrow is the first day of the new year. As soon as you peel open your eyes in the morning, the first thing you have to say to me is: 'Amah, good tidings!' Will you remember that? You have to remember, the entire year's luck is at stake. Don't you dare say anything else! After you've said that, you also have to eat some lucky tangerine." She then picked up the tangerine and waved it a few times before my eyes. "Then this year 'round, will be smooth and sound."

Even in my dreams I still remembered it was New Year's Day. I woke up especially early the next day, and once I was awake and about to sit up, she immediately pushed me back down with her outstretched arm. When I looked at her in surprise, I saw her gazing at me anxiously.

Then, beseechingly, she shook my shoulders. I suddenly remembered:

"Amah, good tidings to you!"

"Good tidings to you! Good tidings to everyone! You're so clever! Good tidings to you, good tidings to you!" She then looked quite delighted, and as she laughed, she shoved a piece of something cold into my mouth. After I got over the shock, I suddenly remembered that this was the so-called "Lucky Tangerine." The trials I had to endure on New Year's Day now behind me, I could finally get out of bed and go play.

She taught me many other life principles. For example, when someone dies, you shouldn't say the person "died" but ought to say the person "aged." You shouldn't enter rooms where people had died or given birth. When a grain of rice falls on the floor, you best pick it up and eat it. Never try to duck under the bamboo pole used for hanging pants to dry. . . . Other than these, I've just about forgotten all the rest, except for the bizarre New Year's Day ritual, which I remember most clearly. In short: they were nothing but the most tiresome of trivialities. Thinking of them now, I still find them to be extraordinarily annoying affairs.

Yet, for a time, I also felt an unprecedented respect for her. She often told me about the "Long-Hairs." By "Long-Hairs," it seemed, she was referring not just to the army of Hong Xiuquan,[43] but to all bandits and thieves—that is, with the exception of the Revolutionary Party, which had yet to come into existence. The Long-Hairs she spoke of were extremely scary, and their language was unintelligible. She said that when the Long-Hairs entered the city, my whole family fled to the seaside, leaving behind only a gatekeeper and an elderly female cook to keep watch. Later, it turned out that the Long-Hairs did indeed enter our home, and the old maidservant called them "Great Kings"—it was said that this was how one should address the Long-Hairs——and told them she was starving. A Long-Hair laughed and said: "Then I'll give you this to eat!" He threw a round object over to her, which still had a small queue attached to it—the gatekeeper's head. The cook lost her wits from then on, and whenever the matter was brought up afterward, her face would immediately turn ashen and she would gently pat her breast and say: "Oh my, scared the bejesus out of me, scared the bejesus out of me . . ."

I really wasn't afraid then because I felt that these things had nothing whatsoever to do with me—I wasn't a gatekeeper, after all. She probably guessed what I was thinking and said: "The Long-Hairs would also abduct children like you, abduct them and make them into little Long-Hairs. They would abduct good-looking young women, too."

"Then you would have been just fine." I believed that surely she would have been the safest, since she was neither a gatekeeper nor a child, and wasn't good-looking either. Not to mention that she had many cauterization scars on her neck.

"What rubbish?!" she said sternly. "So you think those like us were useless? We were abducted too. When soldiers outside the city came to attack, the Long-Hairs made us take off our pants and stand, lined up in rows on the city wall, so that cannons couldn't be fired from the outside. If the soldiers tried to fire, the cannons would explode!"

This was beyond my imagination and I couldn't help feeling astonished. I had always thought that she was nothing more than just a bellyful of troublesome etiquette—I would never have guessed that she possessed such marvelous superpowers. From then on, I felt a special respect for her—an immeasurably deep sense of respect. At night when the outstretched arms and legs took up the whole bed, it was, of course, completely forgivable—it was only right that I deferred to her.

Though it gradually wore thin, this respect probably didn't completely disappear until after I found out that she had murdered my mouse. At that time, I sternly cross-examined her and even called her "Ah Chang" to her face. I figured that since I wasn't really going to become a little Long-Hair and I was neither going to attack the city nor fire cannons, I had even less reason to fear an explosion. So what reason was there for me to be afraid of her?

But while I was mourning my mouse and plotting its revenge, I was also hankering after the illustrated version of *The Classic of Mountains and Seas*. This hankering had been kindled by a distant great uncle. He was a chubby and amiable old man who liked to grow flowers and trees such as cloranthus and jasmine, and the rare silk tree supposedly brought back from the north. His wife was just the opposite. She didn't understand the fuss over the plants and once placed a bamboo rod for hanging clothes out to dry over the perfume plant branch. When the branch broke, she even angrily cursed: "Damned plant!" Having no one to talk to, the old man was very lonely, so he was fond of playing with children and at times even referred to us as his "little friends." In the compound where our clan resided, he was the only one with a lot of books, and unusual ones at that. Naturally, he had eight-legged essays and poems that were tested on the examinations, but it was only in his study that I could find Lu Ji's *Commentaries on the Flora and Fauna in the Book of Songs* and many other books with unfamiliar titles. At the time, the book I most loved reading was *Mirror of Flowers,* which had many illustrations in it. He told me that he once had in his possession an illustrated version of *The Classic of Mountains and Seas,* which depicted human-faced beasts, nine-headed snakes, three-legged birds, winged humans, headless monsters whose two nipples served as eyes . . . a pity it was now misplaced.

I wanted to see these illustrations for myself, but I was embarrassed to badger him to find the book since he was somewhat scatterbrained and lazy. When I asked others about it, no one would give me a straight answer. I still had a few hundred coppers left of my New Year's money, but I didn't know how to go about buying the book. The main street where books were sold was quite far from my home, and the one time of the year I could make it there for a visit was in the first month of the lunar calendar—right when the doors of the two bookstores were tightly shut. When I was playing, it didn't matter much, but the moment I sat down to rest, I would think of *The Illustrated Classic of Mountains and Seas*.

Probably because I was so obsessed with it, even Ah Chang asked me what all this fuss over *The Classic of Mountains and Seas* was all about. I had never spoken to her about it since I knew she was no scholar, and I felt that nothing would be gained from bringing it up. But since she came asking, I told her about it.

Two weeks or so, or perhaps it was a month, passed. I still remember clearly, it was about four or five days after she took a leave to go home that she came back wearing a new blue jacket. As soon as she saw me, she handed me a package of books and cheerily said:

"Lad, here's a copy of *The Classic of Moths and Trees*[44] with pictures in it—I've bought it for you!"

It was as if a thunderbolt hit me; my whole body seized up. I quickly took the package and unwrapped it. I hastily flipped through the four small books and, sure enough, the human-faced beasts, nine-headed snakes . . . all of them were in there.

This again inspired in me a newfound respect for her. She was able to accomplish what others were either unwilling or unable to do. She did, indeed, have marvelous superpowers. My resentment against her for murdering my mouse vanished completely from this moment on.

These four books were the first I ever owned and the books I treasured most dearly.

What the books looked like still remains with me now. But based on what remains with me now, however, they appear to be rather shoddily printed. The paper was yellow and the pictures poorly drawn, consisting almost entirely, it seems, of straight lines connected here

Figure 5. The headless creature Xingtian. Reproduced from
"Shenyi dian" (Section on the divine and anomalous), in *Bowu
huibian* (Compilation of a broad array of things), in *Qinding gujin
tushu jicheng* (The Imperial sponsored collectanea of past and
present illustrations and texts), comp. Chen Menglei, Jiang
Tingxi, et al. (Shanghai: Tushu jicheng qianban yinshuju, 1884),
juan 29. Courtesy of the Asian Library, Special Collections and
Archives, Claremont Colleges Library.

and there; even the animals' eyes were rectangular. But they were the books I treasured most dearly, and looking through them, you could actually find human-faced beasts, nine-headed snakes, one-legged oxen, the sack-like creature Di Jiang, and the headless creature Xing Tian, "whose nipples served as eyes and belly button as a mouth" and "danced while grasping a shield and spear."

From then on I began collecting illustrated books in earnest. I acquired the lithographed edition of *Phonetics and Illustrations in the Erya, A Study of the Illustrations of Flora and Fauna in the Book of Songs, Collected Paintings from the Dianshi Studio,* and *Compendium of Poetry and Paintings.* I also bought another lithographed edition of *The Classic of Mountains and Seas.* Each volume had encomia following the illustrations, illustrations in green, text in red, which was much more delicate than that woodblock edition. I still possessed this book up until the year before last: it was a reprint in reduced format with commentary by Hao Yixing. But as for the woodblock edition, I can no longer remember when I lost it.

My nanny, otherwise known as Mama Chang or Ah Chang, departed this world probably some thirty years ago now. I never knew her name or her life story. All I know is that she had an adopted son, so she was probably widowed from a young age.

Dark, benevolent, and generous Mother Earth, may her soul rest peacefully in your bosom forever!

March 10[45]

The Illustrated Twenty-Four Filial Exemplars

二十四孝图

I will keep searching the four corners of the earth to find the darkest, darkest, darkest curse to curse all those who oppose and undermine the vernacular. If a soul were to exist after a person's death and I should be sent down to Hell on account of this most malicious heart of mine, I would absolutely not repent. I will, above all else, keep cursing all those who oppose and undermine the vernacular.

Though the books we have supplied our children since the so-called "literary revolution"[46] are pathetic compared to those from Europe, America, and Japan, they still have pictures and explanations; so as long as children are willing to read them, they are, at the very least, intelligible. But there is a faction with ulterior motives that is going all out to put a stop to this, intent on depriving the children's world of even the slightest amusement. In Beijing, the expression "馬虎子Ma huzi" (Ma the tiger cub) is often used to scare off children.

First published in volume 1, issue 10, of the journal *Wilderness* (*Mangyuan*) on May 25, 1926. Lu Xun, *Lu Xun quanji* (Complete works of Lu Xun), 18 vols. (Beijing: Renmin wenxue, 2005), 2:258–268.

Some say it refers to Ma Shumou, who, according to *The Records of Constructing the Canal,* helped construct the Grand Canal for Emperor Yang of the Sui dynasty and steamed children alive. If so, then written correctly, it should be the characters *"麻胡子 Ma Huzi"* (Ma the barbarian), in which case, Ma Shumou would then be a barbarian. But his ethnicity aside, there is a limit, after all, to his ability to devour children—it is restricted to his lifetime. However, the pernicious influence of those who undermine the vernacular is expansive and enduring, surpassing even that of floods and beasts—it can transform all of China into a "Ma the barbarian," into whose belly all children would meet their demise.

Those who conspire to eradicate the vernacular should all perish!

The gentlemen will no doubt shut their ears to this talk as it's a case of "leaping into mid-air and cursing until their bodies are just a mass of bruises—and not stopping even then." Men of letters will assuredly be cursing as well, since in their minds this goes against "literary convention" and consequently would inflict great damage on "personal character." But isn't it the case that "words are the voice of the heart"? A person's writing and his character are of course related. Though this human world has always been filled with strange and outlandish things—among the ranks of professors is a special tribe who "disrespect" a certain writer's character, yet have no choice but to admit that "his short stories are well-written."[47] But I'm not bothered by any of this, because I have, fortunately, yet to climb up to the "ivory tower," so I don't need to tread carefully. Were I to clamber into it by accident, then let me fall off immediately. And as I'm falling and before I hit the pavement, I would still say once more:

Those who conspire to eradicate the vernacular should all perish!

Whenever I see schoolchildren happily reading poor-quality printed matter such as *Children's World,* I am reminded of the finely crafted children's books of other countries and naturally feel sorry for Chinese children. But when recalling my own childhood years and those of my peers, I can't help but feel that the children now are, in fact, the fortunate ones as I sadly mourn our glory days, now long gone. What was there for us to read back then? If there was so much as a single illustration in a book, it would be condemned and banned by our private tutors—"the elder mentors of youth"[48] of the time— we might even have been struck on the palms of our hands. My little classmates, bored to death by reading such things as "In the begin- ning, human nature is good,"[49] could only satisfy their instinctive but not yet fully developed love of beauty by surreptitiously flipping to the first page to look at the picture of the demon-like portrait of Kui Xing (God of Literature), captioned "the literary star shines on high." Day after day, this was all they had to look at, and yet their eyes still lit up with recognition and delight.

Outside the academy, restrictions were relatively lax—at least for me, but probably not the same for everyone. In public, I could, with head held high, read things such as *The Illustrated Book of the Virtuous Deeds of Emperor Wen Chang* and *Records of the Jade Calendar,* which contain illustrations depicting the mysterious forces at work in sto- ries of reward and punishment of good and evil. The God of Thunder and Goddess of Lightning stand on the clouds, as masses of ox-headed and horse-faced beasts fill the netherworld. Not only is "leaping into mid-air" a violation of the rules of Heaven; so much as an inappro- priate word or an incorrect thought would be met with a fair mea- sure of retribution. Punishment is not meted out as a result "of suf- fering some personal slight"; since ghosts and gods rule there, "justice" prevails—bribing with wine or going down on one's knees begging for forgiveness have no effect, so there's really no way out. The Chi- nese cosmos is a difficult place, not just for humans but for ghosts as

well. But places better than our earthly realm—where there are neither "gentlemen" nor "gossip"—still exist, after all.

To be safe, it's best not to praise the Netherworld. This is especially true for those who are fond of dabbing their brushes in ink in
present-day China, at a time when "consistency between words and
deeds" is loftily preached but gossip reigns supreme. We ought to
learn from past examples. I have heard that in response to a young
woman's question, Artsybashev once said: "Only those who can find
happiness in life itself can go on living. Those who aren't able to find
any might as well be dead." Then someone by the name of Mikhailov
sent a letter deriding him: ". . . so with utmost sincerity I urge you to
kill yourself so that you may control your destiny. Firstly, this would
be a logical move, and secondly, your words and deeds would not contradict each other."

This argument is, in fact, like premeditated murder, and it's how
Mikhailov sought happiness in his own life. Artsybashev simply un-
leashed a barrage of complaints; he didn't kill himself. As for
Mr. Mikhailov, we don't know what happened to him in the end.
Having missed this chance at happiness, perhaps he was able to find
something else in its place. Of course, "in times like these, courage
is a safe haven and passion is without a hint of danger."

Yet, I have, in the end, praised the Netherworld, and there's no
way to take it back. Although this puts me under suspicion of being
"inconsistent in word and deed," I can say in my own defense that I
haven't received a single penny in perks from the Lord of the Netherworld or any of the lesser demons. So I might as well keep on writing.

The pictures I have seen of the Netherworld are from old books
owned by my family, not my own. The very first picture book I acquired was a gift from an elder: *The Illustrated Twenty-Four Exemplars*.
Though it was only a slim book, it had captions above the pictures

and fewer ghosts than humans; as it was my very own book, I was delighted with it. It seemed that virtually everyone knew the stories in it, even illiterates like Ah Chang could tell an elaborate tale after a mere glance at one of the pictures. But my initial excitement turned into disappointment. Only after asking someone to recount all twenty-four stories to me did I realize how difficult it was to be "filial." This made me lose all hope in my earlier foolish plan of becoming a filial son.

Are "men by nature, good"? This isn't an issue we need to go into now. Yet, I still vaguely remember how when I was young, I was never deliberately disobedient. In fact, I very much wanted to be filial. But as a boy, I was ignorant and simply used my own perspective to interpret what it meant to be "filial," which I believed meant nothing more than to be "submissive," "obedient," and then to make sure that when I grew up my elderly parents would be well fed. I only realized after acquiring this primer on filial sons that I had been mistaken, and that things were tens and hundreds of times more difficult than I had imagined.

Naturally, among them are stories such as "Zi Lu Carries Rice" and "Huang Xiang Fans the Pillow," which we can emulated. "Lu Ji Saves Tangerines" isn't hard either, so long as there is some rich person around who can treat me to meals. "Why is it the case, Mr. Lu Xun, that as my guest, you are saving tangerines?" Then I would kneel and reply, "My mother is most fond of them, so I want to bring some back to her." The rich man would be filled with admiration, and I would secure my status as a filial son, with minimal effort at that. But things like "Weeping to Make the Bamboo Sprout Shoots" are more questionable. I'm afraid that however sincere I might be, I would still fail to move heaven and earth. If I'm unable to make bamboo sprout shoots with my tears, I would merely lose face. But when it comes to

"Lying on Ice to Seek Carp," my life would be at stake. The weather in my hometown is mild, and even in the harshest winter, only a thin layer of ice forms on the surface of the water. If a child, however light, were to lie on the ice, he would surely break through it with a *whoosh* and fall into the water before a carp could swim over. Of course, one should be ready to give up one's own life, as only then would one's filiality move the gods and unimaginable miracles happen. But I was still young then and didn't understand such things.

What I found most difficult to understand, even repulsive, were two stories: "Old Lai Amuses His Parents" and "Guo Ju Buries His Son."

Even now I can still recall—one, an old man lying on his back in front of his parents, and the other, a baby being held in his mother's arms—the different reactions they elicited in me. Both held a toy called a *"gu-dong* rattle" in their hands. This toy is quite adorable; called a small drum in Beijing, it is also referred to as a *"tao."* According to Zhu Xi: "The *tao* is a small drum with an ear on each side. Grasp the handle and shake it and the ears strike at the drum" and *gu-dong gu-dong* sounds would be emitted. But this toy shouldn't have been in Old Laizi's hands; he should've been leaning on a walking stick instead. His manner is really just pretentious affectation and an insult to children. I never gave it a second look, and whenever I flipped to this page, I would quickly turn it over.

I have long since lost track of that copy of *The Illustrated Twenty-Four Exemplars*. The only one I have in my hands now is a volume illustrated by the Japanese Oda Umisen, which recounts the Old Laizi story as follows: "He was seventy but did not consider himself old. Often dressed in colorful garb, he behaved like an infant in front of his parents. He often fetched water to the hall and would fake a fall to the ground and cry like an infant to amuse them." The story in my old copy was probably similar. What rubbed me the wrong way was this "fake fall." Whether disobedient or filial, children dislike fakery; when they listen to stories, they dislike deceit. Anyone who has paid the slightest attention to child psychology would know this.

But when I checked older texts, it turns out that he wasn't such a hypocrite after all. Shi Jueshou's *Biographies of Filial Sons* recounts: "Lao Laizi . . . often dressed in colorful garbs. Fetching water for his parents to drink, he fell when he got to the hall. Afraid of distressing them, he lay face down and cried like an infant." Compared to recent stories, *The Imperial Records of the Taiping Era* rings more true to life. Who knows why the gentlemen who came later insisted upon changing his actions to "fakery" to make themselves feel better. When Deng Bodao abandoned his son to save his nephew, I think it was a case of "abandonment" and nothing more, but fatuous people had to go as far as to say that he tied his son to a tree so that the son wouldn't be able to chase after him. This is like "making something disgusting amusing," or taking something unreasonable as ethical, slandering the ancients and setting a bad example for posterity. Old Laizi is a case in point: while Neo-Confucians see him as the morally perfect exemplar, he had long ceased to exist in the hearts of children.

The son of Guo Ju playing with his *"gu-dong* rattle," however, certainly deserves sympathy. He was laughing happily in the arms of his mother just as his father was digging a hole to bury him. The caption reads: "The family of Guo Ju of the Han dynasty was poor. They had a three-year-old son and Guo's mother ate less in order to feed him. Ju said to his wife, 'We are so poor we cannot feed mother and our son shares her food. Should we bury the child?'" But the account in Liu Xiang's *Biographies of Filial Sons* is a bit different: Ju's family was wealthy, but he had given the money to his two younger brothers. The child was a newborn, not a three-year-old. The ending was roughly similar: "He dug a pit that was two feet deep and found a pot of gold. On it was written: 'Heaven's gift bestowed on Guo Ju, officials should not confiscate it and people should not seize it!'"

At first I broke out in a cold sweat for this child, able to relax only after the pot of gold had been dug up. However, I no longer dared entertain thoughts of becoming a filial son. I was, in fact, even afraid that my father himself would aspire to become one. Our family circumstances had become dire, and I often heard mother and father fretting over our daily expenses. My grandmother was old and if my father were to follow Guo Ju's example, then the one to be buried would be me, wouldn't it? If things worked out exactly as in the story and he too dug up a pot of gold, then of course this would be a blessing from Heaven. Yet, in spite of my young age at the time, I seem to have understood that such happy coincidences didn't necessarily happen in this world of ours.

Recalling this now, I feel foolish indeed. Because I now know that no one actually performed these old gimmicks. Wire dispatches on rectifying morals are common, but one seldom finds gentlemen lying naked on the surface of the ice or generals leaping out of their cars to carry rice. Not to mention that I have long since grown up and read a few old books and bought some new ones—*The Imperial Records of the Taiping Era, Biographies of Ancient Filial Exemplars, The Population Problem, Birth Control, The Twentieth Century Belongs to Children* and the like—and can come up with many reasons to resist being buried. But that was then and this is now, and at the time I was really quite afraid that a deep pit would be dug, no gold would be found, and I would be buried along with the *"gu-dong* rattle," covered with dirt that would be firmly tamped down—there was simply no way out. From then on, though I knew these things might not necessarily happen, I was always afraid of hearing my mother and father fret over being poor. I was afraid of seeing my white-haired grandmother, believing that the two of us were in a mortal standoff, or at least that she was somehow a threat to my existence. Afterward, these impressions gradually faded as the days went by, but some traces of this feeling lingered on up until she departed the world—this probably is something that the Confucian scholar who gave me *The Illustrated Twenty-Four Exemplars* never would have anticipated.

May 10[50]

Fair of the Five Fierce Gods

五猖會

Next to New Year and other holidays, children probably most looked forward to the temple fairs. Since my home was located in a remote area, by the time the procession came by it would invariably be afternoon, and the lineup would have dwindled and dwindled until only a paltry few remained. More often than not, after craning our necks and waiting for a good long time, all we would see were about a dozen or so people carrying a statue of a god with a gold—or sometimes blue or red—face, running by hastily. And that was that.

I often harbored this wish: that the temple fair *this* time would be more majestic than the last. But the result was always more or less the same—all I would be left with was a souvenir purchased with one copper before the statue of the gods passed by. This whistle—made of some clay, a few scraps of colored paper, a bamboo stick, and two or three chicken feathers—would emit an ear-piercing sound when blown. Called a "Blow *toot-toot*," it would *beep* and *beep* as I blew on it for a good two or three days.

First published in volume 1, issue 11, of the journal *Wilderness* (*Mangyuan*) on June 10, 1926. Lu Xun, *Lu Xun quanji* (Complete works of Lu Xun), 18 vols. (Beijing: Renmin wenxue, 2005) (hereafter *LXQJ*), 2:269–275.

As I look through Zhang Dai's *Dream Recollections of Tao'an* now, I feel that the temple fairs of that time were truly extravagant—even if essays by Ming dynasty writers are prone to a bit of exaggeration.[51] Rituals welcoming the Dragon King to bring about rain still exist, but they are performed simply, with nothing more than a dozen or so people twisting and coiling a dragon about and some village children dressing up as sea monsters. In the olden days, they re-enacted the actual stories, and they were truly marvelous spectacles to behold. Zhang Dai's record of the cast of characters from *The Water Margin* reads: ". . . and so they split off in four directions, searching for a short, dark man, a tall, slender man, a snake, a monk, a sturdy woman, a beautiful and slender woman, someone with an ashen-face, someone with a crooked-head, someone with a red-beard, someone with handsome sideburns, a dark burly man, and a red-faced person with a long mustache. They conducted a thorough search of the city, and if the search turned up empty, they went to the outskirts of the city, the villages, the remote areas in the mountains, and the neighboring prefectures and counties. A handsome price was paid to hire the thirty-six people playing the heroes of Liang Mountain, each one of them spirited and true to life, an orderly file of people and horses in procession. . . ." Who can resist the pleasure of reading such a vivid rendition of ancient personages brought to life? A pity that these kinds of grand displays have long since vanished, along with the Ming dynasty.

Although temple fairs—unlike the *qipaos* of Shanghai and discussions of national affairs in Beijing—haven't been banned by the authorities, women and children are still prohibited from watching them, and the educated, that is, the so-called "scholars," are mostly unwilling to watch them. Only idlers who have nothing better to do would rush to the temple or the *yamen* to witness the fun. My knowledge of temple fairs comes, for the most part, from these men's accounts, not the "eye-witnessing" prized by researchers. Yet I recall one instance where I saw with my own eyes a more spectacular version of the temple fair. At the head, a child riding a horse entered first, announcing the start of the procession. After a while, the pole balancer arrived, a big chubby man, whose back was dripping with sweat, holding a tall bamboo pole with a long banner trailing from it. When it pleased him, the pole balancer would place the pole on top of his head or between his teeth, or even on the tip of his nose. Next came the stilt walkers, stringed-instrument performers carried on a platform, and children riding on horses. And there were those impersonating convicts, dressed in red and in shackles, among them children. At the time I felt that these were all glorious undertakings and that those with an "in" were all blessed with good fortune— I was probably rather envious of all the attention they received. I thought: Why can't I come down with some serious illness so that my mother could go to the temple and make a vow to have me "dress up as a convict" in exchange for my recovery? . . . Yet even to this day, I have made no connections with the temple fair.

One time, I was going to Dongguan to watch the Fair of the Five Fierce Gods. This was a rare and splendid event in my childhood. That was the grandest fair in our county, and Dongguan was also very far from home—over twenty miles outside the city by boat. There were two special temples there. One was the Temple of the Plum Maiden, which, as recorded in *Strange Tales from Liaozhai*, refers to a maiden who had observed a vow of chastity after the death of her betrothed.[52] After death, she became a goddess and snatched away someone's husband. So now, on the seat of the shrine were, sure enough, figures of a young man and woman beaming with delight, much in violation of Confucian propriety. The other was the Temple of the Five Fierce Gods—the name itself was rather unusual. According to sticklers for research, these were the Wutong gods, though there is no definitive proof. The statues were of five men who didn't look particularly fierce at all; behind them, in a single file, were five wives seated in random order, the hierarchal distinctions between them far less rigidly drawn than in Beijing's theaters. This, too, was much in violation of Confucian propriety. Yet, since they were *the* Five Fierce Gods, nothing could be done about it, so naturally we just had to view them as exceptions to the rule.

Dongguan was a long way from town, so everyone got up at dawn. Reserved the night before, the big boat—with three windows inlaid with translucent shell tiles—was already moored by the river dock. Chairs, food, tea-water brewer, and snack trays were loaded onto it one after another. I laughed and skipped, urging them to move faster. All at once, the laborers' faces turned very serious, so I knew something was not quite right. I looked around—my father was standing right behind me.

"Go get your book," he said slowly.

The "book" he was referring to was the primer, *A Brief Mirror of History,* the only book I had at the time.[53] Where we lived, the age children started going to school was usually an odd number, reminding me that I was seven at the time.

Feeling uneasy, I brought my book over. He made me sit with him at the table in the middle of the hall and had me read, verse by verse. I anxiously read on, verse by verse.

There were two verses to a line. After I had read about twenty or thirty verses, he said:

"Have them memorized. If you can't recite them by heart, you are forbidden from going to the fair."

After saying this, he stood up and walked into his room.

It was as if a basin of cold water had been poured over my head. But what could I do? So of course I just read again and again, forcing myself to memorize by rote since I had to recite it all out loud.

"In the beginning, there was Pan Gu, born in the primordial void.
He was first to rule the world, to separate the formless chaos."

This was the kind of book it was, and all I can remember now are these first four verses, the rest all forgotten. Of course, the twenty or thirty lines I was forced to memorize are among those I have forgotten. I recall hearing someone say at the time that reading *A Brief Mirror of History* was much more useful than reading the *Thousand Character Classic* or the *Hundred Surnames,* because one could glean from it a general sense of the history from ancient to contemporary times.[54] Having a general sense of the history from ancient to contemporary times is, of course, a good thing, but I didn't understand a word of it. "In the beginning, there was Pan Gu" was just "In the beginning, there was Pan Gu," and so I read on and memorized it. "In the beginning, there was Pan Gu." Alas! "Born in the primordial void." Alas!

All the necessities had been loaded. The chaotic bustle of the home transformed into a solemn silence. The morning sun was shining on the western wall and the weather was clear. Mother, the laborers, Mama Chang, *aka* Ah Chang, not one of them could rescue me. All they could do was to wait silently as I memorized and recited aloud. In the pervasive silence, it was as if iron tongs had sprouted from my head, grasping onto the verses "Born in the primeval void" and the like. I also heard the sound of my own voice quivering as I nervously recited, like a cricket in late autumn, chirping in the night.

They all waited. The sun rose even higher.

I suddenly felt as if I had a good grasp of things. So I stood up, walked into my father's study with the book in hand, then recited it all in one breath—and then it was over and done with, as if it were all a dream.

"Not bad. Go then." Father said, nodding his head.

Everyone sprang into action at once, and their faces all broke out in smiles as they walked towards the dock. One of the laborers, carrying me high above his head as if congratulating me on my victory, quickly strode ahead to lead the way.

But I wasn't as jubilant as they were. After the boat set off, the scenery along the waterway, the snacks in the boxes, and the festivities when we arrived at Dongguan—nothing seemed of any great interest to me.

Even now, everything else is completely forgotten, vanished without a trace, except for the episode of reciting *A Brief Mirror of History*—still as clear in my mind as if it had happened yesterday.

To this day, when I think of it, I still wonder why my father had to make me memorize those lines at that particular moment.

May 25[55]

Wu Chang
[Life Is Unpredictable]

無常

If the gods paraded about on the day of the temple fairs possess the power to grant life and death—no, the phrase "power to grant life and death" is not quite appropriate, as it seems that all gods in China have the power to kill people off at their whim. . . . Or, to phrase it more appropriately, if they, like the City Gods and General Yue, can control people's fate, then you will find some unusual characters in their entourage: ghost attendants, ghost kings, and Wu Chang.

These ghosts and spirits seem to be impersonated mostly by coarse folk or villagers. The ghost attendants and ghost kings wear red and green garments and are barefoot, their blue faces painted with fish scales—or maybe dragon scales, or scales of some creature or other, I'm not altogether sure. The ghost attendants hold steel tridents in their hands, the rings on them jangling when shaken. The ghost

First published in volume 1, issue 13, of the journal *Wilderness (Mangyuan)* on July 10, 1926. Lu Xun, *Lu Xun quanji* (Complete works of Lu Xun), 18 vols. (Beijing: Renmin wenxue, 2005), 2:276–286. Wu Chang is the ghost that, according to folk legend, snatches people's souls at the moment of death.

king carries a small tiger-head talisman. According to legend, the ghost king walks on only one foot, but he is, after all, impersonated by a mere villager. So though his face has scales of some creature or other painted on it, he still has to walk on two feet. Thus, the spectators aren't all that awed by these ghosts and don't pay them much heed—that is, with the exception of the old ladies reciting Buddhist sutras and their grandchildren who, fully considerate of all parties, still follow the proper etiquette, making a show of "fearfully awaiting orders" in their presence.

As for us—I believe for myself and many others—we most wanted to see Wu Chang. Not only is he lively and funny, but the mere fact that his whole body is white as snow in the midst of the sea of red and green makes him stand out like "a crane among a flock of chickens." As soon as people catch a glimpse of the tall white paper hat and the tattered palm-leaf fan in his hand from afar, they tense up slightly and get excited.

Of all the ghosts and spirits, he is the one people are most familiar with and fond of, the one they encounter most regularly. Behind the worship halls of the City God Temple and the Dongyue Temple is a dark room called the "Chamber of Hell." Through the dimness are barely perceptible figures of various ghosts: the hanged ghosts, the fallen-to-death ghosts, the injured-by-tiger ghosts, the failed examinee ghosts . . . But as soon as you enter, the tall white object you see right away is Wu Chang. Though I paid my respects to this "Chamber of Hell" once on my own, at the time I was too afraid to take a good look. I have heard that he holds an iron chain in one hand because he is the messenger in charge of summoning living souls. Legend has it that the layout of the "Chamber of Hell" in the Dongyue Temple in Fan Jiang was quite extraordinary. At the entrance was a live plank. As soon as someone entered and stepped on one end, the effigy of Wu Chang on the other end would fly over and throw an iron chain securely around your neck. After someone literally died of fright from it, the plank was nailed down tight. So by the time of my childhood, the plank had already ceased to budge.

If you really want to get a clear look at Wu Chang, there's a picture of him drawn in *Records of the Jade Calendar*.[56] But *Records of the Jade Calendar* has both an abridged and unabridged version, and any unabridged version is sure to have his image. He is dressed in mourning clothes, a straw sash tied around his waist, feet in straw sandals, and a string of paper money is hung around his neck. He holds a palm-leaf fan, an iron chain, and an abacus in his hands. His shoulders are raised up, but his hair is let down loose. The outer edges of his eyebrows and eyes curve downward, like the character "eight" (八). On his head is a rectangular hat, wide at the brim and narrow at the tip. Calculated to actual proportions, it should be about two feet high. On the front, right at the spot where a jade stone or pearl would be affixed to the melon caps worn by the Qing loyalists—young and old—are four characters, written vertically: "Happiness at first sight." However, in another edition, what's written are the characters: "You, too, have arrived." These four characters are also sometimes seen on the tablets hung in front of the Judge Bao temples. As for who wrote the characters on his hat, whether it was he himself or the King of the Netherworld, I haven't found an answer.

In *Records of the Jade Calendar* is also a spirit that is the antithesis of Wu Chang who wears similar clothing, called Death-Is-Destiny (*Si You Fen*). He also appears in the temple fair processions, but his name is mistakenly identified as "Death-Is-Unpredictable" (*Si Wu Chang*). Black-faced, dressed in black, no one likes to look at him. He also appears in the "Chamber of Hell," standing eerily, his chest facing the wall, a literal case of "running into a wall." Everyone who goes in to light incense sticks has to rub his spine, which supposedly rids one of bad luck. When I was a child, I also rubbed this spine, but it seemed like I was never quite able to escape bad luck. Perhaps if I hadn't rubbed it, my luck would have turned even worse now—yet another thing that I haven't been able to verify through my research.

I haven't studied the classics of Hinayana Buddhism either, but based on what I've heard in passing, in the Indian Buddhist classics, there is the god Yama and the Ox-Headed Demon, both of whom are in charge of Hell. As for this messenger, Mr. Wu Chang, who summons the souls of the living, it seems that there isn't any evidence of his existence in ancient times, but what is commonly heard are phrases such as "Life is unpredictable" (*huo wu chang*). It could be that this idea was given a concrete form after it was transmitted to China. So Wu Chang could, in fact, be a Chinese creation.

But why do people tense up a bit and get excited as soon as they see him?

Literary scholars and prominent men can easily transform a locale into a "model county" by claiming it as their birthplace with a wave of their brush. My hometown was once praised by Mr. Yu Zhongxiang at the end of the Han dynasty, but that praise came much too early. Later, it could not escape the label of the place that produced "Shaoxing legal experts."[57] However, it is not the case that all of us—men, women, the elderly, and the young—are "Shaoxing legal experts"; many other types of "inferior people" exist as well. You can't really expect these inferior types to come up with such clever nonsense as "Just now we are walking a narrow, perilous little path; on the left is a vast, boundless marsh, while on the right is a vast, boundless zone of shifting sand, with our destination at a remote distance far ahead, shrouded in a light fog."[58] But quite unintentionally, they see the path toward "the destination shrouded in a light fog" very clearly: betrothal, marriage, bringing up children, death. But this, of course, applies only to my particular hometown, with people from "model counties" being another case entirely. Many of them—the "inferior people" from my humble hometown—live and suffer, have been slandered and defamed, and know from experience that there is only one assembly where "justice" is preserved in the human world. This assembly itself is "at a remote distance," so they can't help being drawn to the Netherworld. Most people feel that they have suffered mistreatment. The "estimable gentlemen" now alive are only able to deceive the birds, for if you ask the ignorant masses they will reply without a second thought: "Fair judgment can be found in the Netherworld!"

When you think of life's pleasures, life is certainly worth cherishing; but when you think of its sorrows, Wu Chang is not necessarily an unwelcome guest. Whether one is from an aristocratic or humble background, wealthy or poor, when the time comes, all "meet the King of Hell empty-handed"—the aggrieved can appeal and the guilty are punished. Who's to say that "inferior people" haven't engaged in self-reflection? What do I have to show for the life I have lived? Have I "leaped into mid-air"? Have I "been treacherous to others"? In Wu Chang's hands, there is a big abacus and nothing good will come of putting on airs. We expect pure justice for others, but even in the Netherworld, we hope to find some personal connections for ourselves. It is Hell after all—the King of Hell, the Ox-Headed Demon, even China's own creation, the Horse-Faced Demon, are single-mindedly devoted to one job only, to faithfully administer justice, though they haven't published any grand essays in the papers. But before becoming ghosts, those who are honest with themselves when they contemplate the distant future sometimes still can't resist the thought of finding some clemency in the overarching realm of public justice. At this time, our Wu Chang appears quite endearing. One should reap maximum benefit while incurring minimal harm—our ancient philosopher Mr. Mo Que referred to this as a "small gain."

You can't really tell how endearing Wu Chang is from the clay figures in the temple or the ink printed on the pages of a book—it's best to go to the opera. But not just any ordinary opera, you have to watch the "grand opera" or the "Maudgalyāyana opera." Zhang Dai, too, has described with exaggeration the bustle of the Maudgalyāyana opera in *Dream Recollections of Tao An*[59] as lasting two or three days. It was no longer the case by the time of my childhood. Like any other grand opera, it started at dusk and ended at dawn the following day. These operas were performed to honor the gods and avert disasters. The plays always had an evil character who meets his demise at dawn the following day when his "evil ways have runneth over" and the King of Hell issues a writ for his arrest. This is when Wu Chang, brimming with liveliness, would appear on stage.

I still recall myself sitting in a boat below the stage, and the spectators' mood was different from usual. Normally, as the night wore on their spirits flagged, but this time people became more animated. The tall paper hat worn by Wu Chang, originally hanging at one corner of the stage, had been taken inside. A special musical instrument was also being readied so it could be blown forcefully. This instrument resembled a horn, long and thin, about seven or eight feet in length. It could be that ghosts are particularly fond of hearing it, as the instrument isn't used when no ghosts are involved. When blown, it makes the sound *"Nhatu, nhatu, nhatututuu,"* so we called it "Maudgalyāyana's bugle."

Amidst the fixed gaze of many people eagerly awaiting the fall of the evil character, Wu Chang would appear, his costume even simpler than in the paintings, with neither chain nor abacus. Just a coarse fellow dressed all in white limping around, with a powdered face and red lips, his eyebrows black as lacquer—no one could tell whether he was laughing or crying. But as soon as he appeared on stage, he lets out one hundred and eight sneezes and one hundred and eight farts before telling his life story. It's a pity I no longer remember clearly, but one part went along these lines—

> The Great King issued a writ for me to go arrest the scab-head next door.
>
> When I asked, it turned out to be my cousin's son.
>
> What illness does he have? He has typhoid, accompanied by dysentery.
>
> Which doctor has he seen? Chen *la* Nianyi's son from Xiafang Bridge.
>
> What kind of prescription was he given? Monkshood, cinnamon, added to that, achyranthes root.
>
> After taking the first dose, cold sweat broke out.
>
> After the second, both feet stretched out stiff.
>
> I said *nga* aunt is weeping with grief, temporarily revive him in the world of the living for just a moment.
>
> The great king accused me of taking a bribe, then had me tied me up and thrashed forty whips!

The character *"zi"* (in *laizi,* scab-head) in the narrative is pronounced with a glottal stop. Chen Nianyi was a famous doctor in Zhejiang. Yu Zhonghua had written him into *Sequel to Outlaws on the Marsh* as an immortal. But his son, it seems, was not so illustrious. *"La"* indicates possessive and *"er"* as in son is read as *"ni,"* an old pronunciation; *nga* means "mine" or "ours."

In Wu Chang's description, the King of Hell doesn't seem particularly clever—he quite unexpectedly misjudges Wu Chang's personal character—rather, ghostly character. But since he still knew how to "revive him in the world of the living for just a moment," he didn't lose his reputation as a "clever and just god" after all. But this punishment imprinted upon our Wu Chang an indelible sense of injustice. As soon as it was brought up, his eyebrows furrowed even more deeply, he clasped his tattered palm-leaf fan tightly, and as he turned his face toward the floor, he started dancing like a duck floating on water.

Nhatu, nhatu, nhatu—nhatu—nhatututuu! Maudgalyāyana's bugle also seemed to be sounding out its inconsolable grievance over this injustice. Wu Chang thus decided:

> Now no one will be spared!
> Be you behind a bronze or iron wall!
> Be you kin of royalty!

"Though resentful, he doesn't blame others." Though he no longer shows an ounce of mercy, it was because he had no choice in the matter, as he was under the surveillance of the King of Hell. Of all the ghosts out there, only he has any human feeling. If we don't turn into ghosts that would be that; but if we do, then he is naturally the only one we can form a close bond with.

Even now, it is chiseled in my memory how I would often, along with the "inferior people" in my hometown, happily look into the eyes of this ghostly yet human, rational yet sentimental, dreadful yet endearing, Wu Chang. And to appreciate the tears and laughter on his face, the insolent words and witty talk from his mouth . . .

The Wu Chang that appears in the temple fair processions is a little different from the one on the opera stage. He has physical movements but no speech, and he follows on the heels of a clown-like character carrying a dish of food. Wu Chang wants to eat, but the clown won't let him. Two other characters are added, referred to as the "wife and child" by the estimable gentlemen. All "inferior people" have a common fault: that is, they want to give others what they want for themselves. Even ghosts aren't allowed to feel lonely, so ghosts and gods are just about all matched up in pairs—Wu Chang was no exception. First there was the pretty, if a bit rustic, woman whom everyone called Sister Wu Chang. From this we can infer that Wu Chang belongs to our generation—no wonder he doesn't put on the airs of an eminent professor. Then there was the child, wearing a small tall hat and tiny white shirt. Though still small, both shoulders were already hunched, and the outer tips of his eyebrows drooped. Obviously, this was young Master Wu Chang, but everyone called him "Ah Ling," which seemed a bit disrespectful. If one were to venture a guess as to why, it may have been because he was the son of Sister Wu Chang by her former husband. But then why did he look so similar to Wu Chang? Alas! Matters related to ghosts and gods are difficult to elucidate, so we can only set them aside and refrain from discussing them for the time being. As for why Wu Chang didn't have sons and daughters of his own, it's easy to explain in this day and age: since ghosts and gods can foresee the future, he was afraid that once he had many children, those given to gossip would spread rumors of how he had accepted rubles.[60] So he not only researched the subject but had actually long since been practicing "birth control."

This episode involving the dish of food is called "Sending Off Wu Chang." Since he is the summoner of human souls, it is the custom that whenever someone dies, people have to respectfully send Wu Chang off with food and wine. As for not allowing Wu Chang to eat, it isn't actually as it appears—it's just a prank pulled during the temple fair. But everyone thinks of pulling pranks on Wu Chang because he is straightforward, outspoken, and humane. If you are searching for a true friend, he is a most fitting candidate.

Some say that he was a living person who went to the Netherworld. That is, he was originally a human being who, in his dreams, would go to the Netherworld to serve as a messenger—hence his humanity. I still recall a man who lived in a hut not far from my home who referred to himself as "Walking Wu Chang." Lighted incense and candles were often placed by his door. But it seemed to me that the ghostly aura on *his* face was even more pronounced. Could it be that once one becomes a ghost in the Netherworld one's human aura becomes enhanced? Alas! Matters related to ghosts and gods are difficult to elucidate, so we can simply set them aside and refrain from discussing them for the time being.

June 23[61]

From the Garden of Myriad Grasses to the Three Flavors Studio

從百草園到三味書屋

Behind my house was a large garden with the fabled name "Garden of Myriad Grasses." It has long since been sold now, along with the house, to Zhu Xi's descendants.[62] Even that last time I saw it, seven or eight years ago, I am almost certain that nothing but some weeds were growing there. But at one time it was my paradise.

No need to mention the emerald green vegetable plots, the glistening stone wall surrounding the well, the gigantic honey-locust trees, the purplish-red mulberries, nor the continuous trilling of cicadas among the trees, the fat wasps hiding among the rape blossoms, the agile skylarks suddenly scurrying between the blades of grass and flying off into the clouds—just the area around the foot of the short mud wall in itself held endless sources of amusement. Insects sang in

First published in volume 1, issue 19, of the journal *Wilderness* (*Mangyuan*) on October 10, 1926. Lu Xun, *Lu Xun quanji* (Complete works of Lu Xun), 18 vols. (Beijing: Renmin wenxue, 2005), 2:287–293.

low tones, and crickets played their zithers here. Sometimes you might encounter a centipede when you turned over a broken brick. Also blister beetles—when you pressed down on their spines with your finger, you would hear a *pop* as it released a puff of vapor from its rear. Knotweed and creeping fig vines wrapped around each other; the creeping fig bore fruit resembling a lotus pod, and the knotweed had swollen, tuber-like roots. It is said that some knotweed roots resemble the human form, which, if eaten, could turn you into an immortal. So I frequently uprooted them, one after another, damaging the mud wall as a result, but I never saw a human-shaped root. If you weren't afraid of thorns, you could also pick raspberries that were like little balls made of tiny coral beads, sweet and sour at the same time, but far superior in color and taste to mulberries.

I never ventured into the tall grass, as legend had it that a big red-banded snake resided in that part of the garden.

Mama Chang once told me a story: Once long ago, there was a scholar who lived in an ancient temple, devoting himself to his studies. One night, he was enjoying the cool breeze in the courtyard when he suddenly heard someone calling him. He responded and looked around and saw the face of a beautiful maiden above the wall, flashing him a smile and then vanishing. He was delighted, but an old monk who had come for a nightly chat saw through the ruse. The monk said that the scholar's face had taken on a demonic aura, so he must have encountered a "Beautiful Maiden Snake"—a monster with the body of a snake and head of a human that had the ability to call people by name. If one responded to it, it would come in the evening and devour that person's flesh. Naturally, the scholar was frightened to death, but the old monk told him not to worry, gave him a small box, and said that so long as it was placed by his pillow, he could sleep without a care. Though he did as he was told, the scholar was—*of course*—still unable to fall asleep. Indeed, at midnight, it did appear—*sha sha sha!*—a sound of what seemed like wind and rain could be heard outside. He was just curling himself up into a ball in terror when he heard a *whoosh* as a golden ray of light flashed out from beside his pillow. Then all went quiet outside and the golden ray came flying back into the box. And after that? After that, the old monk told him that it was a flying centipede that had the ability to suck out snake brains, and the Beautiful Maiden Snake had been killed by it.

The moral of the story: If a strange voice calls your name, don't, by any means, respond to it.

This story made me realize the precarious nature of human life. When taking in the cool breeze on summer evenings, I would often feel a little anxious, afraid to look above the wall, and long all the more to get my hands on a box like the old monk's that contained a flying centipede. I often felt this way when I walked to the edge of the tall grassy area of the Garden of Myriad Grasses. To this day, I still haven't managed to get my hands on such a box, but then neither have I encountered a red-banded snake or the Beautiful Maiden Snake. To be sure, there have often been unfamiliar voices that have called out my name, but none belonged to the Beautiful Maiden Snake.

The Garden of Myriad Grasses was rather lackluster in the winter, but it was an entirely different matter after a snowfall. When pressing snowmen (imprinting the shape of one's body into the snow) and making snow arhats, one needs appreciative onlookers. Since this was a desolate place with scarcely a trace of human presence, it wasn't a suitable spot for such things—it was only good for catching birds. It wasn't feasible, however, when the snow was sparse; one could only do so after the snow had covered the ground for a day or two, after the birds had gone through a period without food. I would sweep aside a patch of snow to expose the ground and use a short stick to prop up a large bamboo sieve, scatter some grain husks underneath it, and tie the stick to a long string. I would hold onto the string from afar and watch for the birds to descend and peck at the food. When they went underneath the sieve, I would tug the string and trap them inside. What I caught, however, were mostly sparrows. I also caught white-cheeked wagtails, but they were so anxious in temperament that they couldn't be kept alive overnight in captivity.

Runtu's father taught me this method, but I wasn't very good at it. I could clearly see the birds go under the sieve, yet when I tugged on the string and ran over to look, there would be nothing there. After a lot of effort, I would catch a mere three or four sparrows. Runtu's father was able to catch several dozen in no time at all and put them into a sack where they would chirp and collide against one another. When I asked him the secret of his success, he smiled and said calmly: "You're too impatient, you don't wait for the bird to make its way to the center."

I don't know why my family wanted to send me to the private academy—and the strictest academy in our whole town at that. Maybe it was because I had uprooted the knotweed flowers and ruined the mud wall, or perhaps it was because I threw a brick into the home of our neighbors, the Liangs, or maybe it was because I stood on the stone wall surrounding the well and jumped off it . . . but there was no way for me to know. In sum: I would no longer be able to frequent the Garden of Myriad Grasses. Adieu, my crickets! Adieu, my raspberries and creeping figs . . .

I would head out the door, go east for just a few hundred yards, cross a stone bridge, and arrive at my teacher's home. I would enter through a black-lacquered bamboo gate. The third room was the study, and in the middle of the wall hung a placard that read "Three

Flavors Studio," beneath which was a painting of a plump spotted deer resting under an old tree. There was no memorial tablet to Confucius, so we performed our rituals facing the placard and the deer. The first bow was to Confucius, the second to our teacher.

When we bowed the second time, the teacher would smile amiably and return our bow from off to the side. He was a tall, skinny old man, his hair and beard streaked with gray, and he wore large spectacles. I respected him very much, because I had long heard that he was one of the most upstanding, unpretentious, and erudite men in our town.

I don't know where I heard this, but apparently Dongfang Shuo[63] was also very erudite, and he knew of an insect, called the *guaizai*, or "Strange Indeed." It had metamorphosized from the grievances of wronged souls and would disappear when sprinkled with wine. I wanted to know the story in detail, but Ah Chang didn't know about it, as she was, after all, not very knowledgeable. Now I had my chance—I could ask the teacher.

"Teacher, this insect called 'Strange Indeed'—what is it all about?" I asked hurriedly, after the new lesson ended and right before being dismissed.

"I don't know!" He seemed very displeased and an angry look appeared on his face.

It was then that I realized students shouldn't ask about such things—the only thing we were supposed to do was study. Since he was an erudite scholar, surely it wasn't a matter of him not knowing. "Not knowing" simply meant that he was unwilling to tell me. Those older than I were often like this, something I had encountered many a time.

And so I just studied, at noon-time practicing calligraphy, and in the evening composing rhyming couplets. The teacher was very strict

with me the first few days but lightened up later, though he gradually assigned more books for me to read and added more characters
to the lines of the couplets I had to compose—from three characters
to five, and finally to seven.

There was also a garden behind the Three Flavors Studio. Though
it was small, you could climb up the flower terrace to pick wintersweet and search the ground or the osmanthus trees for cicada cast-
ings. The best occupation was to catch flies to feed the ants, which
could be done ever so quietly without so much as a peep. Yet it would
not do when too many of my classmates sneaked out to the garden
at once or lingered there for too long, as the teacher would yell out
from the studio: "Where did everybody go?"

And so one by one, we would return in a steady stream, although
returning all at once wouldn't do either. He had a ferrule, but didn't
use it often, and also a rule of punishment by kneeling, but he didn't
resort to that often, either. Normally he would just glare at you a few
times and say in a loud voice:

"Keep on reading!"

And so everyone recited passages at the top of their lungs—what
a cacophony! Someone would recite: "Is benevolence far from us? If
I desire benevolence, it will come." Someone else would recite: "To
mock someone with missing teeth, say 'the dog's den is wide open.'"
Yet another would recite: "On the ninth of the month, the dragon
hides itself, waiting for an auspicious time." And still another: "Rich
and poor soil are mixed together there. Sacrificial objects include
mats, tangerines, and pomelos" . . . The teacher also recited aloud,
and as our voices grew softer and quieter, he alone would be left
reading out loudly:

"Iron scepter in hand, he directs things in an elegant and free
manner, all are amazed . . . the golden goblet overflows, with utter
pleasure, he imbibes a thousand cups without getting drunk . . ."

I wondered if this were not an exceedingly good piece of writing, because whenever he read to this part, he would always smile, raise and shake his head, tilting it back further and further.

It suited us very well when the teacher was completely absorbed in his recitations. Some of us would place helmets made of paper glued together on our fingernails and perform puppet shows. I would take paper made of bamboo, place it over an illustration from a novel, and trace the picture, just as I would trace characters when practicing calligraphy. The more books I read, the more drawings I made. Although not entirely successful in my studies, I accomplished quite a bit in my drawings, the best being some of the portraits from *Sequel to the Water Margin* and *Journey to the West,* all gathered into a thick volume. Afterward, I sold the volume to a wealthy classmate because I needed money—his father owned a store that made tinfoil used for funerals. I've heard that he has since become the manager of the shop and is soon to be promoted to a member of the local gentry. The drawings have probably long since disappeared.

September 18[64]

Father's Illness

父親的病

It was probably over ten years ago when the story of a particular eminent doctor spread widely in S City.[65]

His fee for house calls was originally about a *yuan* and forty cents, for emergency calls ten *yuan,* night calls double that, and for trips outside the city, double yet again. One particular night, a family that lived on the city outskirts summoned him after their daughter suddenly developed an acute illness. By this time, he had already become so wealthy that he couldn't be bothered, so he refused to go unless paid 100 *yuan.* So they had no choice but to do as he wished.

When he arrived, he cursorily examined the patient and said: "It's not serious." He wrote a prescription, took the 100 *yuan* and departed.

The patient's family seemed to be very wealthy—they summoned him again the next day. As soon as he arrived at the gate, he was greeted with a smile by the master of the house, who said: "After taking the medicine you prescribed last night, she got a lot better, so

First published in volume 1, issue 21, of the journal *Wilderness* (*Mangyuan*) on November 10, 1926. Lu Xun, *Lu Xun quanji* (Complete works of Lu Xun), 18 vols. (Beijing: Renmin wenxue, 2005), 2:294–300.

we asked you to come again for a follow-up visit." As before, he was led into the room. The old maidservant gently pulled the patient's hand out from underneath the bed curtain. Upon palpating it, he found it was ice cold and without a pulse. He then nodded his head and said: "Oh, I understand this illness." He calmly walked to the table, took out a sheet of paper used for prescriptions, raised his brush and wrote:

"On presentation of this note, pay the exact sum of 100 Mexican dollars."[66] Underneath was his signature and stamp.

"Sir, it appears that this illness is pretty serious, so I'm afraid you may need to prescribe stronger medicine," the master of the house said from behind him.

"Fine," he said. He then wrote another prescription.

"On presentation of this note, pay the exact sum of 200 Mexican dollars." Underneath was his signature and stamp.

With this, the master of the house took the prescription and courteously escorted him out.

I had to deal with this eminent doctor for a period of two whole years, as he paid house calls on my father every other day. Though he was already very famous by then, he hadn't yet become so wealthy that he couldn't be bothered, but his consultation fee was already one *yuan* and forty cents. Nowadays in cities, a consultation fee of 10 *yuan* per visit isn't out of the ordinary, but at the time, one *yuan* 40 cents was a huge sum and wasn't so easy to come up with—not to mention that his visits were every other day. He probably was, indeed, somewhat extraordinary, and public opinion had it that the formulas he used for his medicines were unique. I didn't know anything about the medicines themselves, I only felt some of the "adjuvants" in his prescriptions were hard to come by. Whenever he changed to a new prescription, it would create a great deal of work for us. First medicine had to be purchased, then we had to search for the adjuvants. He didn't use things like two slices of fresh ginger or ten bamboo leaves—tips removed. At the very least, it was things like aloe root dug up by the river, or sugar cane that had weathered three years of frost—which took at least two or three days to find. But the strange thing was that there wasn't anything that we weren't able to purchase or find in the end.

According to public opinion, his ingenuity lies here. Once, a patient for whom no medicinal herbs were effective encountered a Mr. Ye Tianshi, who added just one adjuvant: a leaf from a parasol tree. With just one dose, he recovered immediately. "A cure requires careful consideration." Actually, it was autumn, and the parasol tree is always the first to detect autumn's ambience. Prior to this, no medicine had worked, so he may have used the autumn weather to activate something, the *qi* of the ambience affecting the patient's *qi*, so that. . . . While I didn't really understand any of this, I was still full of admiration, as I knew that elixirs were necessarily hard to come by. Those searching for immortality would even go as far as to risk their lives and dispatch themselves into remote mountains to gather them.

This went on for two years, and we gradually grew better acquainted, almost to the point of considering each other friends. Father's edema got worse by the day until he was practically bedridden. My faith in things like sugar cane that had weathered three years of frost also gradually diminished, and I was no longer as enthusiastic as I had been in the past when it came to collecting the adjuvants. One day, right around this time, he came to examine my father again, asked about his symptoms, and then very earnestly said:

"I have exhausted my knowledge. There's a Dr. Chen Lianhe here whose abilities are superior to mine. I recommend having him come take a look—I can write a letter to him in that regard. The illness isn't serious, but in his care the recovery will be much faster . . ."

It seemed that no one was in good spirits that day. Still, I respectfully saw him off to his sedan chair as before. When I returned, I saw a strange expression on my father's face as he discussed the matter with everyone—the point being that there was probably no longer any hope for his illness. The doctor had been seeing him for two years to no effect and had come to know him so well that he, naturally, would feel a little embarrassed. So when the illness became critical, he recommended a new doctor to take his place so as to sever the relationship completely. But what other choice was left to us? The only other eminent doctor in the city was, in fact, this Chen Lianhe, so the following day we summoned him.

Chen's consultation fee was also one *yuan* and forty cents. But the former eminent doctor had a round and chubby face, while this one's face was long and fat—they were quite different in this respect. The medicines prescribed were also different—the former eminent doctor's could still be handled by one person, but this doctor's were difficult to manage on my own, as his prescriptions always included some special powder *and* some unusual adjuvant.

He never called for aloe root or sugar cane that had endured three years of frost. More often than not it was "a pair of crickets," with a notation on the side written in small characters: "Must be mated, from the same nest." It seemed that even insects had to be chaste; remarriage or finding another mate after being widowed disqualified them from even being used medicinally. But these assignments were not all that difficult for me—setting foot in the Garden of Myriad Grasses, I could easily find ten pairs of crickets. I would string them together, throw them into boiling water—mission accomplished. There were, however, things that no one had heard of, such as "ardisia." We asked the herbalist, we asked country folk, we asked purveyors of medicinal herbs, we asked the elderly, we asked scholars, we asked carpenters—all of them just shook their heads. It only occurred to me later to ask my distant uncle, an old man who was fond of gardening. When I ran over to ask him, it turned out that he did, indeed, know. A small shrub that grows beneath trees in the mountains, it bears small red fruit like coral beads and is commonly referred to as "Never-Grows-Large."

"What you search for all over, appears when you search no more." Having found the adjuvant, there was still the special pill: the "Broken Drum Leather Pill," made from the leather of old drums that had been damaged by constant beating. Edema is also known as drum swelling, using leather from a worn-out drum would naturally "beat" the illness. When Gang Yi from the Qing dynasty prepared to attack the "foreign devils" [*yang guizi*] he hated, he used the same logic in training his "tiger spirit battalion," [*hushen zhen*] as tigers [*hu*] eat sheep [*yang*, homonym for "foreign"] and the spirits [*shen*] could defeat devils [*guizi*]." It was a pity that this miraculous medicine was sold in only one place in the entire city, a good mile and half from our home. But at least, unlike the ardisia, it didn't have to be found in the dark, as Dr. Chen earnestly instructed us in great detail after writing out the prescription.

"I have a kind of tablet," Dr. Chen told us on one occasion, "that when placed on the tongue will surely be effective. Because the tongue is where the spirit of the heart sprouts from . . . it isn't very expensive either, only two *yuan* a box . . ."

My father reflected silently for a moment, then shook his head.

"There's been no effect, even with this medicine I've prescribed," Dr. Chen said on one occasion. "I think we should summon someone to see if there's some grievance the spirit world is holding against you.

Doctors can cure your illness, but not your destiny, right? Of course, this may be something that occurred in a past life . . ."

My father reflected silently for a moment, then shook his head.

"The nation's best can revive the dead"—when we pass by doctors' gates, we often see placards making such claims. They have toned it down a bit since, even doctors themselves now acknowledge that "the forte of Western doctors is surgery, while that of Chinese doctors is internal medicine." At the time, however, not only was there no Western doctor in S City; no one could even imagine that such a thing as a Western doctor existed under heaven. So people could only arrange to be seen by the descendants of the Yellow Emperor and Qibo.[67] At the time of the Yellow Emperor, however, there was no distinction between shamans and doctors, and even now their disciples still see ghosts and believe things such as "the tongue is where the spirit of the heart sprouts from." This is the Chinese people's "destiny," and even the most eminent doctors have no way of curing it.

My father was unwilling to put the miracle tablet on his tongue and couldn't think of how he may have offended the spirit world, so, needless to say, of what use could taking a hundred-day course of Broken Drum Leather Pills be? It still didn't "beat" the edema and in the end, father could only lie in bed, gasping for air. We asked Dr. Chen to come yet again, and this time it was an emergency visit, so it was ten *yuan*. As before, he calmly wrote out a prescription, but he no longer called for the Broken Drum Leather Pill, and the adjuvants were no longer as unusual, so it took only a relatively short time for the medicine to be cooked up. However, when we poured it down my father's throat, it just dribbled out from the corner of his mouth.

From then on, I no longer had to deal with Dr. Chen, only at times coming across him on the street whizzing by in a speedy sedan chair carried by three bearers. I've heard that he's still healthy, practicing medicine while also editing some sort of journal on Chinese medicine, battling it out against the Western doctors who are good only at surgery.

There are indeed some slight differences between the Chinese and Western mentality. I've heard that when a parent's death is close at hand, China's filial sons will buy several pounds of ginseng, simmer it into a broth, and force it down them, in hopes that the parent may live a few extra days—even half a day longer would be good. One of my medical school professors had instructed me on a doctor's ethical responsibilities: heal those who can be healed, those who cannot, allow to die without suffering. But of course, he was a Western doctor.

My father's labored breathing went on for a fairly long time, and it was all I could do to listen to it. No one, however, could help him. At times, a thought would unexpectedly flash across my mind like a bolt of lightning: "Better to quickly stop breathing . . ." Then I would immediately feel that I shouldn't have had such a thought and that I had committed a sin. Yet, at the same time, I felt this thought was justified, as I loved my father very much. This is how I feel even now.

In the morning, Mrs. Yan, who lived on the same lane, came by. She was a woman thoroughly versed in etiquette and said that we shouldn't just wait around doing nothing. And so we changed his clothes. Then burned paper ingots along with something called *The Goddess of Mercy Sutra* into ashes, and wrapped them in paper for him to clench in his fists.

"Call out to him, your father is drawing his last breath. Quickly, call out to him!" Mrs. Yan said.

"Father! Father!" I started calling out.

"Louder! He can't hear you. Quickly, why aren't you calling out?!"

"Father!!! Father!!!"

His face, which had calmed down, suddenly tensed up. He opened his eyes ever so slightly, as if experiencing some pain.

"Call out! Call out!" she urged me.

"Father!!!"

"What? . . . don't shout . . . don't . . ." he said softly and then started drawing rapid breaths. After some time things returned to normal, and his breathing calmed down.

"Father!!!" I kept calling out until he drew his last breath.

Even now I can still hear this voice of mine from then, and every time I hear it, I feel this was the greatest wrong I ever committed against my father.

October 7[68]

Trivial Recollections

琐记

Mrs. Yan has long since become a grandmother—maybe even a great-grandmother—by now. But at the time she was still young, with only one son who was three or four years older than I was. Though harsh with her own son, she was kind to other children. No matter what trouble we got into, she never tattled to our parents, so we especially liked playing in or near her home.

To give just one example: In the winter, a thin layer of ice would form over the surface of the water vats. Seeing this after getting out of bed in the early morning, we would eat it right away. One time we were caught by Fourth Mistress Shen, who cried loudly: "Don't eat it, you'll get a stomachache!" My mother heard this ruckus and ran out. We were given a scolding and forbidden from playing for quite some time. We deduced that the culprit behind all this was Fourth Mistress Shen. So whenever her name came up, we didn't use a respectful term of address; rather, we came up with a nickname and called her "Stomachache."

First published in volume 1, issue 21, of the journal *Wilderness* (*Mangyuan*) on November 10, 1926. Lu Xun, *Lu Xun quanji* (Complete works of Lu Xun), 18 vols. (Beijing: Renmin wenxue, 2005), 2:294–300.

Mrs. Yan, however, would never have done this. If she had seen us eating the ice, she would surely have laughed amiably and said: "Good, have another piece. I'll keep a tally to see who eats the most."

But there were also things about her that displeased me. Once long ago when I was still very young, I happened to go to her house. She was reading a book with her husband. As soon as I walked in, she shoved the book in my face and asked: "Look here, do you know what this is?" I saw pictured in the book a house with two stark naked people, who looked as if they were fighting—yet, it didn't look entirely like they were fighting, either. As I puzzled over this, they burst out laughing. I was very displeased, feeling as if I had suffered a great insult, so I didn't go over there for two weeks or so. Another time was when I was already over ten years old. I was competing with a few kids to see who could spin around the most number of times. She stood on the side counting: "Good, eighty-two! Spin another, eighty-three! Good, eighty-four! . . ." But Ah Xiang, who was mid-spin, suddenly fell right when his aunt walked in. Mrs. Yan then immediately said: "See, you fell, didn't you? You wouldn't listen to me, I told you over and over again not to spin . . ."

In spite of this, the children still liked going to her place. If we banged our head into something and then went to our mothers with a big bump, the best we could expect would be a scolding and then some ointment; the worst would be no ointment, our heads knuckled a few times, and a scolding. Mrs. Yan, however, would never blame us. Instead, she would immediately make a paste from alcohol mixed with powder and apply it to the lump, and tell us that it would not only stop the pain but also prevent scars from forming in the future.

After father passed away, I still frequented her home, not to play with the kids but for leisurely chats with Mrs. Yan or her husband. At the time I felt there were so many things I wanted to buy—books to read or food to eat—except I didn't have the money. The topic came up in conversation one day, and she remarked: "Just take your mother's money and spend it—isn't it yours after all?" I replied that mother didn't have any money. She then said that I could sell off her jewelry. When I told her that there was no jewelry, she said, to my surprise: "Perhaps you haven't paid much attention. Just search through every corner of the drawers of that big chest, you're bound to find some pearls and the like . . ."

These remarks sounded quite a bit off to me, so I stopped going over to her place yet again, but sometimes I really was tempted to open that big chest and give it a good rummage. About less than a month after that, I heard a rumor to the effect that I had stolen things from the house and sold them off, which really made me feel like I had fallen into cold water. The source of the rumor I knew well enough. If this had happened today, as long as there was a place to publish it, I would chastise the rumormongers and expose them for what they are, but at that time I was too young. Once I heard the rumor, I felt as if I really were guilty of the crime, and I was afraid to look people in the eye, afraid to receive my mother's caresses.

Fine, then, just leave!

But where to go? I had long been familiar with the faces of the folks of S City,[69] and there was nothing remarkable about them; it seemed as if I could even read their minds. I felt I had to search for different kinds of people, the very people whom folks from S City denounced, be they beasts or demons. At the time, the object of the town's scorn was a school that hadn't been open long, called the Chinese and Western Academy. Aside from Chinese, it also taught a bit of Western language and mathematics. Yet it had already become the target of public criticism. Some scholars well versed in the works of the sages even went so far as to compose an eight-legged essay ridiculing it by combining lines from *The Four Books*. This famous essay circulated throughout the town, and everyone took it as an amusing topic of conversation. I only remember the beginning of the first part, which went: "Master Xu said to Master Yi: 'I have heard of using Chinese ways to transform the barbarian, but not of being transformed by the barbarian. But things are different nowadays: when the bird-like twittering of foreign tongues is heard, it is now considered elegant language.'"

I've forgotten what followed—likely arguments similar to those made by the champions of "national essence" nowadays. But I, too, was dissatisfied with this Chinese and Western Academy, because only Chinese, mathematics, English, and French were taught. Seeking Truth Academy in Hangzhou offered more state-of-the-art coursework, but the tuition was expensive.

Schools that didn't require tuition were in Nanjing, so naturally I just had to go there. I don't know what the first school I enrolled in is called nowadays, but it seems that for a time after the revolution it was called the Thunder and Lightning Academy, a name reminiscent of "the *Taiji* Formation" and the "Primordial Force Formation" from *The Investiture of the Gods*. Anyway, as soon as you entered the Righteous Phoenix Gate, you would see a signal-mast that was over two hundred feet tall and a chimney of unknown height. And the lessons were easy, with virtually four full days of the week devoted to English: "*It is a cat.*" "*Is it a rat?*" One whole day was spent on reading Chinese: "The gentleman said: 'Ying Kaoshu can be said to be a filial exemplar. He loved his mother and extended his love to the Duke of Zhuang.'" A whole day was spent on Chinese composition: "On 'Know Thyself, Know Thy Enemy, and Be Invincible in Battle,'" and "On 'Ying Kaoshu,'" "On 'How Clouds Follow the Dragon and the Winds Follow the Tiger,'" and "'Endure Hardship, Accomplish Anything.'"

When I first entered, I naturally qualified only as a third-level student. My bedroom had a desk, a stool, and a bed, which consisted of two wooden planks. Things were different for the first and second-level students: they had two desks each, two or three stools, and one bed made of as many as three planks. They would strut proudly into the lecture halls carrying a stack of big, thick Western books. The third-level students, limited to English primers and four volumes of *The Zuo Commentary*, dared not look them squarely in the eye. Even if empty-handed, they would place their arms akimbo like crabs so that students in the lower levels wouldn't be able to walk past them. It's been a long time since I've seen this crab-style pose adopted by eminent bureaucrats, but four or five years ago, I unexpectedly discovered someone in a beat-up reclining chair in the Ministry of Education in just this pose. Yet, this old fellow was *not* from the Thunder and Lightning Academy, which goes to show how prevalent this crab-attitude is in China.

Most endearing was the signal-mast. And this wasn't because it stood erect and served as some kind of symbol or other, as one of our Eastern neighbor's China hands claims; it was more because it was so tall that crows and sparrows could only perch on the wooden slats halfway up. If you climbed to the top, you could see Mount Lion nearby, and at a distance No Sorrow Lake—but whether one could really see that far off, I really can't recall clearly now. And it wasn't dangerous either, as a net had been set up underneath, so that even if you were to slip, you would be like a small fish caught in a net. Besides, I've heard that no one has yet fallen since the net was set up.

At one time there had also been a pond where students could learn to swim. But two young students had drowned there, and by the time I arrived the pond had long been filled in. Not only filled in, but a tiny shrine to Guan Yu had even been built on top of it. Next to the temple was a brick oven for burning paper with writing on it, above the opening to which were four characters inscribed horizontally: "Respectfully conserve used paper." What a pity that the two drowned ghosts had lost their pond and, unable to find substitutes to take their place, were forced to wander about the area, in spite of its being under the control of "the demon-slaying Lord Guan Yu." The school administrators were probably kind-hearted people, so every year on the fifteenth day of the seventh month, they would invite a group of monks to the covered athletic field to chant and provide food for the hungry ghosts. A fat, red-nosed monk wearing a hat embroidered with an image of the Vairocana Buddha would gesture with his hands and chant: *Hui zi luo, pu mi ye hong, yan hong! Yan! Ye! Hong!*

Only at this time of year did these "alumni" who had been under the control of the Lord Guan Yu for the whole year reap some benefits—though I didn't really know just what kind of benefits they were. At times like these, I would often think to myself: better be careful as a student.

Things just didn't feel quite right, yet I couldn't describe what wasn't right about it. But now I've found the words that come close to describing it—something along the lines of "pestilential aura" fits the bill. So I had to get away. Nowadays, it's not so easy getting away, as the ranks of "estimable gentlemen" will accuse you of cursing your way into a contract, or of throwing a "celebrity scholar" tantrum, and subject you to some proper-sounding witty remarks. But it didn't matter all that much then, as the stipend that students received in the first year was only two ounces of silver and in the first three-month trial period, only five hundred cash. So there was no problem whatsoever, and I went to take the entrance exam for the School of Mining and Railroads—or maybe it was called that—I can't recall very clearly and I don't have my diploma on hand, so I have no way of verifying. The entrance exam wasn't hard and I was accepted.

This time, it was no longer "It is a cat," but "Der Mann, Die Weib, Das Kind." Chinese was still the same old "Ying Kaoshu can be said to be a filial exemplar," to which was added *Annotated Philology*. There were also slight differences in the essay topics, for example "On 'Sharpening One's Tools Is the Key to Good Craftsmanship'" was something I hadn't written about before.

Other than these subjects, there was also what was called science, earth studies, and the study of metals and rocks . . . all of which were very novel. But here I need to state this: the latter two subjects are what we now call geology and mineralogy, not courses on ancient geography or ancient bronzes and epigraphy. Sketching rail profiles, however, was somewhat bothersome—the parallel lines were especially annoying. But in my second year, the school director was a progressive. He often read *The Chinese Progress* when riding in his carriage and devised his own topics for the Chinese exams, which were quite different from those of the other instructors. Once it was "On Washington," and the Chinese instructor, trembling with fear, came to ask *us:* "What is this thing called Washington? . . ."

So reading new books became fashionable. I found out that a book called *Evolution and Ethics* was available in China, so I went to the southern part of the city to purchase it on a Sunday. It was a thick, lithographed edition printed on white paper, costing exactly five hundred cash. As soon as I flipped it open, I saw very finely written characters, and the first passage read:

Huxley was alone in a room in his house in southern England. Mountains in the background and facing the open plain, it was as if the entire vista of the countryside lay before him. He imagined: What was it like here two thousand years ago before the Roman general Caesar arrived? It must have been nothing but barren wasteland.

Oh! It turns out that there was a Huxley in this world who sat in his study having those thoughts—and how novel his thoughts were! I read the book in one sitting, and words such as "competition" and "natural selection" appeared; Socrates, Plato also appeared, as did the Stoics. The school had set up a periodical reading room. It of course had *The Chinese Progress,* but also *Collection of Translated Works* as well—the first-rate calligraphy in the style of Zhang Lianqing on the cover was an appealing blue.

"There's something not quite right about you, child. Take this essay and read it, copy it down and read it," an elder in my family said to me sternly as he handed me a newspaper. When I took it and had a look, it read: "Your lowly subject Xu Yingkui humbly reports . . ." I no longer remember a single sentence from the essay. In short, it denounced Kang Youwei's reforms, and I don't remember whether I actually copied it down or not.

I still didn't feel that there was anything "not right" about me. Whenever I had free time, I carried on as usual, eating sesame griddle cakes, peanuts, hot peppers, and reading *Evolution and Ethics.*

But we also went through a very troubled period. That was in my second year, when we heard that the school was to be shut down. This wasn't surprising. In the first place, the academy had been set up because the Viceroy of Jiangnan and Jiangxi at the time (probably Liu Kunyi) heard that the prospects for coal mining in Green Dragon Mountain were good, so he tried his hand at it. By the time the academy had been set up, the mine had already fired the original mining engineer and replaced him with someone who didn't quite know what was going on. The reasons being: first, the salary of the former engineer was too expensive; second, they felt that opening up a coal mine wasn't all that difficult. Before the year was out, they couldn't quite figure out where all the coal was. In the end, only enough coal was recovered to keep the two water pumps going—that is, the water was pumped out to dig out the coal, and the coal was used to pump the water, so the income and expenses canceled each other out. Since there was no profit from the mine, there was naturally no need to keep the mining and railroads academy going, but for some reason it wasn't shut down. In my third year, when we went down to look at the mine pit, the situation was really quite dismal. The pumps were still going of course, but the pit had accumulated about half a foot of water, and water was dripping from above as well; the few miners working there looked like ghosts.

Graduation, naturally, was something everyone looked forward to. Yet once graduation came around, I felt at a bit of a loss. Having climbed a mast a few times, needless to say, doesn't half qualify one to be a sailor. Did we know how to extract gold, silver, copper, iron, or tin after listening to a few years' worth of lectures and going down to the mining pits a few times? I really found myself at a complete loss—it was hardly as easy as writing an essay on the adage "Sharpening One's Tools Is the Key to Good Craftsmanship." The outcome of having climbed two hundred feet up the sky and crawled two hundred feet underground was that I was still completely incompetent. My knowledge was a matter of "searching above the blue skies, below beneath the underworld nothing could be seen, hazy it was so." Only one path remained: to go abroad.

Figure 6. Lu Xun in Japan, 1903. Reproduced from Zhou Haiying, *Lu Xun jiating da xiangbu* (Lu Xun family album) (Beijing: Tongxin, 2005), 10.

Our plan to study abroad was approved by the bureaucrats and five of us were dispatched to Japan. One student decided not to go because his grandmother had wept her heart out, so there were only four of us left. Japan was so different from China, how were we to prepare ourselves? A student who had graduated a year ahead of us had travelled to Japan, so he ought to have some idea about the conditions there. When we went to seek his advice, he told us earnestly:

"Socks made in Japan are absolutely unwearable, you need to bring plenty of Chinese socks. In my opinion, the paper currency is no good either—you should just change all the money you take with you into their silver coins."

All four of us followed the commands. I don't know about the others, but I changed all of my money to silver dollars in Shanghai and also brought ten pairs of Chinese socks—white socks.

What happened after? In the end, we were required to wear uniforms and leather shoes, so the Chinese socks were utterly useless. One yen silver coins had long been out of circulation in Japan, so I lost money changing them into half yen coins and paper currency.

October 8[70]

Professor Fujino

藤野先生

So this was all there was to Tokyo.[71] Cherry blossoms radiating at the peak of the season in Ueno, seen from afar, resembled light puffs of crimson-colored clouds. But under the blossoms, there was no shortage of clusters of cram-course students from the Qing empire.[72] The long queues coiled on top of their heads made the crown of their caps rise majestically like Mount Fuji. Some others undid their queues and coiled the hair flat on top of their heads; when they removed their caps, the hair gleamed like a young lady's chignon, which they would toss about with a few twists of the neck. Truly an exquisite sight.

The gatehouse of the Chinese student hostel sold some books, so it was still worth going there from time to time. In the mornings, a few Western-style rooms there were also fine for resting. Come evening, however, the floorboard of a particular room would invariably reverberate with earthshaking pounds *"dong, dong, dong!"* and the whole room would fill with smoke and dust. Ask those in the know and they would reply: "They are learning to dance."

This essay was originally published in volume 1, issue 23, of the journal *Wilderness* (*Mangyuan*) on December 25, 1926. Lu Xun, *Lu Xun quanji* (Complete works of Lu Xun), 18 vols. (Beijing: Renmin wenxue, 2005), 2:313–320.

Why not go elsewhere for a look?

So I made my way to the Sendai Medical Academy. Not long after departing from Tokyo, we arrived at a transit station with "Nippori" written on it. Somehow, I still remember the name to this day. I remember only one other stop, Mito, the place where the Ming loyalist Zhu Shunshui died in exile. Sendai was a mid-sized market-town, extremely cold in the winter, and at the time no Chinese students were studying there yet.[73]

It's probably the case that the scarcer the good, the more it is prized. When sent to fruit stands in Zhejiang, cabbages from Beijing are hung upside down with a red string tied around their roots and referred to respectfully as "Shandong vegetables." When wild aloe from Fujian arrives in Beijing, it is immediately escorted into a greenhouse and addressed by the beautiful name "Dragon Tongue Orchid." When I arrived in Sendai, I, too, received such preferential treatment: not only did the academy not charge tuition, a few of its staff even expressed concern over my room and board. At first I lived in a guesthouse next to the prison. It was already quite cold in early winter, but there were still many mosquitoes. So I resorted to covering my whole body in a quilt and wrapping my clothes around my head and face, leaving only two nostrils exposed for breathing. The mosquitoes had nowhere to insert their beaks into this space of continuous breathing, so I was able to sleep peacefully. The food wasn't bad either. But there was one teacher who felt that the guesthouse, which also prepared meals for the prisoners, wasn't a suitable place for me to live and repeated this to me over and over again. Though I felt that the guesthouse preparing the prisoners' meals had no bearing on me, it was difficult to rebuff good intentions, so I ended up having to look for another more suitable place to live. And so I moved to another guesthouse far from the prison, but the pity of it was that I had to drink unpalatable taro-root soup—every day.

From this time on, I encountered many new teachers and heard many novel lectures. The anatomy course was co-taught by two professors. First was osteology. A thin, dark gentleman with a mustache the shape of the character "eight" (八), wearing spectacles and carrying a pile of books of various sizes, entered. After setting his books on the lectern, he introduced himself to the students, speaking in a drawn-out voice with a distinct cadence:

"I am called Fujino Genkurō . . ."

A few people in the rear of the classroom started snickering. He then lectured on the history of the development of anatomical sciences in Japan. His stack of large and small books included the earliest works to the most recent publications in this field of study. Among the earliest were a few books bound with thread and reprints of Chinese translations. Their translations and study of modern medicine, it turns out, did not precede the Chinese.

The snickering students sitting at the rear had been held back after failing the class the previous academic year; having already been at the school for a year, they were well-versed in various anecdotes. They regaled the new students with the history of each professor. This Professor Fujino was said to be rather careless when it came to his attire—at times he would even forget to wear a tie. In the winter he would be cold and shivering in his old overcoat; one time on the train he was mistaken for a pickpocket by the conductor, who warned all the passengers to be vigilant.

There was probably some truth to what they said—I saw him once, with my own eyes, enter the lecture hall without a tie.

After a week had elapsed, likely on a Saturday, he had his assistant summon me. When I arrived, he was seated in the center of the lab, surrounded by human bones and a good many detached skulls. He was doing research on skulls then, the results of which were later published in the school journal.

"Are you able to copy down my lectures?" he asked.

"I can take down parts of them."

"Let me have a look!"

I handed him my lecture notes, which he took and returned to me two or three days later, telling me to hand in my notes for him to look over once a week from then on. When I retrieved my notebook and flipped it open for a look, I was taken by surprise and felt, at the same time, a sense of both unease and gratitude, for it turned out that my notes had been supplemented and corrected with red ink from beginning to end. Not only were there additions of things I had missed, but every grammar error had also been corrected. This went on until he finished teaching all the subjects he was responsible for: osteology, angiology, neurology.

It was a pity that I was not very diligent then and at times even rather headstrong. I still recall an instance when Professor Fujino summoned me into his lab and flipped to a particular diagram in my lecture notes. Pointing to a blood vessel below the arm, he said to me amiably:

"See here, you moved the position of this blood vessel slightly. Of course, the alteration does indeed make it more pleasing to the eye, but anatomical illustrations aren't works of art, and we can't just change how things actually look. I've corrected it for you this time, but in the future, you have to copy everything as it looks on the blackboard."

Yet, I still wasn't convinced. While I agreed in reply, in my mind I thought to myself:

"I still drew a fine diagram. As for how things actually look, of course I remember it in my mind."

After the final exams of the academic year were over, I vacationed in Tokyo the whole summer and returned in the early fall. Grades had long been posted—I was in the middle of the pack of over a hundred students, but I hadn't failed. This time Professor Fujino was responsible for teaching practical anatomy and topographic anatomy.

After about a week of practical anatomy, he summoned me again, looking very pleased, and said to me in his cadenced voice:

"I'd heard that the Chinese revere ghosts, so I was worried—I was afraid that you would be reluctant to dissect corpses. Now I can finally rest at ease since this isn't the case."

But there were also times when he made me feel embarrassed. He'd heard that Chinese women had bound feet but didn't know the specifics, so he wanted to ask me how feet were bound and what shape the deformed bones assumed. He even heaved a sigh as he said: "I need to actually see it for myself to understand. How, exactly, is it done?"

One day, the student union representatives for my class came to my dorm asking to borrow my lecture notes. I took out and handed over the notes, but they simply flipped through them once without taking them away. But as soon as they left, the mailman delivered a thick envelope. When I opened it, the first line read:

"You must repent!"

This is probably a sentence from the New Testament but had recently been cited by Tolstoy. This happened to be the time of the Russo-Japanese War, and Old Mr. Tolstoy had written a letter to both the tsar of Russia and the emperor of Japan which started out with this sentence. The Japanese newspapers reprimanded him for his irreverence, and the young patriots were also outraged, but they had unknowingly come under his influence a long time ago. The rest of the letter said in effect that I was able to attain my grade because I knew the questions on last year's anatomy exam ahead of time, as Professor Fujino had marked them on my lecture notes. It was an anonymous letter.

It was only then that I recalled the matter from a few days before. A meeting was to be held among students in my class, and the student representatives had written an announcement on the blackboard, the last sentence of which read: "Everyone please attend—it's important not to leak this," with a circle added beside the character "leak" for emphasis. Although I thought the circle was ridiculous at the time, I didn't take it to heart in the least, and it was only afterward that I realized the character was a jab directed at me, as if to say that I was the recipient of questions leaked by the instructor.

I then reported the matter to Professor Fujino. A few classmates who knew me well shared my sense of injustice, so they went together to reprimand the student representatives for their lack of courtesy in checking my notes under false pretenses and also asked that the results of their investigation be published. The rumor was ultimately quashed, but the student representatives agitated for the retrieval of their anonymous letter. In the end I returned to them the letter written à la Tolstoy.

China is a weak country, so naturally the Chinese must be intellectually deficient; left to their own devices, they couldn't possibly attain marks above sixty. No wonder they were suspicious. But after that, I suffered the fate of having to witness the scene of a Chinese man executed by firing-squad.[74] In my second year, there was an added class in bacteriology. The forms of all the bacteria were shown on slides. When we completed one section of the lesson before the class period was over, some slides on current events would be shown, which naturally all depicted Japan's victories over Russia. Perversely enough, however, there just had to be a few Chinese squeezed into the scene: a Chinese spy for the Russians had been captured by the Japanese and was about to be executed by firing squad; the flock of people who surrounded to witness the scene was also Chinese, and in the lecture hall, there was me.

"*Banzai!*" they all clapped and cheered.

This cheering occurred regularly after each slide was shown, but to me the sound this time was especially grating. After I returned to China, I saw idle onlookers cheering drunkenly as they watched criminals being executed by firing squad. Alas, nothing can be done! But at that particular place and time, my thinking underwent a transformation.

At the end of my second year, I sought out Professor Fujino to tell him that I would no longer study medicine and that I would be leaving Sendai. A pained expression appeared on his face, and it seemed as if he were about to speak, but in the end, he said nothing.

"I'd like to go study biology. All the knowledge you have taught me will still come in handy." The truth is, I hadn't decided to study biology, but seeing how dejected he looked, I told a lie in hopes of comforting him.

"I'm afraid that the anatomy and other classes taught as part of medical studies won't be of any great help in studying biology," he said with a sigh.

A couple of days before my departure, he summoned me to his house, handed me a photograph of himself, on the back of which had written two characters: "惜別 *xibie*" (regret at our parting). He also said he hoped that I, too, would give him a photo. But I hadn't had any photos taken at the time, so he asked me to send him one in the

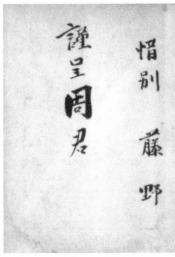

Figure 7. Photo of Fujino Genkurō, which he gave to Lu Xun as a parting gift. "Regret at our parting" is inscribed on the back. Reproduced from *Lu Xun wenxian tu zhuan* (Illustrated biography and documents of Lu Xun) (Zhengzhou: Daxiang chubanshe, 1998), 36.

future and to correspond with him regularly and inform him of my circumstances thereafter.

After I left Sendai, I didn't have any photos taken for many years. And because I was at sixes and sevens for some time, to tell him of my situation would no doubt just have brought him disappointment, so I didn't even have the courage to write a letter. As the months and years went by, it became even harder to know where to begin, so while the thought of writing occurred to me from time to time, I found it difficult to take up my pen—which remains the case even now, as I have actually never sent him a letter or a photograph. From his perspective, there was basically no news of me whatsoever after my departure.

But for some unknown reason, I often think of him. Among those whom I consider my teachers, he is the one who gave me the most encouragement and the one I feel most grateful to. I often think of how his ardent hopes for me, his tireless teaching, were, on a smaller scale, for China, in hopes that China would develop a modern medical science; on a larger scale, it was for scientific research, that is, in hopes that modern medical science would be transmitted to China. In my mind and in my heart, his character is a great one, even though his name isn't known to many people.

I had the lecture notes he corrected bound into three thick volumes, planning to keep them as lifelong mementos. Unfortunately, when I was moving seven years ago, a box was damaged in transit and I lost half the books in it, which, by happenstance, included the lecture notes.[75] When I instructed the transport company to look for them, I received no response. All I have left is the photograph, which remains to this day hanging on the eastern wall across from my desk in my residence in Beijing. Whenever I feel tired in the evening, right when I want to slack off, I look up and in the lamplight catch a glimpse of his thin, dark face, as if on the verge of saying something in that cadenced voice. This immediately arouses my conscience and emboldens my courage, and I then light a cigarette and resume writing a few more things bitterly despised by the "estimable gentlemen" and their ilk.[76]

October 12[77]

Fan Ainong

範愛農

At our guesthouse in Tokyo, we normally read the papers right after getting up. Students mostly read things like the *Asahi News* and *Yomiuri News*. Those keen on getting the latest social gossip read *Niroku News*. Early one morning, the first thing we saw was a telegram from China that went something like this:

> Governor En Ming of Anhui assassinated by *Jo Shiki Rin,* assassin captured.

After the initial shock wore off, everyone—faces flushed with excitement—started talking about it with one another, trying to identify the assassin and the three Chinese characters of his name. Yet the Shaoxing natives whose readings weren't limited to textbooks knew who it was right away. It was Xu Xilin. Returning to China after studying abroad, he served as chief inspector general designate of Anhui in charge of law enforcement and was in the perfect position to assassinate the governor.

First published in volume 1, issue 24, of the journal *Wilderness (Mangyuan)* on December 25, 1926. Lu Xun, *Lu Xun quanji* (Complete works of Lu Xun), 18 vols. (Beijing: Renmin wenxue, 2005), 2:321–332.

Everyone then speculated that he would be subjected to extreme punishment and that his whole clan would be implicated. Not long after, news that Miss Qiu Jin had been killed in Shaoxing also reached us, and that Xu Xilin's heart had been cut out, fried, and eaten by En Ming's personal guard.[78] Everyone felt outraged. A few people then held a secret meeting to raise travel funds. At this moment, it would have been convenient if a Japanese *ronin*—who would tear up some dried squid, down it with wine, and after some heroics, set out to escort Xu's family members—appeared.

As was the custom, the native-place association held a meeting to mourn the martyrs and curse the Manchus. Afterward, someone proposed sending a telegram to Beijing to denounce the inhumanity of the Manchu government. The crowd immediately split into two factions: one wanted to send the telegram, the other opposed it. I wanted to send a telegram, but right after I said this, a slow, dull voice followed up:

"The killed have been killed and the dead have died, so what's the point of sending some bullshit telegram?"

This fellow was big and tall in build, had long hair and eyes which showed more white than black,[79] as if looking scornfully at those around him. Squatting on the mat, he contradicted just about everything I said. I found this odd from the get-go, taking special note of him, and only at this time asked around about him. Who was this speaker and why was he so cold? Someone who knew him told me: It's Fan Ainong, a student of Xu Xilin's.

I was outraged and thought he was absolutely inhuman. His own teacher had been killed, and he was afraid even to send a telegram! So I insisted on sending a telegram and started arguing with him. The result was that the majority supported sending a telegram, and he gave in. After that, we had to elect someone to draft the telegram.

"Why vote? Of course it should be the one who proposed sending it~~" he said.

I felt that his remark again targeted me, but it was not entirely unreasonable. I then proposed that this solemn and stirring essay ought to be written by someone intimately familiar with the martyr's life. Since his relationship with the deceased was far closer than others', he would feel even more grief-stricken and indignant, so his essay would surely be more moving. And with this, we started arguing again. The result was that he refused to write it, and I refused as well—I don't know who assumed the task in the end. After that, everyone went their own way, leaving behind one person to draft the telegram and one or two assistants waiting to dispatch it after it was completed.

From then on I felt that this Fan Ainong was not just odd but also despicable. Previously, I had felt that the most despicable people in the world were the Manchus; it was only then that I realized that they were only second in line, the most despicable being Fan Ainong. If China weren't going to have a revolution then that was that, but if there were to be one, then the first thing to do would be to get rid of the likes of Fan Ainong.

This opinion of mine later seemed to gradually fade in intensity until I completely forgot about it, and we didn't see one another other again from then on. It wasn't until the year before the revolution, maybe toward the end of spring when I was working as a teacher in my hometown, that I unexpectedly saw someone in the parlor of a friend's home. We stared at each other for no more than two or three seconds, then simultaneously exclaimed:

"Oh, oh, you're Fan Ainong!"

"Oh, oh, you're Lu Xun!"

I don't know why, but we both started laughing, laughing at each other and feeling sorry for ourselves. His eyes were the same as before, but strangely enough, he already had some gray hair after just a few years. Perhaps he had had it before, but I just hadn't noticed. Dressed in a riding jacket and tattered cloth shoes, he looked destitute. Speaking of his experiences, he said that he had run out of money for tuition in the end and could no longer study abroad, so he returned home. After returning to his hometown, he was met with scorn, ostracized and oppressed, barely able to hold his own. Now he had ensconced himself in the countryside, tutoring a few grade school children down in the country to make ends meet. But because he found it suffocating at times, he would take a boat into town.

He also told me that he was now very fond of drinking, so we drank. From then on, whenever he came into town, he would always call on me, and we became very well acquainted. After getting drunk, we would often engage in crazy talk that was silly beyond measure—even my mother, who heard us on occasion, would burst out laughing. One day, I suddenly remembered the old matter that occurred at the native-place association meeting in Tokyo and asked him:

"That day you went out of your way to contradict me, even deliberately so, it seemed—what was the reason for it?"

"You mean you still don't know? I always detested you—not just me, but all of us."

"Did you already know who I was before then?"

"Of course I knew. When we arrived at Yokohama, wasn't it you and Ziying who came to pick us up? You looked down on us, even shaking your head at us, remember?"

After some thought, I recalled—though it had all happened seven or eight years ago. At the time, Ziying had come to meet me, saying that we were to go to Yokohama to pick up the newly arrived students from our hometown. As soon as the steamer docked, we saw a large swarm of people, about a dozen in all. Once on shore, they took their luggage to customs for inspection. The inspector rifled through the trunks and at once picked out a pair of embroidered shoes for bound feet. He then set aside his main task, picked them up and scrutinized them closely. I was very displeased and thought to myself: why would these pricks bring things like this? I may have unconsciously shaken my head at that time. After the inspection and a brief rest at the inn, we had to board the train. Who would have thought that this educated bunch would then start insisting on giving up their seats to one another in the train carriage—A wanted B to sit in this seat, B wanted C to sit in that one. Before they had finished their ritual of deferment, the train started moving, the carriage lurched forward, and three or four of them immediately fell over. At the time, I was again very displeased and thought to myself: "Making distinctions in status even for seating arrangements on a train . . ." I might have unconsciously shaken my head again. It had never occurred to me until today that among the group of people offering seats to one another was Fan Ainong. Not only was Fan Ainong among them, but even now I feel ashamed to say the group included the martyrs Chen Boping, who died in battle in Anhui, and the murdered Ma Zonghan. A couple of others were later imprisoned in dark cells, not to see the light of day until after the revolution, and their bodies bore life-long scars of the torture they suffered. But I was completely oblivious at the time, shaking my head as I sent all of them off to Tokyo. Though Xu Xilin had been on the same boat, he was not on the train because he and his wife had debarked at Kobe and taken the overland route.

I thought I might have shaken my head on these two occasions, but I didn't know which instance they had seen. There was a racket when they offered their seats to one another, and it was quiet during the inspection—so it must have been at customs. When I asked Ainong, that turned out to be the case.

"I really don't understand why you guys brought those things. Whose were they?"

"Who else but our teacher's wife's?" He flashed the whites of his eyes at me.

"When she arrived in Tokyo, she would have had to pretend to have big feet, so what's the point of bringing these things?"

"Who knows? Go ask her."

Our financial circumstances had become even more strained by early winter, but we still drank wine and told jokes. Then the Wuchang uprising suddenly took place, followed by the liberation of Shaoxing. The next day, Ainong came into town wearing a felt cap like those often worn by farmers, smiling in a way I had never seen before.

"Old Xun, let's not drink anymore today. I want to see the liberated Shaoxing—let's go together."

And so we went for a walk through the streets—white flags were out as far as the eye could see. Though outward appearances had changed, the core remained the same, since it was a military government made up of a number of the old provincial gentry: the main shareholder for the railroad became head of administration, the money shop manager had become the artillery commander. The military government didn't last long, however. As soon as some of the youth raised a ruckus, Wang Jinfa brought in soldiers from Hangzhou—though he might have come anyway even if there had been no ruckus. After he showed up, he was surrounded by idlers and newly joined members of the Revolutionary Party and reigned as

Military Governor Wang. In less than a couple of weeks, the people in the *yamen* who had initially worn cotton clothing started wearing fur-lined robes, though the weather hadn't even turned cold yet.

In addition to my rice bowl—the position as principal of the Normal School—Governor Wang gave me 200 *yuan* in school funds. Fan Ainong served as dean and continued wearing that same old cotton robe of his. But he no longer drank much and had little free time to chat. He handled administrative duties and taught classes at the same time and was really quite diligent.

"Things are still not going well, thanks to Wang Jinfa and his ilk," a young man who had sat in my lectures the year before said vehemently when he came calling on me. "We want to launch a newspaper to keep watch on them. But the organizers want to use your name, along with that of Mr. Chen Ziying and Mr. Sun Deqing. It's for society's sake, so we know you won't turn us down."

I agreed to his request. Two days later, I saw a flier announcing the paper's publication, and there were, indeed, three organizers. Five days later, I read the actual paper, which began by abusing the military government and its staff, and after that it abused the governor, his relatives, his comrades from his hometown, his mistresses . . .

After two weeks of such abuse, word came my way—because we had swindled him of money and then hurled abuse at him, the governor was going to send some men over to gun us down.

No one else took this seriously, but my mother was most anxious and implored me not to go out. But I went out as usual, explaining to her that Wang Jinfa wasn't coming to gun us down. Though from Bandit Central, he wouldn't murder people as rashly as all that. Also, the funds were used for the school, which he surely knew, so it was nothing but talk.

As it turned out, no one came to kill us. When I wrote a letter requesting funds, I received another 200 *yuan*. But it seemed that

Wang Jinfa may have been somewhat miffed since he also had the following order passed on: "If you ask again, no funds are left!"

Ainong, however, received some news that made me feel ill at ease. It turned out that "swindling" referred not to the school funds, but to another sum of money given to the paper. After a few days of being abused in the paper, Wang Jinfa had someone send over 500 *yuan*. And so our young men held a meeting. The first issue: to accept it or not? The decision: accept. The second issue: after accepting, hurl abuse or not? The decision: hurl. The reason: after accepting his money, he becomes a shareholder, and if a shareholder misbehaves, then of course he should be abused.

I immediately went to the newspaper office to verify the truth of the matter. It turned out to be all true. I said a few things along the lines of how they shouldn't have taken the money, but the accountant was displeased and questioned me in return, asking:

"Why can't the paper accept capital funds?"

"These funds aren't capital."

"If not capital, then what is it?"

I didn't pursue the topic—I had long since learned a few things about the ways of the world. If I were to go on about how this would incriminate us, he would jeer at how I placed such importance on our worthless lives and how I was unwilling to sacrifice for society; or perhaps the following day I would read in the paper an account of my trembling at the prospect of death.

And then by happy coincidence, Ji Fu wrote a letter urging me to go to Nanjing. Ainong heartily approved but was also quite dejected. He said:

"The situation here is untenable, you should leave as soon as you can . . ."

I understood the meaning behind his unspoken words and made up my mind to go to Nanjing. I went first to the government offices to turn in my resignation, which they naturally accepted. They dispatched a snot-nosed receptionist, I handed over the accounts and my remaining funds of ten cents and two coppers, and with that I was no longer principal of the school. My successor was the chair of the Association for Confucian Studies, Fu Lichen.

The newspaper case was resolved two or three weeks after I arrived in Nanjing—the office was ransacked by a band of soldiers. Ziying was in the countryside so he was fine, but Deqing happened to be in town, and he suffered a dagger wound to the thigh. He was furious. Of course this must have been painful, so one can't really blame him. After his fury dissipated, he took off his clothes and had a photograph taken to show off the approximately one-inch knife wound he had sustained. He also wrote an essay describing the circumstances, disseminating it widely to publicize the brutality of the military regime. There probably aren't many people who would collect this kind of photograph nowadays—it was too small, and the knife wound had shrunk so much it was barely visible. Without added explanations, someone looking at it would most certainly have mistaken it for a pornographic photo of some slightly insane and promiscuous personality. If General Sun Chuanfang had come across it, it would most likely have been banned.[80]

By the time I moved from Nanjing to Beijing, the chair of the Association for Confucian Studies had managed to eliminate Ainong's position as dean. He reverted to the Ainong of pre-revolutionary days. I wanted to find him some work in Beijing, which was very much what he wanted, but there were no openings. He ended up having to rely on an acquaintance for room and board and often wrote me letters. As he grew more destitute, his language became ever more miserable. He was ultimately obliged to leave the acquaintance's house and wander about here and there. Not long after, I heard, out of the blue, a piece of news from someone from my village: he had fallen into the water and drowned.

I suspect that he had committed suicide. He was an adept swimmer and wouldn't have drowned so easily.

As I sat alone in the guesthouse in the evening feeling extremely sad, I then wondered if this news was true, yet, for no apparent reason, I also felt that it was indeed most reliable—even though I had no proof. I couldn't do a thing about it, so I just wrote four poems which were later published in some newspaper. I have now almost forgotten them completely, remembering only six lines from one poem, the first four lines of which read: "Drinking wine, opining on the times / you, a man who took little wine / it was as if the whole universe were drunk / and you, slightly tipsy, drowned yourself." I have forgotten the two lines in between, but it ended with "old friends have all scattered like clouds / those that remain are little more than specks of dust."

Only after returning to my hometown did I find out more details. Ainong was unable to find any kind of work because people despised him. Though he found it hard to make ends meet, he still drank at the invitation of friends. By this time he hardly had any contact with others. The remaining few people he saw with any frequency were some relatively younger men he had met later in life. Yet it seemed that they, too, were unwilling to listen to more of his complaining, which they felt was not as amusing as his jokes.

"Maybe tomorrow I will receive a telegram, and when I open it, I'll find that it's Lu Xun summoning me," he often said.

One day, several of his new friends made plans for a boat outing with him to watch the opera. It was already past midnight, gusty and raining hard on the way back. He was drunk but determined to go up on the gunwale to relieve himself. The others tried to dissuade him, but he wouldn't listen, saying that he wouldn't fall. But he fell and though he knew how to swim, never surfaced again.

The next day they fished out his corpse. They found it among the water chestnuts, standing upright.

Even now I still don't know if he lost his footing or committed suicide.

After he died, he left nothing behind but his wife and a young daughter. A few people wanted to raise a small sum of money to fund his daughter's future educational expenses, but once this was proposed, members of his clan began squabbling over the custodial rights to it—even though no actual funds had been raised. People felt it was pointless, so the notion vanished without a trace.

I wonder how his only daughter is doing now? If she is in school, she probably should have graduated from high school by now.

November 18[81]

Afterword

後記

In the beginning of the third piece, where I discuss *The Twenty-Four Filial Exemplars,* I said that the name "馬虎子" (*Ma huzi,* Ma the tiger cub) used in Beijing to frighten children should be written as "麻胡子" (*Ma Huzi,* Ma the barbarian), as it refers to Ma Shumou, whom I took to be a barbarian. I now know that I was mistaken, as the character "胡" ["barbarian"] should be written "祜," which is Shumou's given name. See the piece entitled "Not Ma the Barbarian 非麻胡" in the second volume of the Tang Dynasty Li Jiweng's *Collection for Idle Musings.* The original reads:

> It is common to frighten children by saying: "Ma Hu 麻胡 is coming!" Those who don't know the origins of the phrase believe he is a god with a bushy beard who was a Regional Inspector, but this isn't the case. General Ma Hu 麻祜 of the Sui dynasty, commissioned by the emperor Tang to build a canal at the Bian River, was cruel and abusive. He had an imposing

First published in volume 2, issue 15, of the journal *Wilderness (Mangyuan)* on August 10, 1927. Lu Xun, *Lu Xun quanji* (Complete works of Lu Xun), 18 vols. (Beijing: Renmin wenxue, 2005), 2:333–350.

air of authority, inspiring such awe that the children would terrorize each other by saying: "Ma Hu is coming!" The children's pronunciations were inaccurate, and [the fourth tone] "Hù" was changed to [the second tone] "Hú" (barbarian). This is just like the case of General Hao Pin of Jing in the reign of Xian Zong; the barbarians so feared him that they would say his name to stop children's crying. And in Wu Zong's reign, commoner children would scare each other by saying: "Governor Xue is coming!" These are all similar cases—isn't this proven by the story of Zhang Liao, courtesy name Wenyuan, in the *Records of the Wei*? (Original annotation: The Temple of Ma Hu is located in Suiyang. Li Pi, Governor of Fufang, his descendent, erected a new tablet in his name there.)

It turns out that my knowledge is similar to those in the Tang dynasty who "don't know the origins of the phrase." I truly deserve to be mocked by someone from a thousand years ago—all I can do is force a bitter smile. But I don't know whether the tablet in the Ma Hu temple is still in Suiyang or if the tablet inscriptions are recorded in local gazetteers. If they still exist, we should see an account of Ma Hu's achievements that contradicts the one recorded in the account *Record of the Construction of the Grand Canal*.

I wanted to locate some illustrations for this book so my friend Chang Weijun collected plenty of materials for me in Beijing, some of which I had never seen before. Like *The Illustrated Two Hundred and Forty Filial Exemplars* (the character "卌" is used instead of the characters "四十" for "forty") by Hu Wenbing from Xiaozhou published in the fifth year of Guangxu (1879). The original book has the following annotation: "the character 卌 is pronounced as '*xi*' as in the character 習 (practice)." I really don't understand why he didn't just use the number forty and made things so complicated. He removed the story I objected to, "Guo Ju Buries his Son," a few years before my birth. The preface states:

> *The Twenty-Four Exemplars* printed by this workshop is a fine one. However, the matter of Guo Ju burying his son violates the rules of reason and compassion and should by no means serve as a model. . . . I have presumptuously taken it upon myself to edit the volume. Stories of those who crossed boundaries of decorum in pursuit of a name for themselves have been removed and only ones that do not violate propriety and can serve as models for everyone have been chosen. They are grouped under six categories . . .

The courage and decisiveness of this old mister Hu of Xiaozhou truly inspire my admiration. But this view of his had probably been shared by many others long before—it's just that most didn't dare to cut things out or write about it so resolutely. For example, *The Illustrated Hundred Exemplars*, printed on the eleventh year of the Tongzhi period (1872), contains a preface by Zheng Ji of Jichang, which notes:

> Currently public morals have been eroding and customs have degenerated; people do not understand that filial piety is part of one's nature, but to the contrary, take it to be a separate matter altogether. They pick out the ancients' stories of throwing oneself into the stove and burying one's child and deem them cruel and unreasonable acts, also interpreting cutting off one's flesh and disemboweling oneself as harming the body given by one's parents. Little do they know that filial piety is found in the heart, not in outward manifestations. There is no one way of fulfilling one's filial duties, just as there are no

set ways of being filial. What the ancients considered filial piety may no longer be suitable to current times, just as the filial sons today may find it difficult to emulate the ancients. Because the times and places differ, people and things may vary, but all share the desire to fulfill one's filial duties. Zixia said: One has to do one's utmost to serve one's mother and father. So when asked about filiality, how could the Confucian response be the same in all cases?

In the Tongzhi period, some people clearly regarded matters such as burying one's child as "cruel and unreasonable." As for what exactly this Mr. Zheng Ji of Jichang meant, I still can't quite fathom, but perhaps it's something along these lines: these are things we need not emulate today, but there's no need to say that they are wrong either.

The origins of this *Illustrated Hundred Exemplars* is a bit unusual because it was produced after the author read "Yanzi of eastern Guangdong's" *New Poems on a Hundred Beauties*. While Yanzi valued sensuality, the author valued filial piety, and one can see how passionately he defended morality. Though it was "edited by Yubao zhenlan pu of Kuaji," and I do share some affection for a fellow provincial, I must be honest and say: it isn't all that brilliant. For example, regarding the reference to Hua Mulan joining the army, his annotation reads: "*History of the Sui.*" No such book exists at present. If what he meant was *The Records of the Sui,* no account of Mulan joining the army is in there either.

Yet, in the ninth year of the Republic (1920), the Shanghai Book Company actually went out of their way to produce a lithographic reprint, adding two characters to the title: *Complete Illustrated Biography of One Hundred* **Male** *and* **Female** *Exemplars.* There's a line written

in small print on the first page: "Good Models for Family Instruction."
They also added a piece, a preface entitled "A Prudent Estimation of
the Major Errors by Wang Ding of Jiangsu," which contained within
it the same kind of lament that Mr. Zheng Ji of Jicang offered in the
Tongzhi period.

> A pity that since Westernization has spread to the East, men of
> learning prattle on arrogantly about notions of freedom and
> equality, with morals in decline and the popular mentality de-
> generating by the day. People have become profligate and
> shameless, stopping at nothing, taking on risks in hopes of get-
> ting promoted by sheer luck. In our age, few try to spur them-
> selves on, cultivate an upstanding character, or are disciplined
> and practice self-respect. The cruelty and irrationality of this
> world is like Chen Shubao's heartlessness. If we go on like this,
> how will we end up?

It's possible that Chen Shubao may have been foolish enough to
seem completely heartless, but it would be a bit unfair if we ascribe
to him the words "cruel and unreasonable." This is how some people
assess "Guo Ju's Buries His Son" and "Li E's Throws Herself into the
Furnace."

As for people's hearts and minds, however, it seems they have,
indeed, declined in some ways. Ever since the appearance of *The
Secrets of Men and Women* and *New Ideas on Intercourse between Men and
Women,* there has been many a book title in Shanghai starting with
"Men and Women." Even *The Illustrated Hundred Exemplars,* which was
supposed to "rectify people's hearts and purify customs," has added
these words. This is probably something that Mr. Yu Baozhen Lanpu
of Kuaji, who was dissatisfied with the *New Poems on a Hundred Beauties* and taught filial piety, would never have foreseen.

To go from speaking about filial piety, "the preeminent of all virtues," and suddenly bring up matters of "men and women" seems a bit flippant—even degenerate. But while we're at it, I'd still like to take the opportunity to say a few words—of course, I'll try my best to be brief.

We Chinese, even when it comes to "the preeminent of all virtues," I dare say, still can't avoid associating it with matters related to men and women. In times of peace, idlers abound; on the occasion that a person who "dies in the name of benevolence or sacrifices his or her life for righteousness" may have been too preoccupied to follow decorum, one can always count on the living bystanders to scrutinize them in detail. The story of Cao E—throwing herself into the river in search of her father and, after she drowned, was found afloat embracing his corpse—is recorded in the official histories and quite well known. But people took issue with the word "embrace."

When I was young, I heard the elders in my hometown tell it this way:

> . . . at first, the deceased Cao E and her father's corpse were face to face in an embrace when they floated up to the surface. But the passersby who saw this all laughed and said: *Ha ha!* A maiden so young embracing such an old geezer! The two corpses then sank again; after a while, they floated back up to the surface, this time back to back.

Well and good! In a country known for ritual and propriety, how difficult it is even for a young deceased filial daughter—alas, Cao E was only fourteen—to float to the surface together with her father's corpse!

I examined *The Illustrated Hundred Exemplars* and *The Two Hundred Volume Illustrated Exemplars,* and the illustrators were very clever.

The Cao E they drew hadn't yet jumped into the river but was crying by the riverbank. *The Illustrated Twenty-Four Filial Daughters* (1892) drawn by Wu Youru, however, had precisely the same scene of the two corpses floating to the surface together, and it had them drawn "back to back," as in the top part of diagram 1 [Figure 8]. I think he,

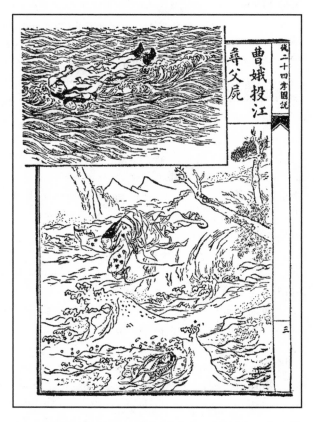

Figure 8. Cao E jumps into the river. Reproduced from *Hua zhe Lu Xun* (Lu Xun the artist), ed. Wang Xirong (Shanghai: Shanghai wenhua chubanshe, 2006), 48.

too, probably knew of the story I had heard. In *The Later Illustrated Twenty-Four Filial Exemplars with Explanations,* also illustrated by Wu Youru, there's a drawing of Cao E in the midst of throwing herself into the river as well, as in the bottom part of diagram 1.

As for all the illustrated stories instructing filial behavior that I've seen up to the present, quite a few depict filial children's encounters with thieves, tigers, fire, and storms—nine out of ten instances, the situation is dealt with by either "weeping" or "kowtowing."

When will there be an end to China's weeping and kowtowing?

As for the method of illustration, I believe the most simple and classical is the Japanese Oda Umisen's version, one that was long ago printed in *The Collected Paintings of the Dianshizhai* and become "naturalized as a Chinese product," so it's easy to come by. Wu Youru's drawings are the most exquisite as well as the most inspiring. But he isn't quite suited to drawing historical illustrations. Having resided in the Shanghai foreign concessions for a long period, he was thoroughly steeped in its culture and most adept at drawing contemporary scenes like "An Evil Madam Abusing a Prostitute" or "Hoodlums Extorting People"—all depicted so vividly, people can almost see Shanghai's foreign settlement come to life on paper. But his influence has been particularly harmful. Recently, in many illustrations for novels and children's books, women are often drawn like prostitutes and children like little hoodlums, largely on account of having seen too many of Wu Youru's illustrated books.

And stories of filial sons are, comparatively speaking, even more difficult to illustrate because they are on the whole much more cruel and heart-rending. Take for example the story "Guo Ju Buries His Son": no matter what, it's hard to depict the scene in a manner that would delight children and make them voluntarily lie down in a grave pit.[82] Then there's "Anxious After Tasting Feces," not easily depicted in an enchanting manner either.[83] There's also Lao Laizi and "Pulling Pranks to Amuse the Parents"—though the inscribed verse says that "the whole household permeated with joy," the illustrations rarely depict a cheerful family atmosphere.[84]

I have now selected illustrations from three different sources and put them together in diagram 2 [Figure 9]. The top one is taken from *The Illustrated Hundred Exemplars* drawn by "He Yunti of Chen Village," which illustrates Lao Laizi "fetching water to the hall, lying on the ground and crying like an infant after faking a fall." It also shows "both parents breaking out in laughter." The small section in the middle I traced from *The Twenty-Four Filial Exemplars with Illustrations and Poems* illustrated by "Li Xitong of Zhibei," which depicts the passage "wearing colorful garb and playing like an infant to amuse his parents." The *"gu-dong* rattle" he holds in his hands represents the idea of "playing like an infant." However, it may well be the case that Mr. Li felt that such a tall, burly old man playing with such a toy wasn't very respectable, so he shrank down Lao Laizi's body as much as he could, depicting him as a child with a mustache. But it still isn't very amusing. As for the mistakes and deficiencies in the sketching, you can't really blame it on the author or me; all you can do is curse the skill of the engraver. On examination, the carver did his engraving in the twelfth year of Tongzhi in the Qing dynasty (1873) at the Hongwen shop on South Provincial Secretary Street of Shandong province. The picture on the bottom is printed by the Shendushan shop in the eleventh year of the Republic (1922) without the name of the carver. It depicts two subjects: one is "faking a fall and lying prone on the ground" and the other is "playing like an infant," both portrayed together, but the part about the "colorful garb" has been left out. The two acts are also portrayed together and the colorful clothing has also been left out in Wu Youru's volume, but Lao Laizi appears

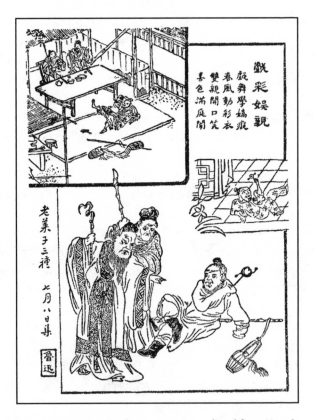

Figure 9. Lao Lai amusing his parents. Reproduced from *Hua zhe Lu Xun* (Lu Xun the artist), ed. Wang Xirong (Shanghai: Shanghai wenhua chubanshe, 2006), 50.

a bit chubbier and his hair is tied in two top-knots—yet it's still not very amusing.

It's been said that there's a fine line between satire and mockery, and I think the same can be said for being amusing and disgusting. When children act coy with their parents, it can be amusing, but it's hard not to find it unappealing when adults do the same. The demonstrative affection that unrestrained spouses show in front of others can sometimes cross the fine line of amusement and quickly turn disgusting. No wonder that no one has been able to draw a decent picture of Lao Laizi's affectations. I would find it insufferable if I were to live, even for a day, in the families drawn in these pictures—just imagine watching this seventy-year-old man fake-playing with his "*gu-dong* rattle" all year round!

In the Han dynasty, people had a penchant for painting or carving images of emperors and kings, the disciples of Confucius, martyrs, chaste women, and filial exemplars inside palaces and on the stone tombs in front of burial plots. There is, of course, no longer so much as a single rafter of the palaces remaining, but sometimes stone tombs can still be found, the best preserved being the tomb of the Wu family from Jiaxiang county in Shandong. I seem to remember Lao Laizi's story carved on the wall, but I don't have a rubbing of it nor *The Selected Inscriptions on Stone and Metal* on hand, so I can't really check. Otherwise, comparing the pictures we have now with those from eighteen hundred years ago would be quite an interesting endeavor.

With regards to Lao Laizi, a passage in *The Illustrated One Hundred Filial Exemplars* reads like this: ". . . There's also a story of Laizi playing with baby birds to amuse his parents: To please his parents, he played beside them with baby birds (Source: *Biographies of Eminent Gentlemen*)."

Whose *Biographies of Eminent Gentlemen*? Ji Kang's or Huangfu Mi's? I still have no books at hand and no way of looking it up. I was only recently able to check the copy of *The Imperial Reader of the Taiping Era* that I bought without a second thought after receiving an extra month's salary, but I didn't find anything in the end. Either I was careless or the account appears in another encyclopedia from the Tang or Song dynasty. But it's not that important anyhow. What I found unusual was the character "雛" (*chu*, baby bird) that appears in the text.

I thought that this "*chu*" might not necessarily refer to a baby bird. Children like to play with clay, silk, or cloth figurines, which in Japan are called *Hina*, written as "*chu*"; there, they often preserve ancient Chinese words. Lao Laizi playing with toys in front of his parents seems more natural than him playing with baby birds. So the English "doll," what we now call "Western baby" or "clay figure" but written as the characters "傀儡" (*kui lei*, puppet) could very well be what the ancients called "*chu*"; later it fell out of use and survived only in Japan. But this is just a conjecture I came up with on a whim—I don't have any solid evidence for it.

It seems that no one has yet drawn a picture of Lao Laizi playing with a doll.

Another set of books I have collected contains images of "Wu Chang" (Life is unpredictable).[85] One is in *The Record of the Jade Calendar to Admonish the World*—or without the last part, "to Admonish the World"; another is *Most Precious Record*—or *Compilation*—*of the Jade Calendar*. In fact, they are almost identical. As for collecting them, I first have to thank Chang Weijun, who mailed me the Beijing Long'guang zhai edition as well as the Jian'guang zhai edition also printed in Beijing; the Siguo zhai edition and a lithographic edition, both from Tianjin; and the Li Guangmin zhuang edition from Nanjing. Next I need to thank Zhang Maochen, who gave me the Hangzhou Ma'nao jing fang edition, the Xuguangji edition from Shaoxing and the most recent lithographic edition. Finally, I myself acquired the Guangzhou Baojing ge edition and the Hanyuan lou editions.

As I said in the preface, there are two versions of these *Jade Calendars,* the original and the abridged. After surveying all the images of Wu Chang, however, I started getting flustered because "Life Is

Unpredictable" is wearing a patterned robe and a gauze hat, with a sword on his back; the one carrying the abacus and wearing a tall hat turned out to be "Death Is Destiny"! Though they may differ in appearance—looking good or evil—and wear different shoes, straw or cloth (?)—these discrepancies are merely byproducts of the illustrator's whims. The captions, however, are of foremost importance, and all say that the figures are "Death Is Destiny." Alas, it is clear that this is deliberately meant to make things difficult for me!

But I'm still not satisfied. First, these books were not the ones I had seen in my childhood, and second, I'm still confident that my memory hasn't failed me. My hopes for tearing out a page to use as an illustration, however, were silently smashed. I could select only one sample from each—"Death Is Destiny" from the Nanjing edition and "Life Is Unpredictable" from the Guangzhou edition. In addition, I had to make do and fill in the gaps by drawing the Wu Chang I remembered from the Maudgalyāyana play and the temple fair, the top illustration in diagram 3 [Figure 10]. Fortunately, I'm not an artist by trade and though the illustration isn't good at all, at least it doesn't seem so bad as to incur readers' abuse. Lacking foresight at the time, some remarks I once made mocking Mr. Wu Youru and his contemporaries might eventually come back to haunt me and make me look like a fool, so I'd now like to offer a few preemptory words in defense, just for the record. But if those are unavailing, then I'll just have to resort to copying President Xu (Shichang's) philosophy: Let things take their course.

Another matter I find unconvincing: I feel that those who promote *The Jade Calendar* don't really understand much about the Netherworld. For example, illustrations of the scenes of the newly dead can be divided into two categories: ones with only a single ghost attendant shown holding a metal pitchfork in his hands and nothing else, called the "Spirit Catcher"; ones with a horse-faced attendant and

Figure 10. Death Is Destiny and Living Wuchang. Reproduced
from Lu Xun, *Lu Xun quanji* (Complete works of Lu Xun),
18 vols. (Beijing: Renmin wenxue, 2005), 2:243.

two Wu Changs—a *yang* Wu Chang and a *yin* Wu Chang—not a Wu
Chang and a Death Is Destiny. Supposing the two were Wu Chang
and Death Is Destiny, their images aren't the same as how they appear in individual portraits. For example, in picture A in diagram 4
[Figure 11], why is *yang* Wu Chang wearing a patterned robe and gauze

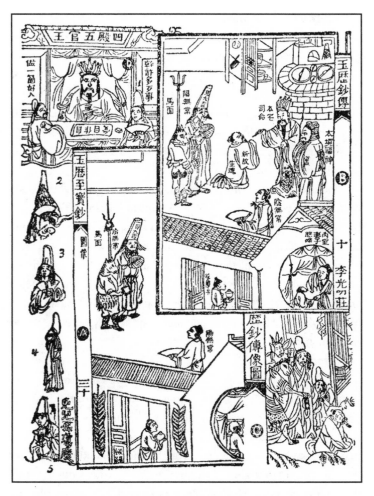

Figure 11. Sketches from *The Jade Calendar*. Reproduced from *Hua zhe Lu Xun* (Lu Xun the artist), ed. Wang Xirong (Shanghai: Shanghai wenhua chubanshe, 2006), 52.

hat? Only *yin* Wu Chang looks similar to the individual portrait of Death Is Destiny, but he too has put down the abacus and holds a fan instead. This may be attributed to the fact that it was summer at the time, but then why would he have grown out such a long beard? Could it be because epidemics are rampant in the summer, and he was so busy that he didn't even have time to shave? The source of this illustration is the Tianjin Suguozhai edition. Here I'd like to note that illustrations in the editions printed in Beijing and Guangzhou are not that different either.

Picture B is taken from the Nanjing Li Guangmingzhuang edition, and the picture is the same as A, but the captions are reversed: the figure that the Tianjin edition noted as *yin* Wu Chang is said to be *yang* Wu Chang, which is, however, consistent with my own view. So, when people from Beijing, Tianjin, or Guangzhou see a figure dressed in white wearing a tall hat, beard or no beard, they call him *yin* Wu Chang or Death Is Destiny; people from Nanjing and I call him *yang* Wu Chang—everyone just does as they please. As they say, names are just referents for things, and they just don't matter all that much.

But I still want to add a bit on picture C, which is from the Shaoxing Xuguangji edition. No captions are above it, so the intent of those circulating it is unclear. When I was young, I often walked past Xuguangji's gate and idly watched them carve illustrations. They only liked to draw round shapes and straight lines, seldom using curved lines, so it's hard to tell just what Mr. Wu Chang really looks like from this engraving. But a "small tall-hat," not found in the other editions, is clearly visible by his side. This is Ah Ling, who, as I have said before, appears in temple fairs. Wu Chang takes his son (?) to work, I surmise, probably so his son can learn along the way, so that when he grows up, he won't change his father's ways.

Other than the summoner of human souls, there almost always appears a character wearing a tall hat standing beside the desk of King Wuguan of the Fourth Court, one of the Ten Kings of the Netherworld. For example, in picture D, sketch 1, the handsome character is taken from the Tianjin Siguozhai edition; in sketch 2, from the Nanjing edition, the character, for some unknown reason, has his tongue hanging out; in sketch 3, from the Guangzhou Baojingge edition, the character has a broken fan; in sketch 4, from the Beijing Longguangzhai edition, the character with a black strip, I can't quite tell if it's a beard or a tongue under his chin, is without the fan; in sketch 5, from the Tianjin Lithography shop edition, also handsomely done, the character is in the Seventh Court, standing next to the desk of King Taishan, which is very unusual.

And, in the pictures with tigers eating people, a character wearing a tall hat holding a paper fan, secretly giving the tiger directions, is always depicted. I don't know whether this is Wu Chang or the so-called "Zhang the Ghost." But none of the "Zhang the Ghost" characters in the operas of my hometown wear tall hats.

Doing research on intangible and unverifiable matters such as souls and spirits is very novel and a most easy way to get ahead. If I were to accumulate materials and begin discussing them, and then compile and print all the correspondences on the topic, I could probably publish three or four thick volumes and thus be promoted to the rank of "scholar." The title "Wu Chang Scholar," however, really isn't all that glorified, so I don't want to keep on doing it. I'll just make a presumptuous conclusion here and now: The ideas in *The Jade Calendar* are crude and superficial. Life Is Unpredictable

(Wu Chang) and Death Is Destiny (Si You Fen) together are symbols of human life. When people are about to die, only Death Is Destiny needs to show up, because his arrival itself shows how "Life Is Unpredictable."

But among the people is a certain kind who call themselves "Travelers of the Netherworld" or "Messengers of the Netherworld," living people who visit Hell for a short time and help out with administrative tasks. Because they help catch human souls and spirits, they are also referred to as "Wu Chang"; because they are living souls, they are also known as *yang,* but as a result, they are implicitly confused with *"yang* Wu Chang." For example, picture A in diagram 4, captioned *"yang* Wu Chang," the character is dressed in ordinary human clothes, clearly indicating that he is just a messenger to the Netherworld. His duty is simply to lead the ghost attendants through the gate, so he stands beneath the stairs.

Since there's *"yang* Wu Chang," a living soul who enters Hell, the title of *"yin* Wu Chang" is conferred upon Death Is Destiny, who plays a somewhat similar role but isn't a living soul.

While the Maudgalyāyana drama and temple fairs are religious rituals, they also serve as entertainment. If the appearance of the messenger of the netherworld is ordinary and too boring, it would be tantamount to no "performance" at all, so they figured they might as well make it more special and let him put on the clothing of "that other Wu Chang," whose origins, naturally, nobody is very clear about either. Yet from then on, this "error" was passed on. So what Nanjingers and I refer to as "Wu Chang" is really a messenger from the Netherworld wearing Death Is Destiny's costume, assuming the name of the "Wu Chang"—such an egregious departure from the original version, it really is quite absurd.

I wonder what the erudite and sophisticated gentlemen within our borders think of all this?

I hadn't originally planned to write an afterword—I had merely wanted to find a few old pictures to use as illustrations. Little did I anticipate that I would be unsuccessful and instead end up making comparisons, and cutting and pasting figures here while making random comments there. That short main text I wrote on and off for almost a year and this short afterword I wrote on and off for almost two months. Hot as the weather is, sweat streaming down my back—a good time to end, is it not? Here I conclude.

July 11, 1927, completed under the western window
of the Eastern Embankment building in Guangzhou

Notes

Introduction

1. Lu Xun 魯迅 was given the name Zhou Zhangshou 周樟壽 at birth. When he enrolled in the Jiangnan Naval Academy in 1898, he adopted the name Zhou Shuren 周樹人, the name he went by thereafter. He adopted a wide variety of pen names, the most well known of them "Lu Xun," first used when he published the short story "Diary of a Madman" (1918).

2. In 1924, Lu Xun was still reeling with the after-effects of his estrangement half a year earlier from his younger brother, Zhou Zuoren (1885–1967), to whom he was once very close. In the same year, the married Lu Xun met his student (later common-law wife) Xu Guangping (1898–1968) at Peking Women's Normal College where he taught at the time. The affair, which commenced in 1925, was a source of joy, confusion, and anguish for Lu Xun. Letters and sources indicate that he was the more reluctant of the two to pursue the relationship and took pains to hide the affair once it commenced. Bonnie McDougall, *Love Letters and Privacy in Modern China* (Oxford: Oxford University Press, 2002), 152–154; Wang Xiaoming, *Wu fa zhi mian de rensheng: Lu Xun zhuan* (A life that cannot be confronted: A biography of Lu Xun) (Taipei: Yeqiang, 1992), 135–138. The unexpected turn of events with Zhou Zuoren and Xu Guangping may have led Lu Xun to reconsider his prior conceptions of "family" and "home" and possibly to his writing the memoir.

3. Lu Xun, "In Memory of Liu Hezhen," in *Jottings under Lamplight,* ed. Eileen J. Cheng and Kirk A. Denton (Cambridge, MA: Harvard University Press, 2017), 74–89; Lu Xun, *Lu Xun quanji* (Complete works of Lu Xun), 18 vols. (Beijing: Renmin wenxue chubanshe, 2005) (hereafter *LXQJ*), 3:289–295. As can be gleaned from the essay, Lu Xun felt a sense of survival guilt and possibly some responsibility for his students' deaths. From 1924 to 1925 he had been embroiled in a bitter dispute between students and the administration of Peking Women's Normal College. He supported the students who advocated for rights to political protest (which included Xu Guangping) against the college administration, then backed by the Beiyang government warlord Duan Qirui, who ordered the killings of the protestors on March 18.

4. Lu Xun used this phrase to describe the works collected in *Wild Grass.* Lu Xun, "Preface to the English Translation of *Wild Grass*" (*Yecao* yingwen yiben xu), translated from Chinese in this volume, *LXQJ* 4:365. The bulk of what Lu Xun considered his creative work—including the stories in *Hesitation* and two of the eight stories later collected in *Old Tales Retold* (*Gushi xin bian,* 1936)—was written within this three-year period.

5. The link between suffering and creativity was a topic of ongoing interest for Lu Xun. His translation of the Japanese writer Kuriyagawa Hakuson's *Kumon no shōchō* (Symbols of agony) was published in 1924. The premise of Hakuson's book is that "the agony and frustration that comes from the suppression of one's vitality is the root of literature and the arts." Translated and quoted from Lu Xun's preface to *Kumon no shōchō* (*Kumen de xiangzheng*) in *Lu Xun yiwen quanji* (Complete translations of Lu Xun), 8 vols. (Fuzhou: Fujian jiaoyu chubanshe, 2008), 2:223. Along this line of thinking, we can read Lu Xun's *Wild Grass* and *Morning Blossoms* as creative unleashings from this fraught period of his life.

6. I borrow this idea of exploring the "beyond" from Jianguo Chen, *The Aesthetics of the "Beyond": Phantasm, Nostalgia, and the Literary Practice in Contemporary China* (Newark: University of Delaware Press, 2009), 20.

Wild Grass

1. Tsi-An Hsia, "Aspects of the Power of Darkness in Lu Hsün," in *The Gate of Darkness: Studies on the Leftist Literary Movement in China* (Seattle: University of Washington Press, 1968), 150.

2. Leo Ou-fan Lee, *Voices from the Iron House: A Study of Lu Xun* (Bloomington: Indiana University Press, 1987), 89.

3. More recently, various scholars have noted the religious aspects of Lu Xun's short stories. Lydia Liu traces the origins of "Prayers for Blessings" (Zhufu) to a story of the travails of the Brahmin woman Bhiksuni Suksma from the *Sutra of the Wise and the Foolish* (*Xianyu jing*). Lydia Liu, "Life as Form: How Biomimesis Encountered Buddhism in Lu Xun," *Journal of Asian Studies* 68, no. 1 (February 2009): 21–54. Ying Lei traces a dialogue on seeds in *The Loner* (*Gu Duzhe*) to a larger debate about the problem of evil between Yogācāra and Tathāgatagarbha schools. Ying Lei, "Lu Xun, the Critical Buddhist: A Monstrous Ekayāna," *Journal of Chinese Literature and Culture* 3, no. 2 (November 2016): 408–417.

4. Disavowing the title of "mentor" and "guide," Lu Xun wrote, "I know for a fact only one destination, and that is the grave." "Afterword to *Graves*," trans. Theodore Huters, in *Jottings under Lamplight*, ed. Eileen J. Cheng and Kirk A. Denton (Cambridge, MA: Harvard University Press, 2017), 32. The original is in Lu Xun, *Lu Xun quanji* (Complete works of Lu Xun), 18 vols. (Beijing: Renmin wenxue chubanshe, 2005) (hereafter *LXQJ*), 1:298.

5. I borrow this idea of exploring the "beyond" from Jianguo Chen, *The Aesthetics of the "Beyond": Phantasm, Nostalgia, and the Literary Practice in Contemporary China* (Newark: University of Delaware Press, 2009), 20.

6. Quoted from John Keats's letter to Tom and George Keats, December 22, 1818, https://www.poetryfoundation.org/articles/69384/selections-from-keatss-letters.

7. David Jauss, "Lever of Transcendence: Contradiction and the Physics of Creativity," in *On Writing Fiction: Rethinking Conventional Wisdom about the Craft* (Cincinnati, OH: Writer's Digest Books, 2011), 112.

8. Lu Xun, *Yecao* (Wild Grass) (Beijing: Beixin shuju, 1927). "Inscriptions" serves as the preface to the volume.

9. Nicholas Kaldis traces the Chinese and Western sources for the development of prose poetry (*sanwen shi*) in *The Prose Poem: A Study of Lu Xun's Wild Grass* (New York: Cambria Press, 2014), 95–142. Sun Yushi notes that the pieces in *Wild Grass* may have been inspired by the prose poems of Baudelaire and Turgenev, which were popular in China at the time. See Sun Yushi, *Yecao ershisi jiang* (Twenty-four lectures on *Wild Grass*) (Shandong: CITIC Press, 2014), 2–18. In the preface to the English translation of *Wild Grass* collected in this volume, Lu Xun referred to the pieces as "small prose pieces" (*xiaopin wen*) and "impromptu reflections" (*suishi de xiao ganxiang*).

10. Two short stories in *Outcry*, "Rabbits and Cats" (Tu he mao) and "The Comedy of Ducks" (Ya de xiju), also have animal protagonists (*LXQJ* 1:577–582, 583–586). After their cohabitation, Zijun, the female protagonist of "Lament for the Dead" (Shangshi) in *Hesitation*, seemingly derives more comfort and solace from the loyal dog Ah Sui and the hens she raises than from her lover Juansheng. As they run out of money, Juansheng persuades Zijun to kill the chick for food and then abandons her dog on the city outskirts for dead (*LXQJ* 2:113–134).

11. "The Dog's Retort," "An Argument," and "The Clever Man, the Fool, and the Slave" bear striking resemblances to Buddhist parables, such as those collected in *The Hundred Parable Sutra* (*Bai yu jing*, originally titled *Stories of Fools, Chi hua man*), for which Lu Xun had a particular affinity. He translated one of the pieces, "The Idiot Talks about Griddlecakes" (Chiren shuo bing) into the vernacular in 1912. See Liu Yunfeng, *Lu Xun quanji buyi* (Supplement to the complete works of Lu Xun) (Tianjin: Renmin chubanshe, 2006), 335–336. Lu Xun edited, wrote a foreword to the sutra, and contributed funds to the printing of a hundred copies of it in 1914. The sutra was published as *Stories of Fools* in 1926. For the foreword, see *LXQJ* 7:103.

12. Roy Chan suggests that one might read *Wild Grass* as a whole as a "nocturnal fantasia"—one long dream, tracing the arc of a drowsy narrator in the first piece and ending with the narrator rousing from his dream in the last piece. Roy Bing Chan, *The Edge of Knowing: Dreams, History, and Realism in Modern Chinese Literature* (Seattle: University of Washington Press, 2017), 40.

13. In the "Afterword to *Graves*" (Xie zai *Fen* hou, 1926), Lu Xun likened writing to a process of "dissection," noting that he dissected himself even more mercilessly than he dissected others (*LXQJ* 1:300). The painful consequences of self-introspection are also apparent in "Diary of a Madman," when the protagonist is forced to confront his own complicity in a cannibalistic culture (*LXQJ* 1:444–456).

14. The scene of a narrator unable to fix his gaze on an image surfaces again in "Dead Fire": "When I was young, I was fond of gazing at the foamy waves stirred up by motor boats and the fiery flames shooting up from blazing furnaces. Not only was I fond of gazing at them, I also wanted to get a clear view of them. Alas they were ever-changing, never keeping a fixed form. No matter how intently I stared, I could never retain a fixed image."

15. Ellen Y. Zhang, Review of Wang Youru's *Linguistic Strategies in Daoist Zhuangzi and Chan Buddhism: The Other Way of Speaking,* published in *Dao* 10 (2011): 403–408, 404.

16. "Perfect interfusion" (*yuanrong wu ai*), a term describing the mutually interpenetrating nature of all phenomena, was central to Huayan (Flower Adornment) Buddhism. The descriptions in "Story of Good Things" resonates with Paul Williams' description of the universe of the *Flower Adornment Sutra*: a "quicksilver universe of the visionary perspective wherein all is empty (or all is the play of omniscient awareness) and therefore is seen as a flow lacking in edges . . . a universe of radiance, and in a wonderful image, it is said to be a world of pure luminosity with no shadows" where "all things infinitely interpenetrate." Paul William, *Mahayana Buddhism: The Doctrinal Foundations* (London: Routledge, 2009), 135–136. Wang Weidong makes a similar link between the dreamscape and the Buddhist notion of perfect interfusion, arguing that "it is in the dissolution of the 'village'—the village of the narrator's memory, the village in the dream, and the village reflected in the water—that the narrator is able to experience the splendid nature of the cosmos." Wang Weidong, *Tanxun "shi xin": Yecao zhengti yanjiu* (Exploring the "poetic heart": A study on *Wild Grass*) (Beijing: Beijing daxue chubanshe, 2014), 141.

17. Lu Xun, "How I Write" (Zenme xie, 1927), in *Three Leisures (San xian ji)*, *LXQJ* 4:18–19.

18. Ibid. The quote starting "When I am silent . . ." is the first line of the foreword to *Wild Grass*.

19. Theodore Huters, "Afterword to Graves," in *Jottings under Lamplight*, 31 (*LXQJ* 1:302). The afterword was written half a year after the last piece in *Wild Grass*.

20. Ibid., 35 (*LXQJ* 1:303).

21. Ibid., 34 (*LXQJ* 1:302).

22. Alan Fox has noted the use of earthquakes in the "omniverse" of the *Flower Adornment Sutra* (*Huayan jing*) "as possible reminders to shake up and loosen or deconstruct fixed ontological commitments." A verse he quotes from the Sutra resonates with Lu Xun's use of trembling in "Tremors": "Then the ocean of worlds of arrays of flower banks, by the power of Buddha, all shook in six ways in eighteen manners, that is, they trembled, trembled all over, trembled all over in all directions." See Alan Fox, "The Practice of *Huayan* Buddhism," in *Chinese Buddhism: Past, Present, and Future* (Yilan, Taiwan: Foguang University Center for Buddhist Studies, 2015), 264.

23. Jonathan Lear, *Radical Hope: Ethics in the Face of Cultural Devastation* (Cambridge, MA: Harvard University Press, 2006), 100. In a letter dated April 11, 1925, written to Zhao Qiwen, Lu Xun writes on "The Passerby": "Insisting on proceeding in spite of knowing that what lies ahead are graves is a way of resisting despair. Because I believe that those who fight to resist despair are up against something difficult, they must be stronger and braver and more tenacious than those that fight on the account of hope" (*LXQJ* 11:477–478). The ideas on radical hope in *Wild Grass* in this section are drawn from the epilogue of my monograph on Lu Xun. See Eileen J. Cheng, *Literary Remains: Death, Trauma, and Lu Xun's Refusal to Mourn* (Honolulu: University of Hawai'i Press, 2013), 230–233.

24. Lear, *Radical Hope*, 100.

25. Lu Xun, "Sudden Thoughts 1" (Huran xiang dao, 1925), *Inauspicious Star* (*Huagai ji*), *LXQJ* 3:18.

26. Lu Xun, "Preface," in *Essays from the Semi-concessions* (*Qiejie ting zawen*, 1935), *LXQJ* 6:4.

27. In part due to his canonization as a revolutionary and realist writer, much scholarship has focused on meticulous political and historical contextu-

alization of the individual pieces, which is not repeated here. See for example, Sun Yushi, *Yecao yanjiu* (A study of *Wild Grass*) (Beijing: Beijing daxue chubanshe, 2007).

28. Critics have noted the possible inspiration for the pieces from *Wild Grass:* from traditional Chinese sources to foreign works such as those of Baudelaire, Turgenev, and Nietzsche (see note 9). Another likely source though less often noted is Natsume Sōseki's dream narratives first serialized in *Asahi Shinbun* in 1908, and later collected in *Ten Nights of Dreams* (*Yume Jūya,* 1909). Lu Xun translated some of the Japanese writer's works into Chinese in the *Collection of Modern Japanese Short Stories* (*Xiandai riben xiaoshuo ji,* 1923) published by the Shanghai Commercial Press and in "How I Came to Write Fiction" (1933) noted that while he was in Japan, Natsume Sōseki was among his favorite writers (*LXQJ* 4:525).

29. Lu Xun's parable of the iron house may have been inspired by the parable of the burning house in the *Lotus Sutra.* Ying Lei, "Lu Xun, the Critical Buddhist," 419.

30. Leo Ou-fan Lee estimates that at least 50 percent of Lu Xun's impressive output of *zawen*—twelve anthologies published in his lifetime and four posthumously—were written between 1933–1936. See Lee, "Eve of the Revolution," *Modern China* 2, no. 3 (July 1976): 288.

31. The "Preface to the English Translation of *Wild Grass,*" written five years after the publication of *Wild Grass,* might have reflected more Lu Xun's literary sensibilities at the time he wrote the preface, by which time he had become a leading voice of the League of Left-Wing Writers and a promoter of proletarian literature. The preface mentions only the pieces written in a "realist" vein while ignoring the more fantastic works in the collection.

32. Y. S. Feng Refers to Feng Yusheng (1899–1957), the translator of *Wild Grass.*

33. 大歡喜 (*da huanxi,* great joy), along with 空 (*kong,* emptiness or void) are originally Buddhist terms that appear with some frequency in *Wild Grass.*

34. While Lu Xun promoted the vernacular, he had a lifelong appreciation of classical poetry and was an accomplished classical poet in in his own right. For a translation of his poems in classical Chinese to English with annotations and commentary, see Jon Kowallis, *The Lyrical Lu Xun: A*

Study of His Classical-Style Verse (Honolulu: University of Hawai'i Press, 1995). "My Lost Love," Lu Xun's sole foray into writing a "modern" poem, is a parody of the esteemed "Rhapsody of Four Sorrows" by the Eastern Han official and poet Zhang Heng (78–139). In the tradition of literary transvestism, which draws its inspiration From Qu Yuan's "Encountering Sorrow," Zhang Heng uses figure of the frustrated lover as an allegory for his relationship with the emperor after palace intrigues left him marginalized. For a comparison with Zhang Heng's original and an analysis of Lu Xun's parodic poem, see Eileen J. Cheng, "The Abandoned Lover," in Cheng, *Literary Remains*, 113–119. Lu Xun's parodic poem reveals his low estimation of the field of modern poetry, showing how far removed modern poets are from the rich tradition of traditional poetry and how the best specimens of traditional poetry are desecrated in modern times. Modern poetry is shown to be little more than sentimental drivel. As Lu Xun notes in "My Relationship with *Threads of Talk*" (Wo yu *Yusi* de shizhong, 1929), the last words of the poem, "Oh, just let her go" was a deliberate mocking of love poems with exaggerated lyrics such as "Oh, oh, I am about to die" which were fashionable at the time (*LXQJ* 4:170).

35. In Buddhism, an arhat (a Sanskrit term translated as 羅漢 *luohan* in Chinese) refers to a being who has reached enlightenment and achieved nirvana.

36. The date completed, noted at the end of the piece, is later than the date of publication and is incorrect. Lu Xun's diary entry on January 28, 1925, indicates that he completed a piece from *Wild Grass*, which could be a possible allusion to "Story of Good Things." See *LXQJ* 2:192n6.

37. *Hehe* appears in roman letters in the original.

38. Referring to Qing troops composed of Han Chinese.

Morning Blossoms Gathered at Dusk

1. One of the most famous examples is the poet-official Qu Yuan (340–278? BCE), who was expelled by court. He adopted a feminine voice in his poems to symbolize his political marginality. Lu Xun was fond of Qu

Yuan's poetry. In lieu of writing a preface to his second short story collection, *Hesitation*, he quotes the following couplet from Qu Yuan's "Encountering Sorrow" (Li Sao): "The road is far and the journey long, I will go to the ends of the earth in pursuit." Lu Xun, *Panghuang* (Beijing: Beixin shuju, 1926).

2. Lu Xun, *Morning Blossoms Gathered at Dusk* (*Zhao hua xi shi*) (Beijing: Weiming she, 1928).

3. Here I draw on Svetlana Boym's definition of nostalgia. She writes: "Nostalgia (from nostos-return home, and algia-longing) is a longing for a home that no longer exists or has never existed. Nostalgia is a sentiment of loss and displacement, but it is also a romance with one's own fantasy." Svetlana Boym, *The Future of Nostalgia* (New York: Basic Books, 2001), xiii.

4. "Preface to *Outcry*," trans. Eileen J. Cheng, in *Jottings under Lamplight*, ed. Eileen J. Cheng and Kirk A. Denton (Cambridge, MA: Harvard University Press, 2017), 19; Lu Xun, *Complete Works of Lu Xun* (*Lu Xun quanji*), 18 vols. (Beijing: Renmin wenxue chubanshe, 2005) (hereafter *LXQJ*), 1:437.

5. The link between suffering and creativity was a topic of ongoing interest for Lu Xun. His translation of the Japanese writer Kuriyagawa Hakuson's *Kumon no shōchō* (Symbols of agony) was published in 1924. The premise of Hakuson's book, in his own words, is that "the agony and frustration that comes from the suppression of one's vitality is the root of literature and the arts." Translated and quoted from Lu Xun's preface to *Kumon no shōchō* (Kumen de xiangzheng) in *Lu Xun yiwen quanji* (Complete translations of Lu Xun), 8 vols. (Fuzhou: Fujian jiaoyu chubanshe, 2008), 2:223.

6. In the autobiographical prefaces to *Outcry* and *Morning Blossoms*, Lu Xun's self-critical portraits describe a pattern of escapist behavior—reflected psychically in his predilection for trivial pursuits and physically in his itinerant wandering. Yet, with each new move, the restlessness and sense of being without a home in the world remains. In spite of his self-mocking portraits, however, Lu Xun rejects such escapism in his writing, so much so that he rarely indulges in "nostalgia" or utopic fantasies in the memoir itself. In the last essay of *Morning Blossoms*, the narrator, like other

sojourners in Lu Xun's stories who return to their hometown, finds it disappointing, prompting him to leave yet again. Those who have no choice but to remain, like his friend Fan Ainong, are left to languish. Lu Xun never returned to his hometown after his last visit in 1919 to relocate his mother, Lu Rui (1858–1943), and his wife by arranged marriage, Zhu An (1878–1947), to Beijing. For a detailed examination of Lu Xun's anti-nostalgic depiction of the hometown in his fiction, see Eileen J. Cheng, "The Journey Home," in *Literary Remains: Death, Trauma, and Lu Xun's Refusal to Mourn* (Honolulu: University of Hawai'i Press, 2013), 140–166.

7. Lu Xun writes: "It is true that I often dissect others, but I dissect myself even more mercilessly." "Afterword to *Graves*" (1926), trans. Theodore Huters, in *Jottings under Lamplight*, 32; *LXQJ* 1:300. This same sentiment is repeated elsewhere: "I know myself and I dissect myself even more mercilessly than I dissect others." "In Reply to Mr. Youheng" (1927), trans. Eileen J. Cheng, in Cheng and Denton, *Jottings under Lamplight*, 49; *LXQJ* 3:477.

8. The English "memoir" is an apt term to describe the pieces in *Morning Blossoms*. As Lu Xun notes, the focus of his memoir is on the *memory* of the past rather than the past as it was. For more on the memoir as a particular genre of autobiographical writing, see G. Thomas Couser, *Memoir: An Introduction* (New York: Oxford University Press, 2012).

9. Catherine E. Pease notes the paradox of the voice of the "child" in literature, which is almost always mediated through the adult writer. Catherine E. Pease, "Remembering the Taste of Melons: Modern Chinese Stories of Childhood," in *Chinese Views of Childhood*, ed. Anne Behnke Kinney (Honolulu: University of Hawai'i Press, 1995), 289.

10. While the child in *Morning Blossoms*, in contrast to those he encounters in the adult world, is largely portrayed as innocent and by nature good, the portrayals of children in Lu Xun's writings were by no means uniform. In "Tremors on the Border of Degradation" in *Wild Grass* and in stories such as "Diary of a Madman," "Kong Yiji," and others, children are also portrayed as cruel and predatory.

11. For background on the "discovery" of the child and the political and commercial symbolism that the figure of the child took on from the May Fourth period and after, see Mary Ann Farquhar, *Children's Literature in*

China: From Lu Xun to Mao Zedong (Armonk, NY: M. E. Sharpe, 1999); Andrew F. Jones and Xu Lanjun, eds., *Ertong de faxian: Xiandai Zhongguo wenxue ji wenhua zhong de ertong wenti* (The discovery of the child: The problem of the child in modern Chinese literature and culture) (Beijing: Peking University Press, 2011); Andrew F. Jones *Developmental Fairy Tales: Evolutionary Thinkers and Modern Chinese Culture* (Cambridge, MA: Harvard University Press, 2011).

12. Li Zhi, "'Tongxin shuo" (On the childlike heart-mind), in *Fen shu* (A book to burn) (Beijing: Zhonghua shuju, 1961), 98–99. Li Zhi's thought, and in particular "childlike mind-heart," is explored in Pauline Lee, *Li Zhi, Confucianism, and the Nature of Desire* (Albany: State University of New York Press, 2011), 45–67. A similar celebration of the childlike spirit is seen in the work of German philosopher and writer Friedrich Nietzsche (1844–1900), with whom Lu Xun was quite taken.

13. The term *liren* first appears in Lu Xun's "On the Extremes of Cultural Development" (Wenhua pianzhi lun, 1908). Fearful that the rampant materialism and erosion of moral values he observed in modern Western nations would be transmitted to China, Lu Xun condemned those with a slave mentality (*nuxing*) who advocated blindly following Western ways. Essential to any civilization, he wrote, is the soul and spirit of its people. He called for "cultivating the human," the nurturing of enlightened individuals who, attuned to their inner voice, would dedicate themselves to fighting against oppression and for a just society (*LXQJ* 1:45–64). In "The Power of Mara Poetry," he hailed the Romantic poets such as Byron and Shelley as spiritual warriors who were models of just such genuine persons (*zhenren*). As Lu Xun grew increasingly pessimistic in the mid-1920s, his early preoccupation with the notion of *liren* surfaces in an opposite guise: that is, an insistent focus on the failure to cultivate the human and a "nation of humans" as the Chinese toil on as slaves. See Eileen J. Cheng, "'In Search of New Voices from Alien Lands': Lu Xun, Cultural Exchange, and the Myth of Sino-Japanese Friendship," *Journal of Asian Studies* 73, no. 3 (August 2014): 589–618.

14. Lu Xun's criticism of filial piety, fueled by his own experiences as a "filial" oldest son and his philosophical reflections of what it means to be human, was also much in line with the New Culture movement's antitraditional

stance and promotion of individualism. In an essay written in 1918, Lu Xun called for a new kind of parenting, not the traditional father-and-son relationship based on filial piety and the child's submission to the father but one that focused on the father's deliberate raising of an independent individual. One was not to think of oneself as a "father of a child," but "father of a human": "Suigan lu 25" (Impromptu thoughts 25, 1918), in *Re feng* (Hot air), collected in *LXQJ* 1:312. The following year he proposed overturning the traditional family system's hierarchal structure, appealing to parents to "liberate the children" so that they can grow up to be independent beings. See Lu Xun, "On Conducting Ourselves as Fathers Today" (1919), trans. Bonnie S. McDougall, in Cheng and Denton, *Jottings under Lamplight,* 127–139; *LXQJ* 1:134–149.

15. Keith Knapp notes that the enduring popularity of filial piety tales among all social classes from AD 100 to 1949 "was due to the effectiveness with which they illustrated the paramount cultural value of *xiao* (filial piety), which has shaped nearly every aspect of Chinese social life." Keith Nathaniel Knapp, *Selfless Offspring: Filial Children and Social Order in Medieval China* (Honolulu: University of Hawai'i Press, 2005), 3.

16. Figuratively speaking, the cannibalism in Lu Xun's essay and story refers to the predatory system that he saw as emerging from the social norms that dictated individuals' strict compliance to social hierarchies to maintain harmony and order. In Lu Xun's view, the division of people into categories and assigned roles, along with the lauding of virtues such as filial obedience, nurtured a "slave mentality" and a culture of conformity, alienating people from one another and preventing the development of the genuine person. A vicious cycle then ensued in which people ingratiated themselves with their superiors and oppressed their inferiors. Lu Xun writes: "If we are bullied and abused, we can still bully and abuse others; we can be eaten, but we can also eat others. There is a hierarchy of strict control that cannot be tampered with, nor does anyone wish to tamper with it." "Jottings under Lamplight" (1925), trans. Theodore Huters, in Cheng and Denton, *Jottings under Lamplight,* 148; *LXQJ* 1:227.

17. The devastating effects of this traumatic incident are particularly poignant when read in tandem with Lu Xun's autobiographical essay "The

Kite" (Fengzheng, 1925) collected in *Wild Grass*. The narrator, once the victim of abuse, perpetuates the cycle of abuse. Relishing his physical power and authority as the older brother, the narrator expresses utter contempt for his younger sibling's "childish" fascination with kites and forbids him to fly one. Upon discovering his brother in a shed secretly making a kite, he angrily crushes and tramples it.

18. Judith Butler, *Precarious Life: The Powers of Mourning and Violence* (New York: Verso, 2004), 20.

19. Among the "estimable gentlemen" Lu Xun attacked in this essay are the literary critic Chen Yuan (1896–1970), the writer Lin Yutang (1895–1976), and the poet Xu Zhimo (1897–1931). The roots of his bitter disputes with Chen Yuan and his ilk stemmed from a series of protests between 1924 and 1925 at the Peking Women's Normal College. Lu Xun sided with the students who demand the right to political protest and opposed the restrictive policies of their American-educated principal, Yang Yinyu (1884–1938), who was supported by the minister of education, Zhang Shizhao (1881–1973), and backed by the Beiyang government warlord Duan Qirui (1865–1936). The public outcry over the dispute eventually led to the dismissal of Yang. Lin Yutang, in an attempt to mediate, called for a stop to the attacks against Yang and her supporters and claimed that "drowning dogs should not be beaten." "Dogs • Cats • Mice" harks back to Lu Xun's rebuttal to what he saw as Lin's use of empty slogans such as "fair play" and "public justice" in "Why 'Fair Play' Should Be Deferred" (1926), arguing that "drowning dogs" needed to be beaten, lest they rear their ugly heads from the water again. "Dogs," too are used snidely as analogies for Chen, Lin, and their ilk, most of whom had studied in Europe or America, as "Western lapdogs." See "Dogs • Cats • Mice" in this volume and Lu Xun, "Why 'Fair Play' Should Be Deferred" (1926), trans. Andrew Jones, in Cheng and Denton, *Jottings under Lamplight*, 156–164; *LXQJ* 1:286–297.

20. Lu Xun may have had in mind to memorialize those who had died or no longer figured prominently in his life at the time he wrote his memoir. His mother barely makes an appearance, and there is no mention of his three brothers (one of whom died in infancy) in his memoir.

21. Butler, *Precarious Life*, 34. The quote here refers to the function of obituaries but is relevant to Lu Xun's essays memorializing the lives of others.

22. Ibid, 28.

23. For detailed analysis of how the essay associates Fan Ainong to the lineage of marginalized scholars first drawn up by the Grand Historian Sima Qian (145–86? BCE), see Cheng, *Literary Remains,* 65–69.

24. The uncharacteristic sentimentality of the essay and Lu Xun's laudatory portrait of Fujino may have, in part, been necessary to overcome the rampant anti-Japanese sentiments at the time of writing. It also may have reflected Lu Xun's frustration with his own literary peers—the "estimable gentlemen" he despised. Ironically, it is in Japan and in the realm of imagination that the narrator is able to find a true confidant and a model of the Confucian gentleman. For a detailed analysis of "Mr. Fujino" as an example of discovering "new voices from alien lands" to invigorate aspects of traditional culture and as a model for a new way of relating to others, see Cheng, "'In Search of New Voices from Alien Lands.'"

25. Yang Bojun, trans. and annotator, *Lun yu yi zhu* (*Analects* with translations and annotations) (Beijing: Zhonghua shuju, 1980), 65.

26. Of traditional biographies, Susan Mann observes that "Famous men constantly referred to the lives of mentors, teachers, friends, relatives, or sages (long dead) who had guided their own decisions and inspired their personal visions. 'Those above' were reared to believe that they were responsible, moreover, for 'those below.' . . . So every member of China's late imperial elite was, on the one hand, conscious of models to whom he was indebted and, on the other hand, aware that he himself was a model for others." Susan Mann, "Scene-Setting: Writing Biography in Chinese History," *American Historical Review* 114, no. 3 (June 2009): 63.

27. The ending of "Professor Fujino" derisively mentions these "estimable gentlemen" again: "Whenever I felt tired in the evening, right when I felt like slacking off, by the flickering light I would see the image of his dark and thin face, as if about to say some words of encouragement. This would ignite my conscience, strengthen my courage, and I would light a cigarette and continue to write some things that would raise the ire of those 'estimable gentlemen' and their ilk." As Marston Anderson notes, Lu Xun held intellectuals morally accountable as agents of social order and as arbiters of culture through which societal norms are dissemi-

nated. Marston Anderson, *The Limits of Realism: Chinese Fiction in the Revolutionary Period* (Berkeley: University of California Press, 1990), 86. Lu Xun's relentless attack on these "estimable gentlemen," whom he felt were focused on portraying a world of comfort, was in part a reaction to the success of what he regarded as escapist literature, which leads readers astray from pressing social issues at hand.

28. As is characteristic of Lu Xun's writings, the signs of hope in "Professor Fujino" are tempered almost immediately; the essay immediately following it, the last in the volume, ends with the death and suspected suicide of Fan Ainong.

29. Couser, *Memoir*, 179. Indeed, in the case of "Mr. Fujino," the gift went beyond fame and immortality for the Japanese anatomy teacher in China. The story of Lu Xun and Fujino's friendship has since gained a life of its own, becoming a larger symbol of Sino-Japanese friendship that endures to this day. See Cheng, "'In Search of New Voices from Alien Lands.'"

30. For a detailed, line-by-line translation and annotation in English of Lu Ji's "Wen fu" (Rhapsody on literature, translated as "The Poetic Exposition on Literature"), see Stephen Owen, "The Poetic Exposition on Literature," in *Readings in Chinese Literary Thought* (Cambridge, MA: Harvard University Press, 1992), 73–181. Li Zhi in "On the Childlike Heart" also called for casting aside old aesthetic standards, noting that "all the most exquisite literature under heaven comes directly from the childlike heart." Li Zhi, "On the Childlike Heart" (Tongxin shuo), 98–99.

31. Janet Varner Gunn, *Autobiography: Toward a Poetics of Experience* (Philadelphia: University of Pennsylvania Press, 1982), 104.

32. Lu Xun, "On Conducting Ourselves as Fathers Today"; *LXQJ* 1:135.

33. Refers to the bombers of the warlord Zhang Zuolin (1875–1928).

34. After the March 18, 1926, incident, Lu Xun was blacklisted by the Beiyang warlord government. From the end of March to early May 1926, he was sheltered in various hospitals, and in one instance, was housed in a German hospital room also used as a carpenter's workshop. See *LXQJ*, 236n6.

35. Refers to, among others, the historian, folklorist, and philologist Gu Jiegang (1893–1980).

36. Lu Xun is targeting here Chen Xiying and Xu Zhimo by sarcastically quoting from Xu's essay calling for both parties to put an end to their dispute, since as intellectuals they "bear the responsibility for guiding youth." "Cease the Gossip, Cease the Empty Talk" (Jiesu xianhua, jiesu feihua), *The Morning Post Supplement* (*Chenbao fukan*), February 3, 1926. See *LXQJ* 2:246n2.

37. Xu Zhimo, "To the Readers, Regarding the Correspondence Below" (Guanyu xiamian yi shu tongxin gao duzhemen), *The Morning Post Supplement* (*Chenbao fukan*), January 30, 1926. See *LXQJ* 2: 246n4.

38. In an attempt to mediate the dispute between the supporters and opponents of Principal Yang Yinyu, who had by then resigned from the Peking Women's Normal College, the writer Lin Yutang (1895–1976) argued that in the name of "fair play," criticism of Yang (the "dog that had fallen in the water") and her supporters should be stopped. Lin Yutang, "An Aside on the Style of *Threads of Talk:* Moderation, Invective, and Fair Play" (Chalun Yusi de wenti: Wenjian, maren, yu fei'e polai), *Threads of Talk* (*Yusi*) 57 (December 14, 1925). In response, Lu Xun deemed that these dogs should not be saved but be beaten instead. Lu Xun, "Why 'Fair Play' Should Be Deferred" (1926), trans. Andrew Jones, in *Jottings under Lamplight*, ed. Eileen J. Cheng and Kirk A. Denton (Cambridge, MA: Harvard University Press, 2017), 156–164 (*LXQJ* 1:286–297).

39. Chen Xiying, "Idle Chat" (Xian hua), *Contemporary Review* (*Xiandai pinglun*) 3, no. 53 (December 12, 1925).

40. Snide references to Zhang Yiping's (1902–1946) popular collection of love stories, *Qingshu yi shu* (A bunch of love letters) (Beijing: Beixin shuju, 1925).

41. Refers to the Spring Lantern Festival, which marks the last day of the Lunar New Year celebrations.

42. "Ah" placed before a surname or given name is an informal form of address, usually used for someone younger or subordinate in status, to indicate familiarity or as a term of endearment.

43. Leader of the Taiping rebellion, which lasted from c. 1850 to 1864.

44. In the original, the illiterate Ah Chang refers to *The Classic of Mountains and Seas*—"山海經 Shan hai jing"—incorrectly as the "三哼經 San heng jing."

45. The year was not written on the original piece.
46. Referring to the New Culture Movement, often dated to 1915, when intellectuals called for a new literature written in the vernacular.
47. In a letter to Xu Zhimo, Chen Xiying wrote: "That I don't respect Mr. Lu Xun's character doesn't mean that I would refrain from saying that his fiction his good; likewise, because I admire his fiction doesn't mean that I would necessarily praise his other essays." "To Xu Zhimo," in the "Idle Chats" (Xian tan) column of *Contemporary Review* (*Xiandai pinglun*) 3, no. 71 (April 17, 1926); *LXQJ* 2: 264n7.
48. Lu Xun is sarcastically quoting from Xu Zhimo, "Cease the Gossip, Cease the Empty Talk" (Jiesu xianhua, jiesu feihua), *The Morning Post Supplement* (*Chenbao fukan*), February 3, 1926.
49. The first lines from *Three Character Classic* (*San zi jing*), which children often memorized as part of their early education.
50. The year was not written on the original piece.
51. This piece recounts the circumstances of a temple fair seeking rain from the gods, held in Shaoxing in 1632, as described in volume 7 of Ming essayist Zhang Dai's (1897–1684) most famous work, *Dream Recollections of Tao'an* (*Tao'an meng yi*). See *LXQJ* 2:273n3.
52. *Strange Tales from Liaozhai* (*Liaozhai zhiyi*) is a collection of supernatural tales by the Qing writer Pu Songling (1640–1715).
53. *Brief Mirror of History* (*Jian lüe*), written by Wang Shiyun in the Qing dynasty, is a primer consisting of four-character rhymes about the history of the Chinese empire until the Ming dynasty. Subsequent editions used in the Republican era were updated to include verses up to the fall of the Qing empire.
54. *Thousand Character Text* (*Qian zi wen*), purportedly written by the historian Zhou Xingshi (469–521) of the Southern Liang dynasty, and *Hundred Surnames* (*Bai jia xing*), written in the Northern Song, were both composed of four-character rhymes and popular primers for teaching Chinese character recognition to children.
55. The year was not written on the original piece.
56. An illustrated religious tract depicting the horrors of Hell circulated in the Song dynasty, compiled and printed during the Qing dynasty.

57. Chen Xiying (1896–1970), one of the "estimable gentlemen" Lu Xun repeatedly refers to throughout the collection, used the term *"Shaoxing shiye"* from the Qing dynasty to derisively refer to Lu Xun.

58. Quoted from Chen Xiying's letter "To Xu Zhimo" in the "Idle Chats" (Xian tan) column of *Contemporary Review (Xiandai pinglun)* 3, no. 71 (April 17, 1926); *LXQJ* 2:264n7.

59. Ming essayist Zhang Dai's (1897–1684) most famous work, *Dream Recollections of Tao'an (Tao'an meng yi)*.

60. Lu Xun had been accused of "accepting rubles" on account of his pro-Soviet views.

61. The year was not written on the original piece.

62. Since their home had been sold to someone by the surname of Zhu, Lu Xun here facetiously refers to the new owners as the descendants of the Song dynasty Neo-Confucian scholar Zhu Xi (1130–1200).

63. Dongfang Shuo (154–93 BCE), a scholar official and writer from the Western Han dynasty.

64. The year was not written on the original piece.

65. "S City" refers to Lu Xun's hometown of Shaoxing.

66. The Mexican silver dollar became widely circulated in China after the first Sino-Japanese War (1894–1895).

67. The Yellow Emperor is a legendary sovereign and mythic ancestor of the Chinese race, Qibo, a legendary doctor. The ancient classic text of traditional Chinese medicine, *Huangdi neijing* (Yellow Emperor's canon of internal medicine), attributed to Huangdi and Qibo, was written during the warring states period.

68. The year was not written on the original piece.

69. "S City" refers to Lu Xun's hometown of Shaoxing.

70. The year was not written on the original piece.

71. Lu Xun's essay may have been in part inspired by Natsume Sōseki's essay memorializing his British tutor, "Kureigu sensei クレイグ 先生" (Professor Craig, 1909). William James Craig (1843–1906) was a scholar of Shakespeare and Natsume's tutor while he was studying abroad in London. Lu Xun translated the essay into Chinese as "Kelaika xiansheng," which he included in *Collection of Modern Japanese Short Stories (Xiandai riben xiaoshuo ji,* 1923), published by the Shanghai Commercial Press.

72. Refers to the preparatory Japanese language courses offered at the Tokyo Kōbun Academy designed for newly arrived Chinese students.

73. Another student by the name of Shi Lin was also in Sendai at roughly the same time as Lu Xun. Lu Xun had purportedly shared a room with him, and a photo of the two together is extant. For more details on some of the "distortions" in "Professor Fujino," see Eileen J. Cheng, "'In Search of New Voices from Alien Lands': Lu Xun, Cultural Exchange, and the Myth of Sino-Japanese Friendship," *Journal of Asian Studies*, August 2014: 589–618.

74. In the preface to his first short story collection, *Outcry*, the execution is recounted as a beheading in the preface, rather than execution by firing squad. This inconsistency and the later unsuccessful attempts to locate the actual slide in question have lead some scholars to speculate that Lu Xun may have fabricated this incident. Leo Ou-fan Lee, *Voices from the Iron House: A Study of Lu Xun* (Bloomington: Indiana University Press, 1987), 18; David Pollard, *The True Story of Lu Xun* (Hong Kong: Chinese University Press, 2002), 31.

75. The notes with Fujino's corrections have since been found and reproduced in various Chinese and Japanese sources. For example, see *Lu Xun yu Xiantai* (Lu Xun and Sendai), trans. Jie Zechun (Beijing: Zhongguo da baike quanshu chubanshe, 2005); *Fujino Sensei to Rojin: Seki betsu hyaku nen* (Professor Fujino and Lu Xun: Regret at departure 100 years) (Sendai: Tohoku daigaku shuppankai, 2007).

76. "Estimable gentleman" is an epithet Lu Xun used mockingly to refer to intellectuals from the Contemporary Review Group and the Crescent Moon Society, whose members had predominantly been educated in England and the United States. They include Chen Xiying (also known as Chen Yuan, 1896–1970) and Xu Zhimo (1897–1931), whom Lu Xun was embroiled in "pen-battles" with at the time. See "Dogs • Cats • Mice."

77. The year was not written on the original piece.

78. Six days after Xu Xilin (1873–1907) was killed, his alleged female conspirator, Qiu Jin (1879–1907), was beheaded. Lu Xun affirms Fan Ainong's patriotism and sacrifice by associating his name with the two well-known revolutionary martyrs from Shaoxing. In Lu Xun's eyes, while Fan's death was neither spectacular nor as glorious as his revolutionary counterparts,

his life was no less worthy of recording. For more on Lu Xun's depiction of Fan Ainong, see Cheng, *Literary Remains*, 58–78.

79. Lu Xun's descriptions of Fan Ainong evoke the image of the nonconformist and dissipated poets of the Wei-Jin period, whom Lu Xun much admired. The last epithet is a well-known reference to the eccentric poet Ruan Ji from the Jin dynasty, one of the "Seven Sages of the Bamboo Grove." According to the biography section of the *Jin shu* (History of the Jin dynasty), Ruan Ji had the ability to look at others with the white of his eyeballs," that is, "when he saw literate men who were vulgar in manner, he would look at them with the whites of his eyes." Fang Xuanling, *Jin shu*, 5.1361.

80. In the name of propriety, the warlord Sun Chuanfang (1885–1935) banned the Shanghai Art Academy from using nude models in 1926.

81. The year was not written on the original piece.

82. For more on "Guo Ju Buries His Son," see *"The Illustrated Twenty-Four Filial Exemplars"* in this volume.

83. When his father was gravely ill, the filial son Yu Qianlou is directed by the physician to taste his father's feces to see if it was sweet or bitter. His father dies not long after. *LXQJ* 2:349n19.

84. For more on Lao Laizi, see *"The Illustrated Twenty-Four Filial Exemplars"* in this volume.

85. For more on Wu Chang, see the eponymous essay in this volume.

Lu Xun's Oeuvre

Creative Writing

Nahan 呐喊 (Outcry). Beijing: Xinchao she, 1923.

Panghuang 彷徨 (Hesitation). Beijing: Beixin shuju, 1926.

Yecao 野草 (Weeds). Beijing: Beixin shuju, 1927.

Zhao hua xi shi 朝花夕拾 (Morning blossoms gathered at dusk). Beijing: Weiming she, 1928.

Gushi xin bian 故事新編 (Old tales retold). Shanghai: Wenhua shenghuo, 1936.

Essay Collections

Re feng 熱風 (Hot wind). Beijing: Beixin shudian, 1925.

Huagai ji 華蓋集 (Inauspicious star). Beijing: Beixin shuju, 1926.

Fen 墳 (Graves). Shanghai: Weiming she, 1927.

Huagai ji xubian 華蓋集續編 (Sequel to inauspicious star). Beijing: Beixin shuju, 1927.

Eryi ji 而已集 (And that's all). Shanghai: Beixin shuju, 1928.

Er xin ji 二心集 (Two hearts). Shanghai: Hezhong shudian, 1932.

San xian ji 三閒集 (Three leisures). Shanghai: Beixin shuju, 1932.

Wei ziyou shu 偽自由書 (Fake liberty). Shanghai: Beixin shuju, 1933.

Nan qiang bei diao ji 南腔北調集 (Southern tunes in northern tones).
Shanghai: Tongwen shudian, 1934.

Zhun feng yue tan 准風月談 (Quasi discourses on the wind and moon).
Shanghai: Lianhuan shuju, 1934.

Ji wai ji 集外集 (Collection of the uncollected). Shanghai: Qunzhong tushu
gongsi, 1935.

Huabian wenxue 花邊文學 (Fringed literature). Shanghai: Lianhua shuju,
1936.

Qiejie ting zawen 且介亭雜文 (Essays from the semi-concessions). Shanghai:
San xian shuwu, 1937.

Qiejie ting zawen er ji 且介亭雜文二集 (Essays from the semi-concessions,
volume 2). Shanghai: San xian shuwu, 1937.

Qiejie ting zawen mo bian 且介亭雜文末編 (Essays from the semi-
concessions, final volume). Shanghai: San xian shuwu, 1937.

Ji wai ji shiyi 集外集拾遺 (Supplement to the collection of the uncollected).
In *Lu Xun quanji* (Complete works of Lu Xun). Hankou: Shanghai
fushe, 1938.

Acknowledgments

Yang Xianyi and Gladys Yang's translations of Lu Xun's works inspired this volume. Their translations have been invaluable to the field of modern Chinese literature but have not reached a broad audience. While Lu Xun's short stories have seen multiple translations since the Yangs', *Wild Grass* and *Morning Blossoms Gathered at Dusk*—which include some of Lu Xun's best and most important works—have not. This combined volume, which comes almost fifty years after the Yangs' renderings, aims to provide accurate and lucid translations while preserving the poetic sensibilities of the original works. My hope is that it will give readers of all backgrounds insights into one of China's most brilliant minds and a sense of Lu Xun's versatility and ingenuity as a writer.

For shepherding the manuscript to its present form, I am indebted to many. My gratitude to Theodore Huters for combing through the manuscript and for his meticulous editing. For answering random queries, pointing me to sources, and commenting on introductions and translations, my thanks to: Bao Weihong, Allan Barr, Timothy Wai Keung Chan, Peter Flueckiger, Hu Ying, Huang Xizhen, Andrew Jones, Jon Kowallis, Lam Linghon, Lu Weijing, Christopher Rhea, Tan Chang, Nicolai Volland, Yao Ping, Wendy Yu, Zou Jidong, and Zou Xiuying. In the initial phase of this project I found a warm and quiet haven at the Humanities Studio at Pomona College, tended by its director, Kevin Dettmar, who watered the early seeds of these wild grasses and blossoms. My heartfelt appreciation to Kirk Denton and his graduate students, who commented on my work in their Lu Xun seminar at the Ohio State University in the spring of 2021. I am fortunate to have the help and support of Ji Zhiqiang, research assistant par excellence. The manuscript benefited greatly from the fine editorial touch of John Donohue at Westchester Publishing Services. I could not have asked for better editors or a more professional team from Harvard University Press: Lindsay Waters staunchly supported the project from the very start. Joseph Pomp enthusiastically saw it through the critical last stages.

The work in this volume came in dribbles. During the pandemic, some writing and translating was done in our backyard, with a backdrop of the mountains, and, in the distance, two tall palm trees piercing the "odd and high" sky. The bulk of the work took place on the dining table in the late evenings by lamplight. The shrinking of light and physical space was accompanied by an expansion of the mind, spirit, and imagination. In the quiet of the dark night, Lu Xun's world—populated with humans, fauna, flora, ghosts, spirits, shadows, sentient corpses, snow arhats, and talking flames encased in ice, each struggling to survive in an inhospitable world— would come alive and offer oddly comforting solace: You are not alone.

My gratitude for the support of a community of family and friends and to Ko Honda, by my side through thick and thin. This collection is dedicated to my maternal grandparents, Du Tian'un (呂天恩 1910–1987) and Chua Guan'di (蔡贯治 1915–2003). Their spirits and the many warm childhood memories spent in their company sustain me to this day. I am inspired by my two girls, Ari and Melanie, whose childlike hearts delight in the world— may you always find joy, beauty, and wonder in this uncertain world.